A HIGHER BETRAYAL

A Wayward

Patriot

Thriller

JACK MEYER

First Edition published in 2024 by:
3PPress Publishing Company
3609 Austin Bluffs Pkwy, #31/2
Colorado Springs, Colorado 80918

3PPress.com

Copyright © 2024 by Jack Meyer

Names: Meyer, Jack (John Allan), 1955- author.

Title: A higher betrayal : a Wayward Patriot thriller / Jack Meyer.

Description: First edition. | Colorado Springs, Colorado : 3PPress, [2024] | Series: Wayward patriot series.

Identifiers: ISBN: 979-8-9862931-4-1 (paperback) | 979-8-9862931-6-5 (hardcover) | 979-8-9862931-5-8 (ebook) | LCCN: 2024906788

Subjects: LCSH: United States. Congress. Senate--Elections--Fiction. | Political campaigns—Minnesota --Fiction. | Elections--United States--Fiction. | Elections--Corrupt practices--United States-- Fiction. | Presidents--Corrupt practices--United States--Fiction. | Border security--United States--Fiction. | Artificial intelligence--Political aspects--United States--Fiction. | LCGFT: Political fiction. | Thrillers (Fiction) | Military fiction. | BISAC: FICTION / Thrillers / Suspense. | FICTION / Thrillers / Technological. | FICTION / Political.

Classification: LCC: PS3613.E953 H54 2024 | DDC: 813/.6--dc23

Editor: Cannella Writing Services
Cover design: Lori Ehlke

This is a book of fiction. The events described are imaginary. The organizations and characters are fictitious and are not intended to represent specific organizations, places, or people.

Printed in the United States of America

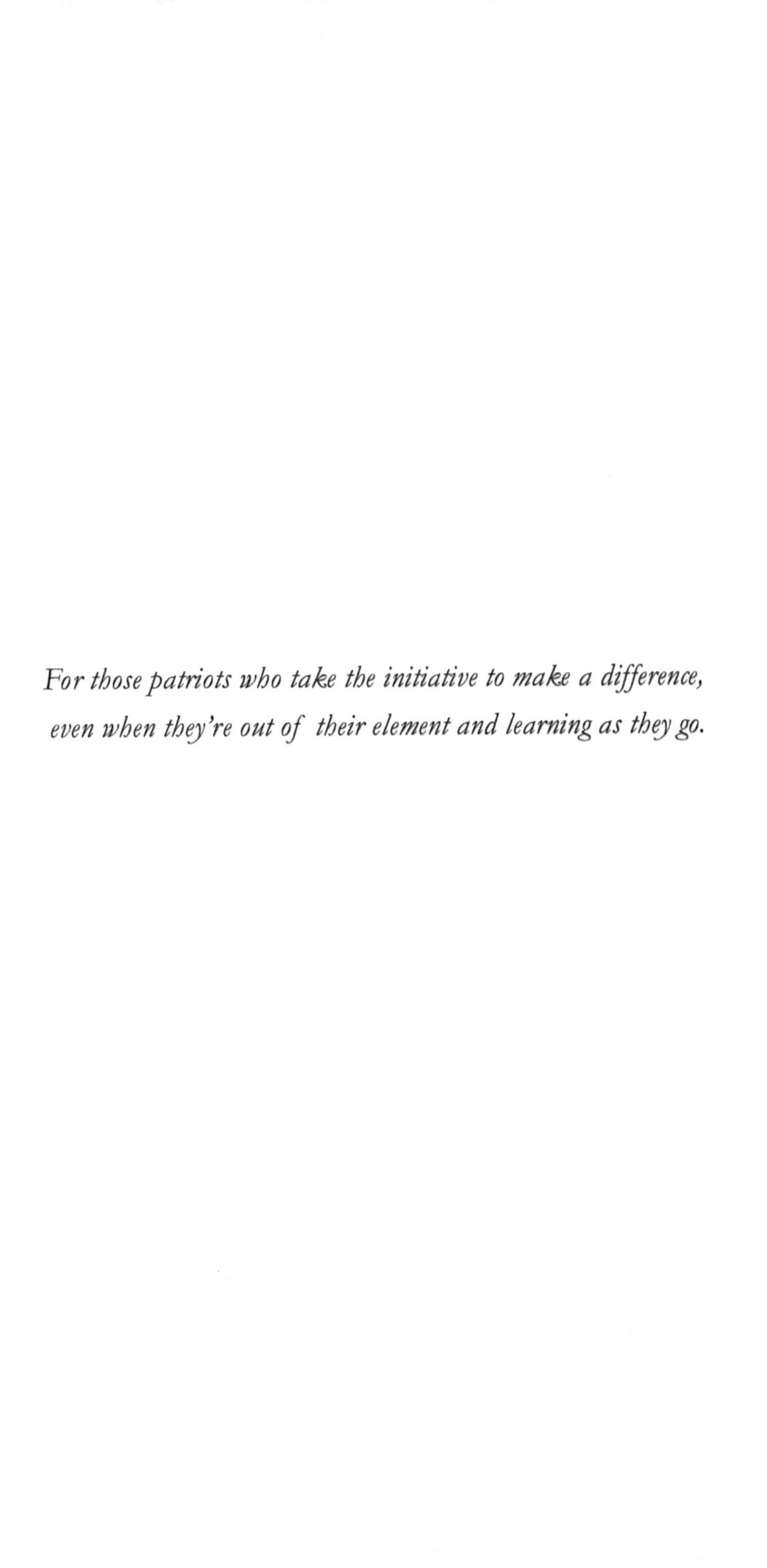

For those patriots who take the initiative to make a difference,
even when they're out of their element and learning as they go.

WAYWARD PATRIOT SERIES

BOOK 2

PART 1

PURSUING THE IMPLAUSIBLE

"Life is either a daring adventure or nothing at all."
– Helen Keller, <u>The Open Door</u>

1

TOM BLADO slammed on his brakes and spun his steering wheel hard right, just missing the slowing truck in front of him. He decided he needed to get his mind off of his upcoming meeting and back to his driving. He took the on-ramp to Interstate 95, north of the Capital. As he entered traffic and adjusted his cruise control to stay with the flow, he pressed the hands-free button on his steering wheel. A tone sounded over the BMW's speaker system.

"Call Patti Blado," he said aloud as he adjusted his sun visor to shield his left window, shading his eyes from the setting sun.

"Hi, hon. Are you on your way home?" Patti answered in her Texas drawl.

"Hey, sugar. I'm afraid I had to change my flight to tomorrow. A whistleblower asked for a meeting tonight. I should get home by three tomorrow afternoon."

"A whistleblower! Can't he wait until after the holidays?"

"You know how it is: When somebody is ready to talk, I need to be ready to listen. If I put them off, they may change their mind. Don't worry. That will give me plenty of time to get my beautifully-wrapped gift for you under the tree."

"I wish you could get off that committee." Patti knew that her husband, the honorable Thomas Blado, United States Senator from Texas and Chairman of the Senate Judiciary Committee, took his job seriously. She had gotten used to such disappointments. "Remember the Carters will be here for dinner."

"Oh, that's right," Tom sighed. "I was hoping we could just snuggle up by the fire on Christmas Eve."

"There'll be plenty of time for that," Patti said playfully. "Hurry home. I'll see you tomorrow."

"See ya tomorrow."

An hour later he left the freeway and meandered through Baltimore traffic. It wasn't quite as bad as normal so close to the holiday. He made his way to Riverside Drive and entered the parking garage for the Royal Suites. After driving around for a few minutes, he finally parked on the fourth level, facing the river. He chuckled to himself. It was like he was providing his car an exclusive view out of the open rail of the garage.

He walked to the elevator and rode to the lobby, where he found the lounge, asked for a table for two, and ordered a scotch on the rocks.

The senator waited for nearly fifteen minutes before getting a phone call.

"Are you in the hotel?"

"I am."

"I'm in room 917."

"On my way," Tom said, leaving a ten and a five on the table to cover his drink.

He walked to the elevator. The doors opened and he stepped in alone, pressing the button for his ride to the ninth floor. He followed the signs and walked down the hallway, registering how soft the posh carpeting felt under his feet. Looking at the room numbers, door by door, he finally reached 917 and tapped lightly.

She opened the door immediately, as though she had been standing on the other side waiting. It was a luxurious suite, with a large sitting area across from one of those electric replica fireplaces intended to look like dancing flames. Too bad fire codes wouldn't allow open flames in such rooms anymore. The heavy drapes on the large window were open to a wide view of downtown Baltimore. A large stand-alone cabinet was against the opposite wall with a mirror above, ornately framed in gold leaf. A chilled wine bottle and a decanter of coppery-colored liquor rested on the cabinet top with a variety of glasses. She walked to the bar and then turned to him and smiled uneasily. "I need a drink. Would you like something? I have scotch and chardonnay."

"Scotch, thanks."

The woman turned her back to him and poured them both a drink. She was tall and not particularly thin, but her shape was well-proportioned. She had dark, closely groomed hair and smooth, brown skin. She turned back to him and handed him the drink, then she walked to the window and looked outside briefly. "I know you need to get home for the holiday, but I really wanted … no, I needed, to see you," she said slowly, taking several sips of her wine.

"My wife was disappointed when I told her I'd be delayed, but she's used to it."

"What did you tell her?"

"I told her that a whistleblower needed to see me."

The woman walked across the room and faced him. "I know it's unfortunate that we have to meet like this, but we both know it's the way it has to be."

She reached out and took his glass and set it on the coffee table next to hers. Then she stood on her tiptoes, put her arms around his neck, and kissed him deeply. Lowering her right hand, she took hold of his necktie and led him into the en-suite. "Come and get your Christmas gift."

\#

Tom quietly got up and dressed at one-thirty in the morning. Trying not to wake her, he slipped out of the ensuite and into the hallway. Once inside the elevator, he was relieved to see that he could go directly to the mezzanine level for the parking garage elevator.

He rode down to the mezzanine and walked across to the other elevator. All was quiet; he saw no one. He stepped in and stood for a minute looking at the control panel, trying to figure out what parking level he was on. As it turned out, the mezzanine was the same as the third floor of the garage. He pressed the button and rode up to the next.

As he walked out into the chilly December air, he was startled to see that there was a vehicle with the trunk open near where he thought his car had been. He cautiously approached the vehicle and was immediately disoriented by the fact that it *was* his car. His spare tire had been pulled out of the tire well and left half in and half out of the trunk. He turned and looked around the parking garage in each direction. He saw nothing. He felt a shiver run up his spine, past his shoulders and up his neck. He didn't know if it was the cold night air or what he was looking at.

He picked up the spare and began to return it to the tire well, then paused and laid it down again. He stepped to the right and looked along the body of his Beamer. Nothing unusual. He walked back the other way and checked the left side. Immediately he saw that the left front tire was flat and that a jack had been placed behind the tire, with the tire iron and jack handle connected. He slowly walked toward the jack.

Suddenly there was a jarring push from behind. Tom tried to look back, but whoever was there was out of his view. He stumbled and lost his balance. The force jettisoned him forward three feet against the four-foot rail. Just before his forward motion stopped, two hands grabbed the front of his shins and pulled his feet out so he continued over the rail. Seconds later his head struck the sidewalk thirty feet below.

2

STAN KAUFFMAN drove his Tesla south on Virginia's highway 286. He drove an electric vehicle, not out of any concern for the environment, but because he loved the speed. It would take him from zero to sixty in 5.4 seconds and top out at 125 miles per hour. Unfortunately, he rarely got to enjoy the rush that came from such speed. He used to be able to get away with it when he was the vice president's chief of staff. He would drive to work at 4 a.m. on some days, and the police would look the other way. Now, he was an ordinary citizen again and needed to be more careful.

He exited the highway onto 654 and drove toward Vannoy Park where his old boss owned a two million dollar home. He showed his ID to the Secret Service detail who was in charge of protecting the former vice president and was waved through. He was expected. He drove slowly up the circular drive to Gerald Donaldson's residence and parked in front. His pace was brisk as he walked to the door, the cold wind stabbing his face. He hadn't bothered to put on a coat. The cloud cover ensured no warmth would come from the sun.

The door was answered by another Secret Service agent. She greeted him with a smile but asked to see inside his briefcase. He placed it on the table in the entry and opened it. The agent ran a wand up and down Kauffman's body. "Thank you sir," she said as she closed the briefcase and handed it to him. "The vice president is in his study." Stan tapped on the door and walked in without waiting for a response. Gerald Donaldson rose from his plush chair beside the fireplace and reached out his hand.

"Hey, man," Donaldson said informally. The two of them had a long friendship that began in law school. Even when Donaldson had been the sitting vice president, they were buddies when nobody else was around. When people were around, Donaldson called Kauffman by his first name, and Kauffman addressed his boss as Mr. Vice President like everybody else.

These days there was no formality. Today, Donaldson looked like a couch potato with his straight black, graying hair uncombed and his flannel shirt tail hanging out of his blue jeans. "Hi, Ger," Kauffman said. "It's Christmas Eve; I thought your kids would be here by now."

"Should be here early this afternoon. We're looking forward to having them. It's been a few years since we've all been able to spend the holidays together. I hate that they have to sweep in at the last minute, but Jason has responsibilities that he has to take care of before they can get away." He walked over to the mahogany sideboard and plunked some ice cubes into a couple of glasses. He filled each glass halfway with Woodford Reserve, handing one to Kauffman and keeping the other for himself. "When do you leave for Philly?" he asked his friend.

"We're driving over this afternoon. Megan's folks are looking forward to the visit. She'll stay a week, but I'll go home Tuesday afternoon."

"For Pete's sake. Take a break for Christmas," Donaldson chided.

"Too many irons in the fire," Kauffman said matter-of-factly. His look changed to one of concern. "Gerry, have you heard about Tom Blado?"

"No. Is he barking about sending out more subpoenas?"

"No. They found his body early this morning at a hotel in Baltimore. It looks like he fell four floors to his death."

Donaldson groaned and his eyes fell to the floor. Looking

back at Kauffman, he asked, "Did he jump?"

"No, it sounds like there is some confusion about what happened. It appears he was in the parking garage changing a flat tire and somehow fell over the rail."

"When did this happen?"

"Sometime overnight."

Donaldson collapsed into his chair and motioned for Stan to do the same. "Was his wife there with him?"

"No. I'm told she was in Austin."

"Any idea why he was there?"

"No. I've only gotten the short version. I'm sure all of that is being investigated."

"That's awful. And on Christmas Eve."

"I'll say," Kauffman agreed. He paused. "It does clear up a significant problem we needed to get resolved."

"Stan, the man's body is barely cold. I can't believe you sometimes," Donaldson scolded.

"I'm sorry, Ger. I guess I've become all politics all the time. Are you going to call his wife?"

"Not right now. I'll give her some time with her family. Once we know a bit more about this, I'll call her. Maybe tomorrow. Can you get me her number and let me know when you have more information?"

"Will do."

"I wonder who they'll tap for the chairmanship of the judiciary," Donaldson said.

"Well, Evans is Vice Chair, so I presume he will be made Chair."

"Hmmm. ... We'll have to see."

"This could be one of the last pieces that we need to fall into place, Gerry. With the sweeping victories the party had in the midterms, you could very well have a sixty-one or sixty-two vote majority in the Senate. The House is a lock as well."

Gerald Donaldson had served as vice president for eight years under President Lloyd Brannon. The voters seemed to be tired of the party in power after eight years, and the opposition was running a populist candidate that people were fawning over. Donaldson had decided not to make a run for president at the time. However, after three years of a bungling administration that had the economy in shambles and foreign policy a mess, people were begging the former vice president to run. He threw his hat in the ring along with three others. They were nearing the primary season, and Donaldson's popularity was high. Polls of registered voters indicated that he was favored by 62% over his rivals, who were all polling at less than 20%. General election polls had him winning over the current president by a twelve-point margin.

"You know, Stan, I thought that the dream I shared with you was just a dream. However, as you say, with Blado gone, we actually have a chance to make it happen."

"You have a good relationship with the Senate majority leader. Do you think you could steer him to put someone even more friendly into the judiciary chairmanship? That would go a long way to help us out."

"It's certainly worth a try, Stan. It's certainly worth a try."

3

THE WHISPER of the wind on the surface of the car and the hum of the tires on the road below had a relaxing effect on Rick Taylor. He dozed as his wife Maggie drove the seventy miles between the afternoon's events. The road was narrow with enough curves and hills that passing another car was out of the question. Every once in a while though, some hot dog in a pickup truck would roar by, betting that no one unseen was coming the other way. When they were wrong, typically they would zoom past and swerve right in front of Rick and Maggie and hit their brakes to avoid rear-ending the car in front. She would roll her eyes, brake, adjust her following distance, and reset the cruise control.

They had left Moorhead at two-fifteen on a sunny February Saturday afternoon, on their way to Thief River Falls for their next campaign event at five. This was one of more than a dozen trips they had made through the backroads of Minnesota in the past couple of months as Rick sought to connect with voters around the state.

#

It was nearly three months earlier that Senator Tom Weimann had announced his intention to retire from the US Senate when his term expired the following January. A week after the announcement, Rick had asked his wife Maggie to go to dinner at Capital Grille, one of the finest restaurants in Minneapolis. This was out of the ordinary, as Minneapolis was nearly an hour and a half drive from their home near St. Cloud, in good weather. They made the drive through snow flurries but on good roads and, over red wine and salad, Rick told her that he had something important to discuss with her.

Maggie had looked at him quizzically. In her mind she thought, *Well this is out of nowhere.* She said, twitching in her seat, "Okay. Tell me."

"I'm not sure if you've picked up on this, but Senator Weiman recently announced that he's not going to run for re-election next year."

"Oh, I wasn't aware of that," she replied, still unsure of where this was coming from.

"Since I heard that, I've developed this incredible desire to run for his Senate seat."

"But ... why?" Maggie asked.

Maggie had been taken aback for good reason. During their seventeen years of marriage, Rick had never expressed an interest in politics before. He had never been active in supporting candidates. His support for his party was always from afar. In fact, he had often shown a level of disgust for party politics. He didn't know the insiders, nor did he show any desire to.

Rick Taylor was born and raised in Mankato, Minnesota by working parents whose Christian faith was the basis for their traditional family values. His mom, a teacher, had taught him how to study and made sure he put a reasonable amount of effort into his schoolwork. As a boy, he never did like the name Patrick. He thought it sounded too "uppity," which was the term he always used. He considered shortening it to Pat, but that name could be either a boy or a girl, so that wouldn't do. In fourth grade he settled on Rick. It was a derivative of his real name, and he thought it suited him. He made the announcement to his parents and his teacher, Mrs. Behm. She called him up to the front of the class and announced that Patrick would now like to be called Rick. It had been Rick ever since.

He grew up to become a lanky young man with deep, puppy brown eyes and unruly dark hair that he combed back. He earned a partial scholarship to the University of North Dakota in Grand Forks. Coeds swooned over him because of his quiet assuredness, good looks, and lopsided smile with broad dimples. Though he dated a little, he remained a serious student and never found anyone special there.

After earning his business degree from UND, he went to work on his MBA at Northwestern, where he met Margaret Trimble, a pharmacy student from the Twin Cities. It was her pretty, girlish face and curly, closely trimmed blond hair that initially attracted him to her. She had a full figure and was tall enough to be able to lay her head on his shoulder when they danced. Her positive aura and incredible sense of humor set the hook and reeled him in. She was self-deprecating, but she could also put Rick in his place with a few carefully placed verbal jabs.

He also loved that someone so smart could be such a gifted musician. Sometimes he would get upset about something, involving her or not, and she would write a little song and sing it to him. It was always funny, and it normally made him realize that he was taking life a little too seriously.

When Rick got his degree, Maggie still had a year to go. She told him she could study pharmacy anywhere, but she wasn't sure she could ever find another tall, dark, and handsome guy with those dimples that she adored. Her parents disapproved of her decision to quit school, but they loved Rick. They were married at her family's church in St. Paul and then moved to St. Cloud, where Rick was offered a job as a financial analyst for a national insurance company.

When they found out that they couldn't have children, they shared some melancholy weeks and decided their love was enough. They chose to open a business together and landed on an insurance company. It was a struggle for a few years, but both worked long hours and were ultimately rewarded for their commitment. Now, fifteen years after they hung out their shingle, they had twelve sales producers working for them and an office manager and two sales assistants. They had reached the point where they were living a comfortable life, though not extravagant. Their company was organized in such a way that they no longer had to sell. However, both enjoyed the work, so they continued to support and grow their customer base.

When Rick revealed his desire to run for office, Maggie tried to push back a bit. She had cautioned him that politics was an insider's game. He just wasn't well enough connected to successfully run a statewide race. Rick, however, was determined, and it was clear that he had been thinking about this for a long time. He spoke with passion about his concern for the country.

"Sweetheart, just six months ago I couldn't have imagined myself running for dog catcher, let alone for the Senate. But the America I've known and loved all my life seems to be changing for the worse. I think about those who have fought and died for our country and how they paid such a great price, and it feels like we are giving away the very freedoms that they secured."

She sat, riveted. She had never heard him talk like this.

"Just think of our government's response to the COVID pandemic. It showed the government for what it's become: a caretaker system that didn't trust the people to do the right thing. It took away so many of the people's rights. Maybe it was just for a time, but it could happen again. All that was needed was an excuse," he had said.

Looking into her eyes he asked, "Don't you feel like freedom itself is slipping away?"

When she didn't respond, he said, "I sure do." He had gone on to talk about trouble in the schools, crime in the streets, and the people who had been elected doing nothing about any of it, and sometimes even making things worse.

By the end of their evening out, Maggie recognized that

Rick was both serious and committed. "Rick, I've never heard you talk like this," she said admiringly. "I love what I am hearing, but this is a big step. A huge commitment. Before we take such a bold step, maybe we should take a couple of days to pray about it."

They were practicing Christians and believed in the power of prayer. Maggie was 100% on board from the start once she heard his reasoning. Rick was so energized, so enthusiastic. He spoke with a sense of purpose that was contagious. She quickly embraced the idea of Senator Rick Taylor, the People's Senator. She believed that he was already giving voice to what millions of people were thinking. She knew that he would work hard to continue to learn what was on their minds and take that to Washington.

Over the next few weeks, they worked together to develop a plan to pull back from the company in order to campaign full time. They each reached out to their network of clients and friends. When they heard Rick speak, the vast majority of them were on board right away. They contributed to the campaign, and Rick was able to recruit and hire an experienced campaign manager and a fundraising manager. The seed of a campaign was planted.

Initially they couldn't afford media, so they started traveling the state and organizing rallies to at least begin meeting people in the smaller counties. This helped them to get a feel for what the people were thinking and reinforced Rick's desire all the more. At almost every stop they would hear, "I was beginning to wonder if I was the only person to think like this. It's like you're reading my mind." They challenged him with, "We need someone with your love for America and your common sense in Washington. If you were elected, could you hold fast to what you're saying now?" Some pleaded with him to hold tight to his values, to their values.

#

Now, Rick took a deep breath, his eyes still closed. "Where are you taking me, Mrs. Taylor?"

She looked at him and smiled. "I'm taking you to Thief River Falls, Minnesota, where they are going to fall in love with their next senator."

Rick stretched his back and neck, sat up straight in the seat, and opened his eyes. "I needed that," he said. "How far out are we?"

"We should be there in half an hour."

He looked at his watch and saw that they would be comfortably early. He grabbed his cell phone and called Jim Gunderson, his campaign manager.

"Hey Rick, where are you?" Jim answered.

"We're about thirty minutes out. Are things ready there?"

Jim said, "Well, not really. Another situation where our volunteers weren't sure how things should go. You know, they seldom see candidates out here for the statewide races."

"Well, I'm sure you're teaching them the ropes. Is there anything you need for us to do differently?"

"No, we'll have things organized. Just be ready to do your dance!"

"Okay, I'll read through your notes on issues of concern in the area. I appreciate your work, Jim."

"I just hope some people show up," Jim said. "See you when you get here."

Rick tapped the end button on the phone and looked at Maggie. "Are you okay? Do you need me to drive the rest of the way?"

Maggie laughed. "I'm fine. You'd better get your act together there. I don't want to drive all this way to watch you tell a bunch of people from Thief River Falls how much you love it here in Rochester."

"Nah, Rochester was last week. Wasn't it?"

"Two weeks ago. Now get to work!"

Rick opened the folder Jim had prepared and went to work.

4

WHEN THEY arrived at the Thief River Falls Community Center, Rick and Maggie sat in the car for a minute scouting out the scene. There was a small group of people near the door. "Is that Jim?" she asked, pointing to the head with short blond hair that rose a bit taller than the others in the crowd.

"I think so," he said. The man looked their way. It was Jim. He excused himself and jogged toward the car. Rick and Maggie met him halfway.

"We've got things all set. There are a good number of people here already, so head in and shake some hands," he said.

Rick and Maggie walked to the door together. This was a routine that Rick demanded. Maggie was his most important partner and supporter, and he insisted that she not be relegated to the background. Rick was comfortable meeting people. He was naturally outgoing and sincerely interested in others and enjoyed visiting with them. The conversation didn't always have to be about politics. If Maggie was not engaged in conversation herself, Rick would introduce her as they walked around. When they arrived early, he made it a point to look around the room and see who was there ahead of time so he could spend time talking with each of them.

The community center was a cinder block building with a pitted, concrete floor. The dingy, cantaloupe-colored walls gave a 1980s vibe. Dusty, plastic plants stood in the corners. A small stage was elevated about a foot above the floor, likely the platform for bands that played for community dances back in the day. The place had an indistinct odor to it, not like mold but like a place where the air didn't circulate much.

As the time came for Rick's talk, Maggie took the stage and thanked everyone for coming. She spoke sincerely and made reference to one or more remarks that she had heard as they visited with the folks. Rick watched and smiled. He looked at Jim and whispered, "She's a natural. She should be the candidate!" Jim nodded and smiled. He knew how lucky they were that Maggie appeared so natural and comfortable in campaign mode.

She gave a smile to the crowd and said, "Please forgive me for going on this way. I just feel like we are old friends already! The real reason I am here is to introduce you to a man whom I have loved and respected ever since we were in college together at Northwestern. I love him for his thoughtfulness, his intelligence that wraps itself around common sense so well, his honesty, and his caring. He has all the qualities that we need in our next senator. I know you are going to love him too. Ladies and gentlemen, the next United States Senator from Minnesota, my husband, Rick Taylor."

The crowd clapped politely. Those who had arrived early smiled, as if Rick was already a friend. Those who came in later reserved any enthusiasm until they heard what he had to say. He began, "Thank you, sweetheart, for such a nice introduction." He looked at the crowd. "Aren't I the luckiest guy in the world?" The crowd clapped, enthusiastically this time, and everyone was smiling.

Rick shared his concerns for the country. Maggie realized that she had been the first to hear his campaign speech as they dined at Capital Grille. He covered the same points each time he spoke. He never bad-mouthed anyone, only described the country he had always loved. He acknowledged the country wasn't perfect but praised her for the progress she had made. He expressed concern that she was losing her way. Rick had developed his message carefully, ensuring that he never questioned the motives of others but described how the direction he saw the country going would take them to a destination that nobody would recognize.

He never referred to notes but spoke from the heart. He didn't stand behind the podium provided but walked the stage. He always asked for a wireless, head-mounted mic and crossed the stage regularly, looking directly at everyone. People could tell that he meant what he said. He included some self-deprecating humor and spoke as if he was chatting with friends, not trying to convince a bunch of strangers that he was their candidate.

After about thirty minutes, Rick invited questions and remained until every one of them was answered, then he thanked everyone for coming and asked them for their vote. He also asked that they talk to their friends about his campaign. He gave them a website where they could stay in touch if questions came to mind and where they could donate if they were inclined to do so.

When he left the stage, he and Maggie returned to the floor where they tried to seek out those who had come in later. They were the last ones to leave, as always.

#

Departing the community center, the Taylors and Jim Gunderson drove the mile to the hotel Jim had booked for the night. After checking in, they walked across the highway to a Mexican restaurant for a late dinner. Mis Amigos was a quaint restaurant with saltillo tile floors. Wrought iron was woven throughout; serapes and Mexican hats were interspersed with pictures of adobe buildings and Mexican peasants on the walls. Colorful tiles trimmed the place. The aroma of spices, especially cilantro, was present. Rick's mouth watered.

They were seated, and all three dug into the chips and salsa as if they hadn't eaten in days. Jim praised Rick and Maggie for their handling of the day's events. "You both are such naturals at this. I can't believe that you haven't campaigned before. Rick, your friendly and comfortable style exudes a charisma that people love. I can't tell you how rare that is."

Jim was an experienced campaign organizer. He had been a political consultant for more than fifteen years. After graduating from the University of St. Thomas with a degree in sales, he got a sales job for a multinational corporation. He was very good at what he did and climbed the corporate ladder quickly, ultimately becoming vice president of product development. He was interested in politics and helped out as a volunteer on several state congressional campaigns. After ten years, he left the company and started his own sales consulting business. His specialty quickly became politics, and he had since worked full time on three statewide campaigns. Rick thought he was lucky to be able to get a guy with his experience to run his campaign.

The waitress took their drink and dinner order, looking at her watch as if to say, *This place closes at nine-thirty, and I don't want to be here after that.*

"Jim, what are you hearing in St. Paul about our campaign?" Rick asked.

"I'm afraid nobody is taking you very seriously. I just can't believe it, but people in the party don't seem to be interested. They have picked Jeff Sands as their guy. They cling to him because he has won a statewide campaign before."

Maggie looked at him incredulously. "A statewide campaign? He ran for an at-large Board of Regents seat for the University of Minnesota! Did he even have an opponent?"

"Well, yes, but not one who knew much about running for office."

"I guess I can understand their way of thinking, but as I recall he's not a great campaigner, is he?" Rick asked.

"He's a terrible campaigner. Not only does he show no personality on the trail, he is about one hundred pounds overweight and looks like he couldn't go two rounds against

Sister Olga Marie. Rick, people really relate to you in these events. If you can get some attention, you can beat this guy."

The waitress brought their drinks and let them know that their meal would be out shortly. Rick took a sip of his beer and said, "Getting people's attention is the issue. I can wander around the hinterlands all campaign long, but it won't do me any good in the big cities."

"Jim, it's going to take money to get Rick recognized in Minneapolis, St. Paul, and other larger cities," Maggie said. "Can you get us in to see people from some of the larger political action committees?"

"I'm afraid it isn't that easy. It's a good ol' boys' network. They are going to put their money where the party tells them."

"That's ridiculous," Maggie whispered with fire in her eyes as she looked around the restaurant at the other patrons. "They would support a poor candidate over a brilliant campaigner just because he stumbled into a win once before?"

"I'm afraid so. That's party politics," Jim said.

"I hate party politics." Rick shook his head. "I would run as an independent if I thought it was possible to win."

"No, you did the right thing by running for the nomination. It will be tough, but it is possible. A long shot, but possible."

"Why do we bother?" Maggie asked.

"Maggie, a campaign is a different thing," Jim explained. "It's a long game. You never know what could happen along the way that will turn everything on its head. A skeleton in the closet, a poor choice of words, a big news event. Anything can happen at any time that could totally shift the momentum. Shift it toward you or away from you. We just need to keep doing what we are doing. Over time people will begin to notice."

"How much time will it take? And will the clock run out on us?" Rick asked as the waitress arrived at the table with their food.

"Greg has some ideas for bringing in more cash. We can talk with him tomorrow and see what he thinks."

"Hiring a full time fundraiser is eating up a lot of our contributions. I hope he is worth his salt," Rick said, pointing his fork at nothing in particular.

"I promise you, it would be impossible to run a campaign without someone like Greg," Jim assured him.

When they finished their meal, Jim paid and they crossed the street back to their hotel. "It was a good couple of days. You should both be proud," he said. "Tomorrow you can head home and get some well-deserved rest. I'll call you in the next couple of days with our schedule for the rest of the month."

5

THE NEXT day they got back home just before noon. It was a cold March day in St. Cloud. Snow was still on the ground from the winter blanket that had been with them since December. Their ranch-style house sat on a heavily wooded lot near the Sauk River. During the summertime when the leaves were on the trees, other homes couldn't be seen from their property except for the neighbor across the street. The privacy suited them.

Rick went into the office that afternoon to meet with the staff. He was pleased to find that all was working well in their absence. Maggie had planned on doing some catch-up work around the house, but found she just wasn't motivated to do chores. Instead she picked up her guitar and enjoyed some peace and quiet, plucking on the strings and singing. She liked all kinds of music, but that day she sang some slower ballads and love songs. Rick arrived home at four-thirty and asked Maggie if she had a plan for dinner.

"I took some steaks out of the freezer. We have some potatoes and salad. How does that sound?"

"Sounds great," Rick said as he leaned over the guitar and gave her a kiss. "I'll take a quick shower and then start the grill."

Maggie set down her guitar. Before going to the kitchen to make the salad, she turned on the TV. Watching local news, she was annoyed to see a brief story from one of Jeff Sands's campaign events. They played a video clip of his speech. *He really is a pathetic campaigner*, she thought. He talks in a monotone voice and shows little enthusiasm.

#

"This election is too important to risk giving the nomination to someone without experience," Sands told the crowd. *"I have demonstrated that I can win a statewide election. This year we are going to do it again. I'd appreciate your vote so I can take your concerns to Washington as your next senator."*

#

Even the nasal tone in his voice is off-putting. She shook her head as she thought back to the previous night's dinner conversation. She thought that the party was supposed to be neutral until they had a nominee. It wasn't only the party big wigs. The news never showed up for Rick's events. They had done fifteen events so far, and she was not aware that there had ever been news coverage other than on the day Rick had announced his candidacy.

After dinner Rick went to his study to check his email and see what the online news organizations were writing about. He believed there were no objective news sources anymore. Every media outlet, whether television, radio or online, had a right or left bias. He tried to keep up with both sides of the political divide so he could form his own opinions. It was vital that he stay informed so that he could address questions relating to current events, including local, national, and international. He couldn't afford to hire advisers to keep him updated and support him in areas where he had no experience.

In the living room, Maggie sat down at her piano. She picked out a little tune and made some notes on a piece of paper she kept nearby. At eight-thirty she wandered into Rick's study where he sat at his desk staring at his laptop. She moved behind him and began rubbing his back, looking for knots and other signs of tension. "How are things going at the office?" she asked. "I hope you don't mind that I didn't go in with you."

He leaned back against her and smiled. "Not at all. They're actually going well. I was a bit concerned that as we have to be gone so much with the campaign, some might feel abandoned or resent being left to do the work without us, but they seem to be thriving on the challenge. They seem proud of the way they are

making things happen on their own. They're also excited about the campaign and asked lots of questions."

"We owe them a lot. I'll think about ways we can show our appreciation. We're blessed to have a wonderful work family."

They moved to the living room couch and chatted about the campaign stops—the people they had met and the impressions they came away with. They sincerely believed that, win or lose, they had been given an opportunity that most people didn't get. They were able to travel the state and meet new people. In a way it gave them a sense of hope, as it appeared to them that most people seemed to maintain level heads. They met few who spewed hate toward one side or the other. In fact, what people seemed to want most was for all of that to go away.

By nine-thirty fatigue caught up with them. They were both in bed and asleep before ten.

6

Stan Kauffman entered the vice president's hotel room for the daily brief. They were in Phoenix for an evening rally the weekend before the Arizona primary. He brought in the weekly event schedule that Donaldson's campaign manager had prepared. Kauffman still acted as a de facto Chief of Staff for Donaldson. The candidate met regularly with the campaign manager, but having Kauffman there to run things down took a load off of the manager.

Once they went through the event schedule, Donaldson stood and walked to the buffet next to the sitting area, opened the cabinet, and took out a decanter of quality bourbon. "Do you have time for a quick one?" he asked.

Kauffman nodded and took the drink. "Just to relax, or is there something you want to discuss?"

"Stan, I have never thanked you for the great job you did coaxing Governor Webb to select George Grimes to fill Blado's Senate seat. Now, running as an incumbent, Grimes's chances of being elected this fall are much better. He will be a big promoter of our border plan."

"It wasn't a tough sell. The governor believes that, if elected, you have the guts to fix the border once and for all."

"I like his confidence. If he only knew how we were going to do it, he'd probably mess his pants," Donaldson mused.

"This is going to be a careful dance, preparing for the border operation without people realizing the scope."

"We'll have to walk lightly for sure. Fortunately, the border mess has gotten so ridiculous that most people are ready for extreme measures."

"Yes, but Ger, I doubt they will be ready for this."

"I concede that. Neither one of us should talk with anyone about this without discussing it first with the other. What's the latest on the investigation into Blado's death?"

"My contacts tell me they are totally baffled," said Kauffman as he returned to his seat on the couch. "It's a really strange situation. Some elements strongly suggest that he was pushed off of that garage, but they just don't have any real evidence. They haven't found the whistleblower that he told his wife about. In fact, they've discounted that story.

"From the autopsy, they determined that he had recently had sex. They retrieved DNA, but it does them no good unless they find a match. He was only seen by a waiter at the lounge, and he was alone. They have camera footage of him going to a room on the ninth floor and then leaving around one forty-five in the morning. There was a woman who checked into that room, but, of course, she checked in under an assumed name. She went into the room with a scarf on and left the same way, not long after he did."

"It sounds like our Tommy boy had a little thing going on the side," Donaldson said. "It had to be murder. There's no way that someone is going to just fall over a rail while changing a tire. I also can't believe that a woman could throw a man Blado's size over a rail."

"Well, all we can do is let the FBI do their thing," Stan said. "It was a stroke of genius the way Leader Moreno sidestepped Evans and placed your pick into the judiciary chairman's seat. You'll get no trouble from him."

"I hope you're right."

7

As of late March, Rick Taylor's campaign continued to struggle. The focus remained on rural areas. Occasionally, Jim was able to arrange small events in larger cities. Rick did well in those settings too, but the media was still ignoring him. The party did not donate to any campaign and declared themselves neutral. "The nomination will be the people's to decide," the Minnesota state party chairman announced. Behind the scenes, however, political action committees were encouraged to contribute to Jeff Sands's campaign, as "he had a winning track record in a statewide campaign." Rick and Maggie rolled their eyes every time they heard the line.

At campaign rallies, Rick was surprised by the number of questions he got on the topic of guns and the Second Amendment. He would respond by saying that he was an advocate of the Second Amendment and, in fact, kept a gun close by at all times. He kept a 9mm handgun in the center console of his truck. He had bought it as tensions seemed to rise with China and Russia. He had read about what an enemy could do to us by exploding a nuclear weapon in the upper edges of the atmosphere. The resulting electromagnetic pulse would melt the wiring and circuits of everything mechanical, including power substations, automobiles, computers, and the like. He envisioned how quickly food would be hoarded and/or used up. He ordered a several months' supply of ready-to-eat meals and bought a gun in the event he would ever need to defend himself and Maggie from panic-stricken people. He had taken lessons on how to use the gun and had gone to a shooting range from time to time in order to stay proficient. Sometimes he wondered if he wasn't a bit paranoid.

The porous southern border was also a major concern to voters he spoke with. While they expressed concern with the flood of immigrants being allowed to come through, they were even more concerned about the smuggling of drugs, especially fentanyl, into the country. Rick's position advocating a strong southern border proved to be popular with the people. Truthfully, however, he didn't feel that he knew enough about the subject. He had heard former Vice President Gerald Donaldson talk of deploying the military on the southern border as he campaigned for president. Rick had serious doubts about that. He had never seen any border agents call for such a thing when being interviewed.

Maggie continued to travel with him on campaign trips. She began taking her guitar on the road with her. When Rick met with potential donors or had other less public meetings, Maggie stayed behind and picked at her guitar. While at home during a three-day break, Rick woke up at six one morning to find Maggie wasn't in bed. He found her sitting on the piano bench in her pajamas with her guitar in hand.

"What happened to my late sleeper?" he asked as he stooped for a kiss.

"I've been working on a little song about your campaign. It's kind of silly, but you know me and music. This idea came to me a few weeks ago, and it's stuck in my head."

"That's great. I'm sure it will be beautiful," he said as he poured himself a cup of coffee. "I'll be right back. I'm going to grab the paper."

It was a drizzly day, and the cold rain was melting some of the winter snow cover. He put on an old pair of loafers he kept by the door and jogged out to the driveway to get the paper, which was wrapped in a plastic bag. As he jogged back, he grumbled that their driveway was so long. The paper delivery person seldom got it even halfway up to the house from the road.

He returned with his wavy brown hair now beginning to drip and his shirt damp. He jumped through the door, closing only the screen door behind him, letting in the outside light to brighten the room. He walked quickly to the kitchen and grabbed a dish towel to wipe the rain off his hair and clothes. He sat in his favorite chair and looked up to see that Maggie had not moved. She was still on the piano bench, guitar in hand. However, she was not playing it. She was giving him 'the look.' It was the look that Rick dreaded. Her curly head was cocked slightly, eyes widened and lips pursed.

"What?" he said with a defensive tone as he arched his back and raised his shoulders. He knew that he had done something wrong. He had no idea what.

"I was telling you about my song and you dismissed it. I felt like a little girl being patted on the head and told, 'That's nice, honey.'"

Rick exhaled and laid the paper on the coffee table. "I'm sorry, sweetie. Tell me about your song."

She began to speak, almost reluctantly. "Well, do you remember how Lee Greenwood wrote "God Bless the USA" as we were going to war with Iraq in 1991? It struck a tone with people. It inspired them. People sang along with pride."

"I do remember. It's still a favorite song of many, even now. I love that song."

"Right. Well, as I listened to your campaign speech, I wondered what kind of song would strike a tone with people now amidst the divisiveness and meanness? People relate to what you have to say. They long for the days when civil discourse wasn't at the root of every conversation. They don't want to hide what they think to avoid confrontation. They just want good schools, safe streets, and an environment in which they can raise their families based on their own values. I really think most Minnesotans don't view our country based only upon the mistakes we've made in our history. I hope they still take pride in America, the most generous, freedom-loving country in the world. Only about 10% of the people are making all the noise on both sides of the political spectrum."

"I think you're right. Most people just want things to be the way they used to be, when they could live in peace and have freedom to live the life they wanted as long as they don't hurt others. People can disagree without hating one another. Everyone believes in the United States. All of the political rhetoric is where the hate is coming from. People are afraid to stand up for what they believe because they will be given some kind of hateful label."

"Exactly. … So, would you like to hear my song?"

Rick smiled with a gleam in his eye and said, "I would love to hear your song."

Maggie grinned, shuffled a bit on the piano bench, straightened her back, and began to strum and then sing.

> *Our heroes fight for freedom,*
> *Their very blood the price they pay.*
> *Now it's ours to keep from*
> *Rolling over, giving it away.*
> *We're smothered with restrictions;*
> *No, our judgment won't suffice.*
> *They'll save us from their dire predictions,*
> *Our liberty the price.*

The tune was simple and yet had a catchiness to it. It sent Rick's mind back to some of the songs he had heard as a kid in the 1970s. Folk songs had been written back then with a political message. They had some success in the Vietnam war era and shortly after. He liked the song. When he heard the refrain, he stared at her with his mouth partially open, a smile taking shape.

> *Reject the plans they make for us,*
> *Can't let freedom slip away.*
> *It's not the time to look to others;*
> *It's now my fight to wage!*

Maggie stopped, her face pink with embarrassment. "I know it's not that good, but it's how you make me feel when I hear you speak."

"Not that good?" Rick said incredulously. "It's great! There is even a call to action in that last part. It encourages people to not just let things happen that they disagree with." Rick pulled himself forward, on the edge of his chair. "I love it. You need to write more!"

"Maggie beamed. "Well, I actually have more verses. Do you want to hear?"

Rick's grin was now stretching from ear to ear, his eyes sparkled, and tears were on the way. This was the kind of thing she did that surprised him and endeared her to him. He nodded with excitement. "Absolutely I do."

"I'm glad you like it," she said sheepishly. She began to strum again.

> *Why must we all be labeled*
> *For every single thought we share?*
> *At one time we were able*
> *To treat each other with more care.*
> *Suspicion now confronts us*
> *For everything we say or do.*
> *Respect is lost for one another,*
> *Can't have a point of view.*

Exactly, he thought as she repeated the refrain. So many people he talked with expressed sorrow for the loss of tolerance for different viewpoints. Maggie continued singing.

Took liberty for granted,
Freedom's all I've ever known.
Dissent and hatred's planted
All around us; internally it's sown.
Inside our nation's schools,
Education's set aside.
Replaced by redirected values,
With parents kept outside.

As Maggie sang the refrain, Rick's mind was whirling. *How could we use this in the campaign?* he wondered. He gazed with amazement at his beautiful wife. He knew she was a talented musician, but she had never considered herself a singer/songwriter. He loved how she had captured the principles that people seemed to care about most and also motivated them to do something. He liked that the song painted a picture of why people were upset and encouraged people to consider whether their elected officials, locally and nationally, were taking things in the direction they wanted.

Maggie finished up with a triple strum, strum, strum. She looked at him and smiled. "Are you sure you like it?" she said with a little more confidence in her voice.

"Maggie, the words to your song even motivate me," he said, now pacing the floor. "We need to get a hold of Jim and see what he thinks. If he won't agree, I'll fire him and we'll *find someone who does*," he said in a metered and melodic way, obviously mimicking the song.

She put her arms around him and planted a big kiss on his lips. "Let's cook a special breakfast," she said, as if daring him to take a risk.

He kissed her back. "Let's do."

#

After breakfast, Maggie practiced her song a few more times, and Rick called Jim. "Jim, I hope you're sitting down."

"Uh, I'm sitting at my bench press," he said, slightly out of breath. "Please tell me you're calling to make my day."

"That I am," Rick assured him. "I want you to sit back and listen to something that Maggie has come up with. We want your honest opinion on this."

"Okay," Jim said slowly.

Rick put his cell phone on speaker and whispered, "Go ahead," with a wink.

She played her short intro and began to sing. She sang the three verses and then paused. "I actually have a fourth verse that I didn't play earlier," she said, and to Rick's surprise she sang a new verse.

> *Our nation built on laws,*
> *Showing stress cracks from neglect.*
> *The death of justice caused*
> *By those who serve us,*
> *Those that we elect.*
> *When those who represent us*
> *Refuse to do our will,*
> *We'll use the liberty we cherish,*
> *And send someone who will!*

As she finished, there was silence on the line. "What do you think?" Rick asked.

Slowly and dramatically Jim said, "I think it's incredible. Have you recorded it, Maggie?" he asked.

She squinted and scrunched up her nose. "No," she said in her hollow Minnesota *ohh*. "Why would I do that?"

"I'm going to find a studio where we can record that, this week if possible. Hopefully tomorrow," he said, serious and deliberate. "Mrs. Taylor, you are going to sing that at the end of every campaign event, starting this Friday."

Maggie's eyes got big, and she tilted her head and stared at

Rick. "Oh come on Jim, it's not that good," she said.

"Oh, yes it is. I am going to find out how to get that recording on Spotify and every other digital music platform there is. People are going to go home from our events, tell their friends, and download a copy so they can share it."

"I think it's great too, Jim, but it's not like she's Carrie Underwood," Rick cautioned.

"No," Jim said patiently, "she is the Joan Baez of the twenty-first century!" He paused. "Okay you two, let me explain this to you. This little song of Maggie's is going to help us in three ways. First, it is totally unique. How many campaigns have you ever seen that had a theme song written just for it, not to mention that the candidate's beautiful spouse sings it? This will be an attention getter," he explained. "The media will love it.

"Secondly, the song is really good, and it is going to hit people in their hearts. They will want to download it and listen to it over and over again. They will play it for their friends. Finally, as people download it, money will be going into the campaign coffers." Jim paused. "Assuming you are alright with that."

Rick and Maggie looked at each other, beaming. "Absolutely," Maggie exclaimed.

"I guess that's why you're the campaign boss," Rick laughed. "I hope you're right." He looked at his wife. "Maggie, I want you to write one more verse focusing on the crisis at the southern border. Can you do that and get ready to record this?"

"I don't know about tomorrow, but I'll be ready by Thursday," she said. "I hope you're not disappointed."

"You're going to be amazing," Jim assured her. "I'll get to work on finding a studio and call you back. Remember Maggie, you are going to do this live at every stop!"

8

AS MAGGIE thought about it, she realized that she wasn't really ready to record the song. Recording a song with just a guitar strumming accompaniment would sound cheap and unprofessional. She called Jim and asked him to let her arrange the studio time so she could get some better accompaniment arranged. She knew what sort of accompaniment would work best for her song and arranged the music for piano, bass guitar, and drum. It was still minimal but gave the song a more professional-sounding introduction and some instrumental sections that would work to dramatize parts where she wanted to build the listeners' emotions.

Much of her work and coordination was done while on the road with the campaign. Though the recording session was put off a week, Maggie followed through on her commitment to sing at the next campaign event on Friday. The afternoon event was in Rochester, the largest city in southern Minnesota. Attendees were in banquet chairs in a hotel ballroom, and a podium stood on a collapsible stage about nine inches high. The room was about three-quarters full. They followed their normal routine, arriving early to meet the attendees. Maggie spoke and introduced Rick, and he gave his regular campaign speech. He was getting good at it. He now knew what things crowds got excited about. He

had become adept at changing his tone to reinforce their feelings. He was able to get the crowd stirred up.

When he reached the end of his talk, he introduced Maggie again. "My friends, Rochester is about to experience a first. You've been kind and patient in listening to me as I shared my vision with you. Now, you are about to be rewarded for sticking with me. You see, Maggie has written a little campaign song.

"Now, this is something new for my wife and she is a bit shy about it. Maybe with a little coaxing from you we can get her to sing for you right now. Ladies and gentlemen, please give some encouragement to Maggie Taylor."

The crowd was generally in a positive mood from Rick's speech, but this was a little bit unusual. They applauded respectfully as Maggie walked to center stage with her guitar and a bottle of water. She took a sip and placed it on a shelf in the podium that had been set up but not used. Rick helped her adjust the mic stand as she climbed onto a stool with guitar in hand.

"Isn't Rick just wonderful?" she asked the crowd as she adjusted herself on the stool. That got more applause. "Don't you think he would represent you well in the United States Senate?" she added, and was pleased to hear more of a cheer this time.

"Ladies and gentlemen, Rick inspires me when he talks about his love for our great nation and his concerns for where we are. So much so that I wrote a song because ... well, that's just what I do when I'm inspired. I hope you like it."

Having worked on the musical accompaniment, she had a better feel for how she wanted to sing it. She had practiced more on the guitar to add more emotion to it. With all of the enthusiasm she could muster, she began. She started out somewhat softly, as if out of reverence to the heroes who had fought for the country. She showed a longing when singing about the loss of civil discourse and even some anger when singing of the things happening that she and Rick believed were taking the nation in the wrong direction.

Rick stood next to Jim off stage and watched. Both were

blown away. This was not the same meek presentation they had heard earlier in the week. This was emotional and inspirational.

Throughout the first verse, a few in the crowd shouted, "Yeah!"

A woman somewhere in the back hollered, "You go, girl!"

With that bit of support, when she came to the refrain, Maggie rocked out. She strummed harder, sang louder, and her head was moving to the beat.

> *Reject the plans they make for us,*
> *Can't let freedom slip away.*
> *It's not the time to look to others;*
> *It's now my fight to wage!*

The crowd roared. People began to stand up as she continued through the next verse. As their enthusiasm built, Maggie's did as well. By the time she had finished the fourth verse, the entire audience was on their feet. As she went into the last refrain, Maggie was astonished when the crowd started to sing along. She smiled and laughed, stumbling over the lyrics, but it didn't matter. The crowd got them right.

When she finished, she heard cheers like she could never have imagined. She stood from her stool and waved at the crowd. She was beaming. Jim leaned in and shouted in Rick's ear, "What did I tell you? This is going to cause a stir like you won't believe."

As Maggie and her adoring fans continued their love affair, Rick stepped up onto the stage. Maggie saw him approach and put up both hands, asking for quiet. As the noise subsided, she plucked the microphone from the stand and spoke to the crowd. "Do you get this? You are going to save this country. You will make the difference. Tell your family, your friends, your co-workers. Tell everybody! Your vote is critical. Know the candidates! Know the issues!"

The applause continued. People nodded enthusiastically..

Maggie turned to Rick and began to hand him the mic. Then her eyes grew wide, and she took back the mic before he could take it. "Oh, and vote for Rick!" she said as an afterthought. The crowd laughed.

Rick laughed too and took the mic. He looked at all of the smiling faces and simply said, "I can't say it any better than that. Thank you for coming, and God bless you all." He put the mic back into the stand, and he and Maggie walked into the crowd as they normally did. Suddenly Jim went running across the stage. The thudding noise echoed throughout the room, and everybody turned to look.

He grabbed the mic and the stand with it. "One more thing, everybody. Maggie will be recording that song, and in a week or two you will be able to get it wherever you download your favorite music."

"What's it called?" someone shouted.

Jim was caught speechless. He looked down at Maggie, who was laughing at him. She shrugged her shoulders. Jim thought for a moment, then shouted into the microphone, "'My Fight to Wage' by Maggie Taylor."

Another cheer went up. On the floor among her fans, Maggie shrugged her shoulders again as if to say, *That'll work.*

#

The scene in Rochester repeated itself Friday evening in Mankato. Those in attendance loved "My Fight to Wage" and were singing along by the end.

That weekend's events were closer to the Twin Cities. The ten-thirty morning speech in Apple Valley was planned in a relatively small location, and their attendance expectations were modest and in line with what they had experienced throughout the campaign. When they arrived at ten, however, the community center parking lot was full and cars were on nearby streets in every direction. It was thirty-eight degrees, and the bright sunshine continued to melt what was left of the winter snow. As they turned into the parking lot, they saw a News Channel 7 van parked in the fire lane near the door.

Jim turned into the lot and stopped. They all looked at one another with smiles on their faces. "The word is out," he said.

Indeed, the word was out. Morning talk radio shows received calls from several people who had attended the rally in Rochester or Mankato and had gushed with enthusiasm over their experiences. The radio hosts probed the callers for more information. "What do you think of Rick Taylor?" they asked. "He's a political neophyte. What impression did you come away with?"

Callers spoke positively, telling the audience that Rick seemed to read their minds as he talked about the issues that concerned them the most. Of course, the conversation always led to the candidate's wife. "The song she sang did the same thing!" one caller said. "She seemed to really motivate the crowd. I walked away telling my wife that if we are going to change what is wrong with this country, it starts with our votes."

"What did he say that made you feel like he knew what was on your mind?" the announcer probed.

"On many topics, such as education and crime, he just wants us to get back to the basics. I want my grandchildren to go to school to learn reading, writing, math, and history. I don't want them to be indoctrinated into whatever cause the teacher espouses. As for crime, I just want bad guys to be held accountable. Right now it seems like criminals are treated like victims while the real victims are just forgotten about."

Jim dropped Rick and Maggie off at the front door and drove away, wondering how far away he would have to park. As they approached the door Rick said, "Let's do this the same as we always do. No media interviews until after we are finished with the rally."

They walked through the door and saw a huge crowd. The venue appeared to be a community center for a large housing development. It was a relatively new structure with a combination of wood floors and carpeting. The bright morning sun shown through large windows, and both had to blink a few times to adjust their eyes. On one side of the building there seemed to be a kitchen bar set up, likely for parties. On the other side of a large opening was a spacious room with pictures on the wall, almost like a gallery. There was no stage. Folding chairs had been set up in the room. All were full, and still a lot of people milled around. The din of the crowd surrounded them completely.

Rick and Maggie smiled at one another again and simply walked in and started to introduce themselves to individuals in the crowd. The interaction with folks was not different from before; there were just a lot more people to get to. They had always been able to meet everyone before, but it became obvious that it would not happen today with a two-thirty rally still to come in Stillwater. They continued to greet people as quickly as they could, forced to take less time for meaningful conversations.

Jim approached Rick in the crowd at 10:25 and motioned him to the area where the microphone had been set up. He also caught Maggie's eye and nodded in that direction. As they looked over the crowd, all they saw were wall-to-wall faces. People filled the side aisles, the back area, and even the carpeted section where the kitchen bar was. Maggie took the microphone and said, "Oh my goodness. Let's pray the fire marshall is busy elsewhere!" The crowd chuckled and quieted down.

She went through her normal routine of introducing her husband. Rick gave his speech, and Maggie received thunderous applause along with some whistles and yelps after her song. As soon as they returned to the crowd, a reporter appeared next to them. Rick told her that he and Maggie would love to talk with her but asked that she give them about fifteen minutes to interact with voters again.

Once they had shaken hands with almost everyone in the crowd, Rick and Maggie found the reporter. The cameraman pointed out where he wanted them to stand and gave the reporter a 'go' sign with his index finger.

"Mr. Taylor, that was quite a little rally. It's unusual to have the crowd singing at one of these events."

"I guess it is," chuckled Rick. "Maggie, my wife, wrote that song as a source of inspiration for voters and to help make my message more memorable."

"Nice job, Maggie," the reporter smiled, moving the microphone toward her.

"Thank you. It was fun to do."

"What gave you the idea to write the song?"

"I just feel so strongly about Rick's message that I want everyone to hear it and remember it. I was hoping this would help."

"Is it online and available for download?"

"Well, yes, it should be by the end of next week," Maggie replied. "But again, it's not really about me and the song. Rick's message is the primary focus."

The interviewer turned back to Rick, "How does it feel to have a celebrity in the family? It appears that the crowd loved Maggie and her song."

Rick smiled. "I love Maggie and her song too. She has been so encouraging and supportive of me in many ways. She's deserving of some recognition." The reporter turned back to the camera and did her wrap up.

After it was all over, Maggie felt badly that from a media perspective, her singing seemed to be of more interest than Rick's candidacy. Jim soothed her fears and said it might be that way for a few days, but what mattered was that it had gotten them on the political map. People were beginning to know who they were. He said, "Now we're going to start booking larger venues and more people will hear what Rick has to say."

As the weeks passed, it was as Jim promised. Initially Maggie was shown on TV singing, and the interviews continued to be all about the song. However, the reporters also began asking more questions of Rick and his candidacy.

Some asked substantive questions about national topics, which Rick handled well. However, those questions also reminded him of topics the media was interested in and motivated him to spend more time doing research to prepare.

The recording was out a week after Maggie's first live performance of the song. They priced it at $4.99 and noted that all sales went to the campaign. It got over a thousand downloads in the first two weeks. As time passed, the number doubled, then tripled. Maggie and Rick were invited to be interviewed on Minneapolis television news and talk programs. They even made it on the popular *Sunrise in Minneapolis* morning talk show. That day, there were 576 downloads.

The next week they were invited onto a popular national morning program. The hosts played a clip of Maggie singing and asked many of the same questions about Maggie and the song. They took the last fifteen seconds to provide Rick the opportunity to tell the audience why he was the best person to be his party's senatorial candidate.

"Mr. Sands seems to be a nice person. However, I have never heard him propose anything that wasn't right down the party line. If I'm elected, I will be an independent thinker. I will represent the people of Minnesota by taking stands that I believe are right for Minnesotans and other Americans, whether they align with the party or not."

9

THE DONALDSON campaign had started traveling on a chartered 737 and used it to head to a rally scheduled in Indianapolis. It was a different kind of aircraft inside. The first-class section was removed, and a plush, private cabin was installed to replace it, including a partition and door for privacy from the people in back. The reporters and other media would pay to fly with the vice president and would be charged the normal rate for commercial travel between points of travel. Donaldson liked the privacy and comfort, and the media liked being as close to him as possible.

Kauffman, who often sat in the back and jawed with the media folks, walked up and tapped on the door to Donaldson's cabin.

"Yep," Donaldson hollered.

"You wanted an update on the senatorial races."

"Yes, that's right," Donaldson said, opening the door and motioning for his friend to sit across from him. Do you think we're going to get our sixty votes in the Senate?"

"It will be tight," Kauffman replied.

"Is what I'm hearing in the media true?" asked Donaldson.

"I'm afraid so. Tucker in Nevada has been accused of fixing a contract for a big donor friend of his. From what I hear, the evidence is significant. I told your campaign team that they should probably distance you from him."

"What about his campaign?"

"I couldn't get anything from his campaign. They were obviously surprised as well."

"What do you think, Stan?"

"I think he may have to resign. Even if that doesn't happen, he will need to withdraw from the race."

"Who would likely replace him?"

"There are several people that could run, but none have very good name recognition. Tucker's race was going to be competitive anyway," Kauffman added. "I think that we should figure Nevada a loss."

"Alright." Donaldson did a calculation in his head. "Are we at risk in other races?"

"Well, we're barely into the race for nominations, so it's early. None of the other races that we're following involve people of questionable character that we know of. But this *is* politics."

"What about Weimann's seat in Minnesota?"

"Weimann has hand-picked his successor. Someone named Jeff Sands. I don't know much about him, but he's won a statewide race before. Weimann said it won't even be close. We'll keep the seat."

"Some Senate candidate is making a bit of a splash up there. I don't think his name was Sands. Which party is he in?" asked Donaldson.

"Yeah, that's a guy named Rick Taylor. He's getting some media attention because his wife wrote a campaign song for him. He's in our party, but nobody knows anything about him. Weimann doesn't think he's a factor."

"Okay," the vice president paused and stared at the coffee table in front of him. "If need be, could your AI team help with any close races? Just to make sure we will have people who will go along with us?"

"What do you have in mind?"

"Using AI to mimic a candidate's voice in order to create a negative backlash to their campaign. Even if it could put them on the defensive for a while, it could make the difference."

"I wouldn't recommend it. People are too aware of the potential negative applications of AI. It would be risky to try it. The party has a good ops research group. It has dirt on almost everyone. I'll make sure it is revealed at a strategically convenient time."

"Thanks, Stan. Let's keep a close watch on it."

10

DESPITE THE publicity Rick's campaign was getting, he was still not being recognized by the state party office, let alone getting any support from them. All the donations from big contributors were going to Jeff Sands's campaign. Even with the thousands of dollars from the sale of Maggie's recording and the increase in small donor contributions that came with the improved attendance at rallies, they could not afford much advertising in major markets.

When Jeff Sands or other prominent players in the party were asked about Rick Taylor's campaign, they would chuckle and say something like, "I'm sure Rick Taylor is a fine guy, but he's just not ready for such heavy responsibility. Now his wife —she seems to be getting a lot of attention. I just hope she doesn't decide to run." Maggie became furious when she heard such drivel. Rick, she knew, would make a better senator than Jeff Sands or anyone else they could pick from their precious party.

One morning in late April, Rick and Maggie met Jim at Connie's Comfort Cafe in Maple Grove. It was their regular meeting spot when not on the campaign trail, and they met there at least weekly to work on strategy and planning and to review their financial status. They had to drive a little farther, but it was worth it. It had a down-home feel, and the food felt like it came straight from a grandmother's kitchen.

When discussing some of the media attention Rick was getting, Maggie referred to the comments about her running for office and became angry. "I think I need to stop singing at the rallies," she growled. "I'm a distraction. Maybe I should stop attending the rallies altogether." Her voice was loud enough to draw attention to their table.

"Calm down," Jim whispered, looking around the restaurant to see how many stares they were getting.

"Calm down?" she hissed in a lower voice. "What do we have to do to give Rick a fair shot at the nomination? How do we get past this manipulated system?"

"Sweetheart, you know you are having a positive impact on the campaign. You're having a positive impact on me. I need you," Rick said in as soothing a voice as he could muster.

"Remember," Jim said, "an election is a marathon. There are still three months before the primary."

"Well, it looks to me like we're so far behind that we'll never catch up," she huffed.

Jim paid the bill, and as they prepared to leave, he tried again. "Rick is getting interviewed more often. He is being taken more seriously by the media and the voters."

"Yeah, if not by the party," she quipped and walked out the door.

#

A week later, when they had a couple of days off between events, the three of them had a conference call. After some scheduling issues got cleared up, Jim announced, "I'm working on getting the media to set up a series of events around the state where both Jeff Sands and Rick would speak. The media is interested, but the Sands campaign not so much."

"What are they saying?" asked Rick.

"They point to a few polls and say it really isn't worth their time to be seen with someone who isn't even a factor."

This got Maggie's ire up again. "They don't want to do it

because they are afraid of him. I'm sure they've sent people to Rick's rallies."

"I'm sure they have," Jim agreed. "At least Sands isn't ignoring Rick anymore."

"Yeah, he's telling people they shouldn't vote for Rick just because his wife can sing!"

Rick scrunched up his nose. "That may be, but at least he feels the need to start attacking me."

"I'll keep working on this," Jim said. In the meantime, just keep doing what you're doing. We're making progress."

#

In early May, while traveling between campaign events, Rick got a call from Frank Moreno, the other US Senator from Minnesota. Not only was he a very senior Senator, he was the Senate Majority Leader.

"Rick, this is Frank Moreno. I just wanted to tell you how impressed I have been with your campaign."

"Thank you, Senator Moreno. I appreciate the compliment, especially coming from someone with your experience."

Maggie, who was driving, turned and looked at Rick with wide eyes. *Now he's getting some attention,* she thought.

"Oh, I'm very impressed. I'm sure you recognize, however, that Jeff Sands is almost sure to win the nomination."

"Oh?"

"Sure, and I don't say that to discourage you in any way. It's just nearly impossible to defeat someone who has won a statewide campaign before, especially when the challenger has had so little statewide exposure himself."

Rick's face reddened. He turned and looked at Maggie and gave her a disgusted look. "Well, we are out to be the exception, Senator Moreno. We're getting more attention all the time."

"Yes, you are," Moreno agreed. "That gimmick you created with your wife has been just great." Rick felt the hair on the back of his neck rise as he heard the condescension in Moreno's voice.

"Listen Rick, I haven't had a great deal of time to check out your position on various things. Where do you stand on the problem with the southern border?"

Rick settled down a bit, appreciating the fact that Moreno was at least acknowledging that Rick might have a position on an important topic like this. "I think it is a national travesty," Rick explained. "That border needs to be sealed as soon as possible. The millions of people crossing the border each year, along with the drugs, pose a significant risk to our nation."

"Yes, I'm glad to hear you say that. You know, Donaldson has the nomination locked up, and I can't even fathom him losing the general election. He strongly believes that it will take the US military to fix that problem. Do you agree?"

"At this point in time, I don't agree. I have never heard someone from US Border Patrol suggest that's the way to go. I think changing the policy and the rhetoric from the Administration would go a long way toward discouraging the migration."

"I don't want to insult you, Mr. Taylor. but I'm afraid you are showing naivety in this area. I strongly encourage you to go to the border and see things for yourself rather than just watching the news."

Rick's eyes nearly popped out of his head as he turned and gave Maggie a look as if to say, *Who is this guy to talk to me this way?* He took a long, deep breath.

"Thank you for your suggestion, Senator Moreno. I'll make every effort to do that."

"Good. Now Rick, when you decide to go, just give me a call on this number, and I will arrange for a member of my staff to accompany you. That way you can easily gain access to everything you need to see."

"Thank you for your thoughtfulness, Senator. I appreciate your call."

"Thank you, Mr. Taylor. Good luck to you."

Rick popped the red 'end' button on his phone and slammed it into the drink holder beside him. Maggie was eager to hear about the conversation. She was trying to keep her eyes on the road and on him at the same time.

"What did he say?"

"That jerk called to try and discourage me. Interestingly enough, he also wanted to know my position on the border. And he didn't like what he heard."

Rick's phone rang again. He sighed.

"Rick, I've got great news. A new poll is out and has you at 32% and Sands at 56%."

"Hey, Jim. That's better, but I wouldn't put it in the category of great news."

"This is just what we need to get Sands to bite on the joint events. I just called the state party chairman and told her what we wanted. She hemmed and hawed about it, but she knew that she had to agree in order to at least give the appearance of objectivity. We even talked dates."

"Now, that is great news! What are you proposing?"

"I suggested three dates in late June and early July. One in the Twin Cities, one in Duluth, and one in Rochester. That will leave about three weeks for the full court press before the August second primary."

"Are we talking debates?"

"No. We are thinking you would each do a regular stump speech, although we're kicking around the idea of each date having a topical emphasis. Maybe one on the economy, one on foreign policy, and another on other domestic issues. Are you okay with that?"

"What kind of domestic issues are you thinking of?"

"The immigration situation, education, crime, and the like."

"Yes. That sounds great."

"Thanks. I couldn't wait to let you know. Let me go now. I've got a few things to tend to before you get here. It's a nice venue. I think you'll like it."

"One more thing while I've got you. Frank Moreno called just before you."

"Hey, you are getting into the big time. Why did he call?"

"He spent the first few minutes giving me backhanded compliments on the campaign and letting me know I can't win. The second half he wanted to know my position on border security. He obviously didn't like what I told him. He says he wants me to let one of his staffers take me on a border tour."

"Hmmm. That's interesting. What didn't he like?"

"He pointed out that Donaldson wants to send troops to the border, and I disagreed. He called me naive."

"Wow. Let me make some phone calls to see if I can learn anything. I wouldn't worry about it."

"Okay. Thanks for the call, Jim. We should see you in about thirty minutes."

"See you then."

11

MAGGIE WAS excited to hear about the prospect of joint appearances with Sands. She felt that it lent credibility to Rick. She also thought that, in personality alone, Rick would blow him out of the water. She continued to be aggravated that so much under-the-table support was given to Sands. The man seemed to get fatter all the time; in television appearances he would sweat like a horse, and he always sounded like he was out of breath. She wondered if he would even live through a six-year term as senator, and then chided herself for thinking it.

They continued their campaign tour in the same way, although in bigger venues and with larger audiences. The spring weather also made it possible to plan more events outside. This helped financially, as large indoor venues always came at a cost. Maggie's singing continued to be a crowd-pleaser. They noticed that frequently people knew the entire song and would sing along with her. She loved that and would often stop singing through some of the refrains, holding her mic out toward the audience and letting them sing it without her.

While enjoying the attention that it brought Rick, she did ask to bow out of some of his appearances. Sometimes it was to handle something in the insurance business, and other times she just wanted a day off. Jim took a picture of Maggie playing and singing and had it blown up to a life size cut-out that stood by itself. On those occasions Rick would tell people apologetically that Maggie was not with them. There was always a disappointing groan. Rick would say, "Maggie really wanted to be here but just couldn't be in two places at the same time. Instead, she sent the next best thing." Jim would walk out onto the stage with the cut-out of Maggie, and they would play the recorded version of the song. The crowd would laugh and sing along. Rick would stand on the stage and mouth the words as the crowd sang the refrain. He figured that if they ever heard him sing, his poll numbers would drop sharply.

Over the next week, Jim was able to nail down the joint appearances. The two campaigns agreed on June seventeenth in Duluth, July second in St. Paul, and July ninth in Rochester. They agreed to the concept of a special emphasis on one topic for each date. They would focus on the economy in Duluth, other domestic topics in St. Paul, and foreign policy in Rochester. Both campaigns thought that approach would increase the likelihood that there would be media coverage. The state party office worked out a deal to have each event covered live by a different television and radio station.

Rick, Maggie, and Jim met for coffee at Connie's. Since it was a sunny spring day, Rick suggested they ride to the meeting on his Harley. He loved riding his motorcycle on a warm day, and they hadn't had much time for it, as busy as the campaign was getting. He especially enjoyed riding with Maggie. Having her snuggled up behind him with her arms around his waist made him feel like her protector. But a morning chill was still in the air, and she convinced him to drive.

Rick pulled into their normal parking space, and they walked in. The smell of the blend of coffee, fried potatoes, and sweet treats got their appetites flaring. Jim was already there and had a table. "Good morning Mr. and Mrs. Taylor," called out Jenny, the manager. They made their way to Jim's table, and she met them there with coffee.

"Thanks for working out the details on the joint events,

Jim," Rick began.

"No sweat! That's why I'm here. However, there are two things that I had to agree to in order to get this done," Jim explained.

"Uh-oh." Rick cringed. "What are they?"

"I had to agree that you would be the first to speak in each session."

"For all three?" Rick asked. "I guess he wants to have a shot at me or defend himself at the end so people will remember it. What else?"

"Sands said he would not agree to Maggie singing her song to close the event."

"What a wimp," Maggie said, rolling her eyes. Then she put on her best pouty face, "Is he afwaid of a widdow gurl?"

Jim cracked up. "I would be too if it was you!"

They all laughed, but then Rick frowned. "Maggie's song is one element that makes my message memorable. Isn't there anything we can do to push back on that?"

"We don't need to push back," Jim said coyly. "You each get thirty-five minutes. You'll just take thirty minutes and give the last five to Maggie."

Rick and Maggie both broke into big grins. "Yes!" said Rick, with a fist pump.

Jim changed the subject. "There's something else I wanted to make you aware of. I made some phone calls about Frank Moreno, Gerald Donaldson, and the southern border issue."

"You must have contacts in high places," Rick commented.

"Well, not so much, but that wasn't even necessary. On the campaign trail, Donaldson talks about sending the military to the southern border all the time. I understand Moreno is quietly pressing to have the sixty votes needed to authorize the use of military force against the Mexican cartels."

"They would need to be declared terrorist organizations before that could happen," Rick interjected as he took a sip of coffee.

Jim nodded. "That's the easy part. That can be done without

action from Congress."

"You know, on the surface, that sounds great as a solution to our problem. Just get a bigger stick," Rick began. "But I don't want to see a war on our southern border. Will he even solicit help from Mexico, or is he just going to invade their sovereign territory and start a war?"

"Well, I can't answer that, but if you really intend to visit the southern border, and I think you should, I would figure out a way to do it with someone who is more objective. I feel sure that Moreno would use the opportunity to manipulate you by showing you only what he wants you to see."

"I hear that. Well, at this point, I have no connections anywhere. I don't even know who I would reach out to in order to arrange a visit."

"We may be putting the cart before the horse here. Let's work on winning you the nomination right now, and if things look positive on that front, then we can figure out who can give you an objective tour."

12

ON THE thirteenth of May and the day before the Maryland primary election, Donaldson was in Baltimore preparing for a rally. He had the nomination locked up but didn't want to give the impression that he took the voters for granted. He wanted Frank Moreno to pay him a visit while he was there. He had nearly two hours before the rally, so he asked the senator to meet with him on his airplane.

Moreno's driver picked him up from his office, and they took the drive to Baltimore/Washington International Airport, now named for the late Thurgood Marshall. Moreno, used to people catering to him, was a bit put out by the request to make the hour-and-a-half drive in rush-hour traffic. However, Donaldson would soon be the President of the United States, so he figured it best to oblige him this request. The two had always maintained regular communication. Moreno had the power to make things happen, and Donaldson knew it. In fact, Donaldson had made certain promises to Moreno if he were able to help him get the authorization of military force in Mexico passed.

They pulled up to the fixed-base operation, and Moreno got out of the car. He was met by the Secret Service and escorted through the lobby of the facility that normally catered to small private aircraft, business jets, and the like. The scream of a business jet caused him to put his fingers in both ears. The smell of jet fuel permeated the air. *What a terrible place to be on a beautiful spring afternoon*, he thought.

Moreno climbed the stairs and was greeted by another Secret Service agent, who escorted him into the vice president's cabin. Donaldson stood and greeted him as an old friend with a handshake and a pat on the back. He asked the steward to get Moreno a scotch. He knew well what the majority leader drank and wanted to take good care of him. Donaldson motioned for Moreno to sit across from him at the small conference table. The steward brought his scotch and they were left alone.

"How are the Senate races looking, Frank?"

"It's much closer than we thought it was going to be," Moreno replied. "John Tucker's resignation in Nevada hurt us badly. Governor Randall's appointment of someone from his own party to temporarily fill the vacancy was a death blow for us on that seat. It was going to be challenging anyway, but now we are running against an incumbent, and that will likely put a nail in the coffin."

"I'm sure you're right. I'm beginning to feel uncomfortable with Minnesota's open seat. I met Weimann's hand-picked successor when I was there last week, and let's just say I wasn't impressed. I also had several people ask me if I had heard about Rick Taylor's campaign. People seem to be excited about him. If he pulls a surprise victory out of the hat, will he play ball with us?"

"There won't be any surprises there. I've arranged for some big names to campaign with Sands over the next couple of months. Taylor's bump in the polls is purely based on his wife's little campaign song. That excitement will die down, and we'll get Sands across the finish line to the nomination. Our party has the general election wrapped up there, and we'll have our sixtieth vote comfortably in the bag."

"Frank, if Taylor wins, will he play ball on the authorization of military force?" Donaldson repeated.

Moreno paused and sipped his scotch. "I talked with him the other day about the border crisis. He recognizes the need for action but currently isn't on board with using the military. Don't worry though, I've already planted the seed to help him understand that he needs to rethink his position. I'm going to get him down to the border with one of my people. He's still brand new to this game, so I'm sure he will be impressionable."

Donaldson frowned. Looking down at the table and then back up to Moreno, he said, "I'm telling you there is excitement in Minnesota over Rick Taylor. I expect you to make sure he is positioned comfortably on my side. Moreno, you've got a lot riding on this. Don't let me down."

"Don't worry, Mr. Vice President. I wouldn't be in the position I'm in if I couldn't be very convincing."

"I sure hope that's true."

They spent the next thirty minutes discussing strategy for winning more Senate seats, then Donaldson thanked Moreno for making the trip. He said, "Why don't you stay and attend the rally with me?"

"Mr. Vice President, I would love to do that, but I have a meeting in an hour and a half. Maybe another time."

"Okay. Thanks again for making the trip."

As Moreno walked out of the aircraft, Donaldson headed to the back passenger cabin and waved for Stan Kauffman to join him. He closed the cabin door and looked at his friend and right-hand man. "See what we can do about getting a campaign together to remove some of the polish from Taylor's image."

Kauffman looked at Donaldson and nodded.

13

JUNE THE seventeenth came upon them faster than they thought possible. Rick had spent hours expanding his focus on economic issues. He and Jeff Sands were in the same party and not that far apart on most things, but Rick had only heard vague ideas coming from Sands. Jim and Rick had worked up a strategy to focus on the details. Rick shouldn't get so deep into the weeds that he sounded wonky, but people needed to gain confidence that he really understood the economic factors. If he could set the stage with sharp information and help voters understand the issues and why they were important, one of two things would happen when Sands spoke. He would either sound like he was just spouting generalities without understanding, or it would sound like he was leaning on Rick's presentation to make his points.

Even though Maggie had been thrilled at the prospect of Rick and Sands being seen side by side, she felt that nervousness in the pit of her stomach for her husband. It wasn't that she lacked confidence in him, but she knew that any mistakes in front of a large crowd and a larger TV audience would be magnified significantly. Also, with the obvious bias of the party, who knows what they might orchestrate to make Rick look bad? She just didn't trust them.

They drove to Duluth on June 16 and went to a couple of shopping centers to meet with prospective voters. They introduced themselves, asked questions about their concerns, and generally tried to leave them with a positive impression on Rick's grasp of the issues and his personal integrity. One gentleman asked, "How do you think we should address the border crisis? It seems that Donaldson's idea of sending troops is the right one to me."

"I understand how you might feel that way," Rick said. "I hear that a lot. However, I don't believe we have to put our troops in harm's way to solve the border problem."

Rick saw a bit of skepticism in the man's eyes. "I want you to know," Rick said, "that I plan to visit the border soon, and I will absolutely have an open mind. I assure you, nobody wants to solve that problem more than I do. I will do the right thing whether it's popular or not with my party or the president."

On the morning of the event they arrived early, as they always did. It was in a park with a bandshell on one end. It was a hot day, and Rick was glad that the event was planned for the morning. He and Sands would both be drenched in sweat by the time they spoke. The current temperature was seventy-nine degrees with no breeze. Mosquitoes were thick in the humid air. Rick wore a long-sleeve shirt and covered himself with bug spray. He smelled like a chemical factory, but at least he wouldn't be swatting at bugs during his speech.

People started to gather, setting up lawn chairs in the grass. Party volunteers were helping people get situated so as many people as possible could comfortably see and hear the candidates. A large speaker system had been set up, and Rick could hear someone saying "one, two, three, check, check."

Jim had some staffers carefully pack Maggie's guitar inside a large box that contained flyers and paper fans with Rick's name and picture on them. This way, he thought, there would be no squawking by the Sands campaign if they guessed the plan. He could tell that Maggie was more nervous than usual. Her hands were fidgety, in and out of her pockets, and she couldn't stand still. He finally said, "Why don't you just go out there and visit with some folks? Relax a little and enjoy yourself. I'll join you in a minute." Her genuine joy at meeting new people was one of the things he loved about her.

Rick mingled a bit but was also asked to do a couple of interviews with television reporters. He was comfortable in these interviews because he didn't try to impress anyone. He answered the questions as clearly and honestly as he could.

The park was just off Lake Superior, and a breeze developed just before the event started, helping to relax people. The state party chairman thanked everyone for attending and introduced Maggie. Once in front of the mic, she was engaging and confident as always. She introduced Rick to enthusiastic applause. Once he began talking, he settled into the role, and the words came just as planned. His voice grew scratchy as he spoke. He sipped at a bottle of water and finished his talk in twenty-eight minutes, leaving plenty of time for Maggie to sing.

"Ladies and gentlemen, I recognize that we are in a little different format today than in our normal campaign stops. I was given thirty-five minutes for my presentation, and I still have a few minutes left. I don't want anyone to go home disappointed, so I am turning over the last five minutes to my wife Maggie."

The look on Sands's face made it obvious that he had not expected this. His campaign manager left and ran across the park to find the state party chairman to cry foul. However, the crowd was already giving Maggie a thunderous round of applause, and there was nothing anyone could do to stop it.

Maggie carried her bottle of water up and placed it on the shelf under the podium. She settled on her stool and looked out to the crowd. "Wow, I've never sang to such a big group before. Just a minute." She reached under the podium and grabbed her water. "I sure hope you enjoy this because you're intimidating the sweat out of me!" Her hand trembled slightly as she took a big swallow.

The crowd laughed. Maggie took a deep breath and began to play. On the first verse, nobody sang along. It was almost like the crowd was trying hard to be polite to Jeff Sands. But by the second verse, they couldn't help themselves. A large contingent in the audience sang along with the refrain as loudly as they could. At the end, the crowd stood up and applauded. Maggie glanced at her watch and jumped up, her guitar in one hand and her water in the other. Before she left the stage, she said, "You must promise me that you're going to give Mr. Sands your careful attention. Then, study the issues yourself and vote! Vote, vote, vote!"

The crowd agreed with a cheer.

The announcer introduced Jeff Sands and he stepped up to the mic. "It's not fair I should have to follow that!" he half-shouted with a smile on his face. Most people heard it as good-natured and a nice compliment to Maggie.

As he made his campaign presentation, his shirt became soaked. Sweat poured from his face. He mopped his face with a handkerchief, drank his entire bottle of water, and asked for more. His speech fell flat, just as they had hoped it would. He spoke in generalities that made him appear to either not really know what he was talking about or not believe the crowd could understand more than the pablum he was spouting. When he spoke about inflation, he talked about how much money the current administration was spending and provided some examples of the spending that he said had fueled inflation. "Remember how Mr. Taylor explained that inflation is caused by the government printing money and borrowing to pay for projects they want to implement? That's exactly what our government has been doing."

Rick and Jim made eye contact at that statement. Jim winked and gave him a faint smile.

Finally, the first match-up was in the books. Rick, Maggie, and Jim met privately after the event was over for a late lunch and debrief. "The guy looked terrible," Maggie said in wonder. "Don't you think that will have an impact on the voters?"

"Yes," Jim said in a somber tone, glancing back and forth at them. "I'm afraid it almost went too well."

Rick's eyes widened. "Too well. What what does that mean?"

"I could see a six or seven-point swing in the polls in the next week. That would put you at around 42% and Sands at 49%. We're becoming a threat."

"Well, that's what we're trying to be, isn't it?" Maggie asked impatiently.

"Yes. However, if they are serious about sticking with Sands, which I believe they are, we are about to see some nastiness coming our way. Rick, I should have asked you this early on, but … do you have anything in your past that they could scrounge up and throw out there to damage your reputation?"

Rick gave the question no serious thought. "There's nothing that they can drum up on me. I'm clean."

"I'm glad to hear that. You'd be surprised what these people can come up with, whether it's true or not."

14

IT WAS as if Jim was clairvoyant. Rick got a phone call from him while at home preparing for his upcoming speech on July second.

"What can you tell me about Lisa Manly?"

"What? Who is Lisa Manly?"

"Someone who told a political hack that she worked for you six years ago and ultimately decided to quit because of sexual harassment. I just got a call from a KNNG reporter that asked for a comment before they put it on their five o'clock news."

Rick stood up from his office chair and began to pace. He felt a tingling in his head. He stared out the window at the lawn that needed to be mowed. "Wait a minute, she did work for us. She did a decent job and left after a year or so for what she said was a better opportunity. I never engage in ... no, I've never *engaged* in sexual harassment, period. She's lying!"

"Rick, I know this is uncomfortable for you, but I have to ask. Did you ever come on to her or make a pass at her?"

"No!"

"Did you ever engage in, let's say, playful rhetoric back and forth that could have been perceived as sexually nuanced?"

"No! She reported to Maggie," Rick countered. "As far as I can remember, I greeted her and treated her in a friendly manner just like all the other staff." He turned from the window and felt his eyes go blurry for a moment. Then he began to pace again.

"Did you ever talk about politics? Were her political views different from yours?"

"I don't talk politics at work. I keep office conversations about work, other than a polite greeting and asking people how their weekend was. I don't recall any discussion with political substance."

"Alright, we need to try and get a jump on this. I need you to … no, I need Maggie to get to your office and see what she can learn. First of all, she needs to find out if any female employee has ever felt uncomfortable from your behavior. Second, we need to find out if anyone who worked with her remembers anything about her politics. Was she a hardliner? What might be her motive for saying something like this?"

Rick stood over his desk and jotted some notes down but was shaking his head while doing so. "I'm going to do this myself. I can't put Maggie in that position."

"Listen to me," Jim said calmly. "You're upset, and rightly so. This is very personal to you, and you want to clear your name. I understand. But if you tackle this, it could come across as intimidating to your staff, or at least others could claim that. Maggie gives it a bit of an arms-length feel. People who have met or seen Maggie love her and could never perceive her as intimidating. Rick, this is important. It isn't fair —it's politics."

Rick sat down and leaned his elbows on his desk. Holding his phone to his ear with his right hand, he rested his forehead in his left. "Okay Jim, I get it."

"We'll get through this, Rick. Oh, and one more thing. Have Maggie ask if anyone would be comfortable doing an interview to defend you."

"Got it. We'll get on this today."

"I'll call the TV reporter back and issue the denial. Rick, one other thing. We don't want to attack Lisa Manly in any way. That will only make matters worse. See what Maggie can learn and call me when it's done."

"Jim, this is the part of politics I hoped to never have to experience. I hate it."

"I do too. Let's just nip it in the bud and continue."

"I guess there's nothing else we can do."

Rick's conversation with Maggie did not go much differently. She didn't believe it. She became angry. She also had no idea what would motivate Lisa Manly to do such a thing. Rick had to be the calming voice this time and encourage her to meet with the staff and be as objective as possible. They decided to go one step further. After Maggie spoke with staff, their manager Ben Wolfe would give them another opportunity to say anything that they may not have felt comfortable saying to Maggie.

Fortunately, nobody from the office was on vacation. Considering the time of year, this seemed like a miracle. The only thing that came up during the meeting was ire. One of their agents, Julie Merten, knew Lisa pretty well. They would go to lunch together and talk about personal things. She remembered that Lisa knew Jeff Sands. It was a bit of a fluke that she remembered it, but she recalled Lisa saying that she and her husband had worked on Sands's campaign for the Board of Regents.

They briefed Jim as soon as Maggie got home from the office. Based upon what they had learned, Jim was not too concerned. "I think this should blow over pretty quickly," he said. "I'll be careful not to disparage Mrs. Manly but let the reporter know that she worked on the Sands campaign previously and suggest that there could be a motive there. I'll reiterate your denial and say that anyone who has worked with you knows that you would never do such a thing. I would guess they may send someone to your office."

"I don't want our people to start getting hounded by the media. How can we avoid that?" Maggie asked.

"Well, I'm not sure that you can. Maybe you can coax your manager to make a statement, if asked. The bottom line is, if a reporter wants to, they will find your employees and approach them. I would just tell them that whether they choose to speak to reporters is totally up to them. Let them know that you're not asking them to defend Rick. It's their choice."

"How should I address this on the campaign trail? What about the joint event in St. Paul?"

"Give me some time to think it through. We'll talk tomorrow."

#

Jim's response to the television reporter had apparently put enough doubt into the news editor's mind that they did not run the story that evening. The charge was made public in a newspaper op-ed piece the next morning, though. Julie Merten stepped forward and asked if she could write a letter to the editor refuting the, in her words, 'bullshit' that she had read that morning. Wolfe thought that would be a good idea but suggested they do so carefully so that neither Rick Taylor's nor the company's image would be tarnished.

Julie drafted her letter and Ben made some minor edits with her approval. Maggie, Rick, and Jim reviewed it as well and would have loved to interject some additional comments but thought it best to have Julie send it just the way it was. They wanted to make sure they couldn't be accused of influencing the employee or putting words in her mouth. Based upon the limited distribution of the charge made against Rick and the letter to the editor refuting its validity, they decided not to address it publicly unless he was directly questioned about it.

The St. Paul joint event went off very much like the first. There was more media than there had been before, likely because the polls were showing that Rick was closing the gap. A reporter did ask Rick about the accusation in the op-ed. He told him that he would never do such a thing and suggested that they look at the letter to the editor another employee had sent.

Jeff Sands looked terrible. He was limping when he arrived. Rick walked over to him and shook his hand. "I see you're limping. Did you twist an ankle?"

"No, it's just a bit of gout flaring up. It's happened before. Painful, but it will go away if I watch my diet."

When discussing domestic issues, there was greater opportunity for Rick to distinguish himself from Sands. On the border issue, Rick explained his reluctance to "blindly follow Gerald Donaldson into a war on the southern border. I grant you that his approach sounds like an easy fix. However, do you really think the cartels can be fought by the military without invading Mexico, a sovereign nation? Are you all right with invading Mexico and the loss of life that will result in such a war, when it has been proven that the border can be sealed without it?"

Sands voiced his strong support for moving the military to the southern border and dealing with the cartels once and for all, wholeheartedly embracing Donaldson's campaign rhetoric.

Rick, Jim, and Maggie met for coffee afterwards to discuss the event and concluded that their strategy was still working. As they prepared to leave, Rick asked, "You're going to join us for the St. Paul's Fourth of July parade, aren't you?"

"I wouldn't miss it," Jim said. "Somebody's got to follow you two celebrities around and hand out flyers."

Maggie put her hands on her hips and cocked her head. "The campaign staff and volunteers have grown to the point that you don't need to do that anymore."

"Sure, I may have some help with it, but why should I miss all the fun?"

Rick patted him on the back. "Great. Be at River Road and Mississippi at eleven."

"No, that's where the parade ends. It starts at River Road and Osbourne at one," Jim corrected.

"That's right. We're getting there two hours before the parade starts and will walk the route north to the starting point. That way we can meet and spend time talking with plenty of people as they gather for the parade."

A big grin came across Jim's face. "You're getting good at this!"

"You know, I really enjoy it. In the past month, I've seen ten thousand faces, and I've liked them all."

"That's an attitude that will get you elected," Maggie said.

15

On the Fourth of July, they met at the agreed-upon point and worked the crowd. It was a perfect day for a parade, though the thermometer was already approaching eighty degrees when they started north. Lawn chairs were set out but were mostly empty as people milled around.

The street was wide and black from having just been sealed. There were no parade sounds, only the muted sound of people greeting each other along the side of the street. Rick and Maggie wore shorts and t-shirts with American flags on them. Jim wore slacks and a polo. They once again lathered up with a combination of sunblock and bug spray. Maggie had thought to bring a pocket-sized pack of damp wipes so they could get the crud off their hands before they started approaching people with handshakes.

Maggie walked on one side of the street and Rick on the other. Because the crowd was still thin, they took the time to step over to the sidewalk and grassy areas where the people were gathering to introduce themselves. Some people knew who they were and some didn't. A few were excited to see them and told them when they had attended a rally. Maggie heard "I love your song" often. Jim and several volunteers followed them both, smiling and handing out flyers. When the parade began, they noted that Jeff Sands was also there, still limping. He was set to walk a few blocks in front of them. By this time, both sides of the street were teeming with people, shoulder to shoulder, behind chairs that were all full now. The sound of high school bands tuning their instruments filled the air. Some of the horses there to pull floats were leaving droppings along the way, and the familiar smell wafted through the air.

As they began walking along, Rick and Maggie switched sides of the street. They shook hands and greeted people, more quickly this time. Volunteers were handing out squishy squeeze balls to children; each one had "Vote for Rick Taylor for US Senate" printed on it.

Ten minutes into the parade, everything stopped. Rick and Maggie assumed it was just a pause created by some glitch along the way. However, the pause continued. The band in front of them stopped playing. The spectators were poking their heads out into the street to see what was happening up ahead. Rick was visiting with some people in the crowd when he began to hear the chatter working its way back. "Jeff Sands fell," one person said. "I heard he collapsed," corrected another.

As soon as Rick heard that he whistled to get Maggie's attention and waved her over. He grabbed her hand, and they jogged forward along the parade route until they got to the point where a small huddle of people gathered. Rick let go of Maggie's hand and approached carefully and respectfully. He whispered to a person watching, "What happened? Is he okay?" The person looked at Rick, then shook his head and motioned with his eyes as if to say, *Look for yourself.*

Rick peered around the man and saw Sands lying on his back in the street with two EMTs kneeling beside him. They had a portable oxygen mask over his nose and mouth. One technician was tearing open a syringe and grabbed a bottle of something to inject Sands with. A woman was kneeling near his knees, crying and holding his hand. Sands's campaign manager knelt next to her with his arm around her. Rick had seen her before at the joint events. She was Sands's wife, Emily.

The crowd nearby was totally silent. They stared, somewhat

in shock but also fascinated by the work of the technicians. Rick looked around at Maggie and gave her a look that said, *This doesn't look good.* Maggie was standing back with both hands over her mouth, tears pouring down her cheeks.

Realizing that there was nothing he could do there, Rick turned around and took Maggie in his arms. He turned her to face away from the scene. Neither spoke. Rick looked down the street and noticed an ambulance was driving up the parade route. He let Maggie go and ran toward it, asking people to move out of the way so it could get through.

Jim stepped forward and put his arms around Maggie and hugged her. "Let's move back; they have things well in hand." Maggie didn't respond, only followed Jim's lead. They walked back and stood behind a float that was stopped in the middle of the road. Maggie swiped at her eyes.

Rick watched as the EMTs hurriedly put Sands into the ambulance. As it drove away, he looked around to find Maggie. Not seeing her, he asked some people in the crowd, "Did you see where my wife went?" Someone pointed back to where she was standing with Jim. Rick jogged over and put his arms around Maggie again. "Jim, how can we get out of here?"

Jim looked up and down the street and side to side. "Not easily," he said.

#

Rick announced that he was suspending his campaign activity for a time, at least until after Jeff Sands's funeral. Maggie was deeply disturbed by all that had happened. They completely stopped talking about the campaign. She mostly stayed home and kept herself busy catching up around the house.

Eight days after Sands's death, a funeral was held at St. Augustine Catholic Church. Rick and Maggie planned to go, but that morning Maggie felt sick. Rick attended the funeral without her. As he stood in line to greet the family, he wondered what he should say. He had barely known Sands at all and had never met his wife or grown children. As he approached Jessica Sands, he said what he hoped people would say to Maggie in this situation.

"I'm so sorry for your terrible loss, Mrs. Sands. I didn't know Jeff well, but I've heard only positive things about him. I was heartened to hear of his Christian faith. I rejoice to know he is in the arms of his Savior, even now. I pray that God gives you and your family strength and comfort."

Emily Sands smiled. "Thank you so much, Mr. Taylor. Your prayers are greatly appreciated. I also want to thank you for the campaign you have run. I never heard of you attacking Jeff, even politically. That speaks volumes to me about your character. I wish you luck with your campaign. I will pray for your success."

A tear ran down Rick's face as he listened. He was truly touched. This was a thoughtful woman to share such kind words in the midst of her grief.

"Thank you," was all he could say.

<h1 style="text-align:center">16</h1>

STAN KAUFFMAN was at Donaldson's house for a meeting with the vice president and his campaign manager. The campaign travel had wound down. Other than a few trips to New York for media appearances, Donaldson was able to stay in and around his home ahead of the August 23 convention.

Donaldson had announced his selection of Marjorie Whittington as his running mate. Whittington was not his choice. He had some friends talk with her about the border issue to see if she might be on board for his border plans. She expressed her willingness to go along with the president's desire to deploy the military at the border, but when asked to assess the relationship between the United States and Mexico and the future of that relationship, it became obvious that she was not aligned with Donaldson. However, some of the battleground states appeared to be closer than they had anticipated, so he was talked into naming her to the VP spot. As governor of Pennsylvania, the campaign hoped that she would deliver the state in the general election.

"Ger, it looks like we're stuck with Rick Taylor as our nominee in the Minnesota race," Kauffman remarked.

"Yeah, that's sad. I would rather have had Sands, but we'll just have to win over Taylor to our way of thinking," Donaldson said smugly. He paused. "We sent Sands's wife something, didn't we?"

"We did. The president also sent someone to attend the funeral."

"Good. He was too young to be taken. He obviously had a lot of physical issues."

"If it was going to happen, it's better that it happened now. Imagine the potential problems if he died in office, and the governor had to appoint someone temporarily. We'd have a newbie to draw into the fold and have to do it all over again the following year," Kauffman said.

"Not so. I have our Minnesota governor in a pretty good place right now. If need be, I'm sure I could have chosen the person to replace him."

"That's good to know," said Kauffman, thoughtfully. "I'll get to work with Frank Moreno on getting Rick Taylor in line."

"By the way," Donaldson said, "let's reach out to some of our better contacts in the FBI and CIA. I want to get some intel relating to Mexico."

Kauffman paused and looked at Donaldson's campaign manager, not sure of what he knew. "Okay," he said slowly. "Do you want me to set that up?"

Donaldson looked at his campaign manager too. "Chris, can you please give us a few minutes?"

Chris Thomas was used to this. He walked out of the study in search of the bathroom. Once Thomas was out of earshot, Donaldson said, "Yes, but before you do, let's talk strategy. Do you think I should meet with them together or individually?"

"Is this about what I think it is?"

"Yes and no. I want to see if we can get a briefing by the CIA on corruption in Mexico. I'm not going to bring them in on the plan, just tell them that I have some thoughts on seriously expanding trade with Mexico, and I would like to understand how deep the corruption runs and whether there is anyone in government and military ranks who can be trusted. I want the FBI to tell me what they have regarding Mexico's federal and state police forces."

"I would meet with them separately," Kauffman said

immediately. "That makes it appear more like a favor being asked to get yourself prepared for the campaign and taking office. You don't want to give the impression that you're planning something specific."

"That's what I was thinking too," Donaldson agreed. "I'm thinking we will need to know who to target and who can and cannot be relied upon as we make our plans."

"Are you sure you want to bring the CIA into this now?"

"Listen, Stan, I'm not going to get into details of the plan with them. But we need to give the planning team and your AI folks plenty of lead time to be ready for our rollout. I want to kick this thing off within one hundred days of taking office. That puts the second phase a few months after that."

"Alright. I will get individual meetings on your schedule as soon as possible. I'll set up the FBI first."

"Sounds good," Donaldson agreed. "Let's try and get it done within the next couple of weeks."

"Got it, boss," Kauffman said as he stood.

17

IT WAS as if heaven had opened the floodgates. After Sands's death, the party communicated with Jim daily. Most of the political action committees began donating to the Taylor campaign, and the focus moved toward winning the general election.

With plenty of resources and advisers available to him, Rick was able to set up a fact-finding trip to the southern border in late July. He made it clear that he wanted a full, unvarnished look at the situation and, if possible, to meet with top level Border Patrol officials to discuss their view of strategies needed to fix the problem.

Rick's visit reinforced his view that the military was not the answer to address the illegal immigration problem. He was horrified to see the massive effort required just to document people as they came across the border and direct them to some other location in the United States, typically those that were sanctuary states or cities that would welcome all migrants. Nobody he talked to thought using the power of the military was the way to go. "What are we going to do, shoot them?" mused Kirk Banfield, the Chief of the Del Rio Sector. "There are three things that have to happen to stop the flow. First of all, the Administration needs to change their rhetoric and policy to indicate that the border will be secured and that people need not even attempt the trip. Second, every person who comes across that border must be sent home, period.

Finally, there needs to be an improved process for people requesting asylum to do so from their own countries," he said forcefully. "Now, how does the military help with those things?"

"What about the border wall, technology, and all that?" Rick asked.

"Those will be a big help in dealing with the few that want to get in without detection. These are the worst of the worst. They will be your drug traffickers, human traffickers, and terrorists. By finishing more of the border wall and utilizing the technology, we can detect and catch them effectively. That is what we're here for," he said. "Now we're just punching people's tickets as they walk through the gate. We have very little time to focus on anything else."

#

As the only person left running, Rick got 96% of the vote for the nomination to be the candidate for the general election. On August third, he got a phone call from Frank Moreno, congratulating him on winning the nomination. "Let's get that border visit scheduled so you can gain a better understanding of that issue."

"Thanks, Senator Moreno, but I was able to arrange a visit a couple of weeks ago. You're right—a person has to see it to believe it."

"I told you that I would arrange that visit. Do you remember that?" Moreno was actually yelling at him.

Rick wondered, *What kind of nerve have I struck there?* He didn't know if Moreno was pissed because he thought his power had been usurped, or if he was upset because he hadn't been able to control what Rick saw. "I know how busy you are, Senator Moreno. An opportunity presented itself, and I took it. Did I do something wrong?"

There was a pause. This time Moreno was more controlled when he spoke. "No, you didn't do anything wrong. I just hope you didn't waste your time. I wanted to make sure you got the full briefing with the right people."

"I think I did. I was able to sit down with Kirk Banfield from the Del Rio Sector."

"See, that's what I mean. Banfield is an idiot who doesn't know what it will take to properly address the problem. He's living in the past," Moreno said with a nastiness that surprised Rick. "Look, Rick, when you come to Washington, and I have full confidence that you will win that seat, you need to understand that in order for us to make progress toward our goals, we need to work as a team. You'll want to take advantage of the knowledge and experience of those of us who have been here for a while. You'll see the benefits once you get your feet on the ground."

"Yes, well, I think I need to focus on the campaign right now. I appreciate your call, Senator."

"Frank, call me Frank. We are soon to be colleagues working for our constituents in the great state of Minnesota."

"Thank you, Frank."

"Rick, you let me know how I can help. I will be in town a few times during the August recess, so if you would like me to campaign with you a bit, let's schedule it. I'll have one of my staffers reach out to you to set something up."

"Thanks, Frank. Why don't you have them call Jim Gunderson. He and his team handle all of the scheduling these days."

"Jim Gunderson. Okay, Rick, Jim it is. Oh, and Rick, maybe I can even get Donaldson up there to give you a strong endorsement. I'm sure he'll have great coattails for senatorial candidates with his big presidential victory."

"Thanks a lot, Frank," Rick said again. "I'll brief my team."

As he hung up the phone, Rick was bewildered by the conversation. Moreno flies off the handle at him, puts down the Del Rio Sector chief, and then behaves like his best friend with all sorts of promises of support. He called Jim and briefed him.

"That's great! If Donaldson makes a stop here and sings your praises, that would be pure gold. Right now, the presidency is his to lose. His endorsement would be valuable."

"I hear you. I'm just a bit put out by Moreno's behavior. He comes across as a control freak. I'm not going to D.C. to be controlled."

"Well, that is going to be your issue to deal with. Mine is to get you to Washington. Once you get there, it's all on you."

"You're a big help," Rick laughed. "But just the same, there is something I'd like you to consider. If I win this thing, I want you to come with me. I will need an adviser who hasn't drunk the Kool-aid yet."

"Rick—"

"Don't answer me now. I just want you to think about it."

18

Dᴜʀɪɴɢ ᴛʜᴇ general election, the Taylor campaign continued to do live events in the same way they had in the primary. However, now the distinction between the two candidates was much clearer. There were a lot of voters from the other party who absolutely did not want Rick Taylor to win the Senate seat. Rick had anticipated this, but the personal attacks still gave him pause. The hateful rhetoric on social media was the worst, so he stayed off of it and allowed his campaign staff to handle it.

Rick was ahead in the polls by early October, and Maggie's song continued to make him the memorable candidate for those who didn't follow politics closely. Yet, she gradually seemed to lose interest in the campaign. She didn't travel for the personal appearances as much and started spending more time with their business. They used her recorded music, and people still bought and downloaded the song online. It had made national news and, as a result, people from all over the country were downloading the song. Jim even got a few calls from other like-minded candidates wanting to use the song in their campaigns. After asking Maggie's permission, he agreed. He knew that the wider the distribution, the more downloads and the more money into the coffers.

After Sands's death, money was not an issue. They advertised a good bit and always included the refrain from the song at the end of each ad. Moreno did attend one event to campaign for Taylor, and Donaldson made a visit and enthusiastically endorsed him later in October. Rick Taylor won the election handily and became the Senator-elect for the state of Minnesota.

The next two months were a whirlwind of activity. Rick was able to coax Jim into accepting a position for at least a year. He didn't want to be in Washington all the time, so he was made a deputy chief of staff with the primary responsibility of managing Rick's Minnesota office. He would spend a couple of weeks a month in Washington.

Rick was still getting used to the fine office he had received. It was smaller in size compared to other senators, but the furnishings were beautiful. The deep blue carpeting was downright luxurious. His large mahogany desk had what appeared to be hand-carved caps on the corners and didn't have a scratch on it, and the wall-to-wall, mahogany credenza and book display case gave the impression of statesmanship. He was offered the opportunity to fully redecorate to his own taste, but he didn't feel right about coming in and immediately spending money wastefully.

Rick knew that he wanted some pictures of Maggie, so he scrolled through images on his phone and found one that he especially liked of her standing on Angels Landing at Zion National Park. It was from a vacation they had taken the summer before he got into the Senate race. Her smile reflected her sense of accomplishment from hiking, and the look in her eyes showed a sense of wonder at the beautiful surroundings. He had the picture blown up and placed in a frame. He placed some other pictures in smaller frames, including one of her playing and singing at one of his campaign events.

He wished she had taken more of an interest in helping him with the space. She would know just the right objects to put on display to represent Minnesota. He had to enlist his new assistant, Carla, to procure some artwork by a painter and a sculptor, both from Minnesota, as well as some ancient tools on loan from the Chippewa tribe from the Red Lakes area.

They also hung a print of a painting of Father Hennepin discovering Saint Anthony Falls and included memorabilia from Minnesota's professional sports teams.

It was difficult trying to put together a staff in D.C. when Rick had no political connections there besides Frank Moreno, but Senator Weimann, the man he would replace, invited him to Washington in November and introduced him to his own staff. During the month of December, Rick and Jim interviewed those staffers who had an interest in working for Senator Taylor. They were careful in their hiring, however, since Rick's approach to the office would be different from Weimann's. Rick was going to work for the agenda that he promised on the campaign trail, even if it didn't necessarily follow the party line. Weimann had always been a *go along to get along* kind of guy. They wanted staffers who weren't afraid to push back against their peers in other senators' offices.

The more people he talked to, the more it became obvious to Rick that the US Senate was run by staffers. Senators were, for the most part, the face of the team. They got the attention and the glory, or criticism, and everyone else did the work in the background. Weimann's Chief of Staff Sandra Dellingham was anxious to go to work for Rick. She and Weimann had not seen eye to eye for some time, and she had considered leaving his staff had he not retired. She viewed Rick as a breath of fresh air—someone who had his priorities straight.

Rick met with Moreno and got a feel for the top issues for the next couple of years. This helped him to focus on hiring legal aides who were knowledgeable on those issues. He also got a few resumes from students looking for internships. He, Sandra, and Jim interviewed a young woman named Lily Gadis who was in graduate school studying artificial intelligence. Sandra advised that they not interview her, suggesting that her education may not be relevant to the position. Rick insisted because he knew that AI was in the news often, and he needed to learn more about it. When they met with Lily, he asked her Sandra's question. "Your education is in high tech. Why would you want an internship that puts you in the bowels of

Congress dealing with administrative minutiae?"

Lily smiled. "Senator Taylor, I've read that the median age in the Senate is over sixty-five years of age. I've also heard that some senators don't even use email. It seems to me that this is a fertile field in which to explore ways that artificial intelligence can be used to improve decision making."

"So you believe that a college intern is going to stroll in and change the United States Senate," Sandra remarked skeptically. "What application do you see for AI in Congress?"

"The opportunities are endless. Decision making requires information. With AI, every man and woman in Congress can gather more information more quickly than people here can possibly imagine."

"So is that what you believe is needed in the Senate? High-speed library access?" Jim asked.

"Well, yes. However, the greatest contribution people like me can make is to save you from yourselves."

"I beg your pardon," Sandra interjected.

"Yes, ma'am. I'm sure the wheels are already turning to utilize AI in both the House and the Senate. When people see the power and potential of AI, there will be a real temptation to turn everything over to it. One of the things I'm focused on are the unintended consequences of AI applications. As people learn about the capabilities, they may become giddy and think it's the low-cost solution to everything. Why do we need people? We'll let AI make the decisions."

"And there's danger in that." Rick said.

"Yes, sir. Computer software, at present, has no values. Let it make all of your decisions for you without human involvement, and you're going to create a sociological mess, perhaps even risking war in a geopolitical context. There is no replacement for human judgment."

Rick liked what he was hearing, and he liked Lily's confidence. "Well, I don't see how we can run this place without you," he said, reaching out to shake her hand. "Welcome to the Taylor team."

Rick had a full team in place by January. The staffers had to learn the rules of the Senate and other administrative minutiae that boggled Rick's mind. Government inefficiency aggravated him, but he knew that he couldn't change that by himself. He simply tried to learn the rules and follow them.

The freshman senators were required to attend a briefing by their party leadership in the Senate. Moreno's emphasis in the meeting was party unity. He explained that "everyone needs to vote together in order to make progress." He likened it to a baseball team. "We all need to work together on the goal that is before us. Compromise will be required of everyone, or else we will be unable to accomplish much of the work you all came to do." He looked at Rick Taylor as he said, "We are all focused on the same goals. Acknowledge that there is more than one way to get there. We need you to get on board the train that is leaving the station."

Rick and Maggie talked regularly on the phone when he was away. Mostly, she caught him up on what was happening in the business, and he talked about all of his new experiences in this jungle called Washington, D.C. He noticed that Maggie listened but didn't really seem interested anymore. They had talked about buying or renting a home near the Capital if he won the election, but now Maggie didn't seem anxious to move. Her mood just seemed to be down.

Rick tried to probe into her change of heart. He sensed something was wrong, but she denied that anything was upsetting her. She offered words of encouragement for him to do the good job that he wanted to do, but she thought her time would be best spent with the business in St. Cloud. Rick rented a small apartment in Virginia without Maggie's input. She seemed too busy to make it to Washington to search for a place, although she did attend the swearing-in ceremony.

19

GERALD DONALDSON became president by a wide margin of votes. The work he had to do in preparation for his new administration dwarfed that of Rick Taylor. The difference was that everything seemed to go smoothly for him since he had ample friends in the Senate to push through his cabinet nominees without delay.

Throughout the general election and prior to his taking the oath of office on January 20, Donaldson's rhetoric on defending the border with the United States military became sharper. His voters loved it because they were simply tired of the open border that the last administration had allowed. With Donaldson being the only candidate offering a solution, they bought into it.

Rick Taylor was still not convinced. He was sure that most voters didn't understand that there were alternatives. Though it made no difference, Rick voted against approving Donaldson's director of national intelligence, secretary of defense, and director of the CIA. His vote was merely a demonstration of his objection to the border policy of the new president, but it did nothing to stand in the way of the president's nominees taking office.

Watching Rick Taylor's votes in the Senate, Donaldson and Kauffman got the message. In the early days of Donaldson's administration, the two met to review actions that would be needed to accomplish the promises for Donaldson's first one hundred days.

"At our first cabinet meeting, I need the secretary of state to issue his declaration that the nine largest Mexican cartels are 'Foreign Terrorist Organizations,'" the new President told Kauffman.

"Are you sure you want to go that route in designating them as terrorist organizations?'

"Sure. All we need to do is have the secretary prepare an administrative report and present it to Congress. If Congress doesn't act to challenge it within seven days, it's done. I like the thought of having Congress on board."

"There's one thing that concerns me with that. If we do it that way, suddenly anyone providing material support to cartels will be guilty of a felony. Once that becomes known, it could seriously hurt the cartels' ability to get people through undetected. They need people on our side of the border to move them into the interior."

"I don't follow."

"If we get too aggressive right away, we are going to curb the flow too much too soon. People will begin to doubt that we need the military on the border. However, if you designate them terrorist organizations through an executive order, we can still freeze their assets, but it will be less restrictive in terms of US citizens who are working for the cartels. It will also let suspected cartel members cross the border more easily. It will show your voters that you are taking action, but it will also keep the flow going so that the military can be justified. The American people won't know the difference."

The president simply looked at Kauffman thoughtfully, a hand cupping his chin.

Kauffman added, "You can still have the secretary of state prepare the paperwork to send to Congress but hold it until the right time. Then, he can submit it, so that the stronger designation is in place before asking Congress for authorization to use military force in the region."

"I wish we could ride on the 2001 AUMF that Congress granted after 9/11, but this is so different that we would surely be challenged on it," Donaldson observed. "Okay, prepare an executive order, and I'll sign it next week.

"Talking about getting an AUMF passed, it looks like Moreno has not been able to corral his new senator from Minnesota," Donaldson continued. "Moreno is sure that he will be needed to allow such an authorization vote to come to a vote in the Senate. I was afraid of this; it is going to be a huge detriment to the plan. I don't know, Stan; this is a hard nut to crack. I'm not sure how we can overcome Taylor's opposition. Tell me you have some ideas."

"Mr. President, we are one vote away from initiating the plan. We may never be in this situation again. This is worth fighting for. When this is done, you will go down in history as the man with the foresight to enlarge the United States of America. You will pull millions of people out of poverty and significantly improve our ability to be self-sufficient. I will fight with everything I have to get the votes."

"Well, we'll have to get Rick Taylor on board," Donaldson said as he looked Kauffman in the eye.

"I've about had it with Rick Taylor already," Kauffman sighed. "I'm going to take this on personally. You are about to make the most significant contribution to the United States of America since the signing of the Constitution. No wet-behind-the-ears senator is going to get in the way."

PART 2

SURVIVING SUCCESS

"Bran thought about it. 'Can a man still be brave if he's afraid?' 'That is the only time a man can be brave,' his father told him."
– George R.R. Martin, *A Game of Thrones*

20

Senator Taylor worked hard to ensure he and his staff got up to speed on the work of the Senate. They established priorities for gathering information on various issues. There was plenty of documentation on everything, but Rick also wanted his aides to meet with those of other senators to gain an understanding of all sides of each issue.

Aides would then brief Taylor, Sandra Dellingham, and Jim Gunderson, who would then have a discussion to establish Rick's position and assign an indicator of strength to it. A ten would indicate Rick saw no possibility that he could change his mind on the issue. A one would indicate that he was on the fence and might be easily persuaded to change, under certain circumstances. When they discussed the use of the military on the border, Rick was a ten. He had heard all the arguments, and none had changed his mind. He would not vote to authorize the use of military force against the cartels.

Rick agreed with Donaldson's executive order that declared nine cartels to be terrorist organizations. That is what they were. They were not tied to Middle Eastern terrorists, but they were guilty of human trafficking and the selling of children and adults to be put to work as sex slaves, and they were involved in the killings of tens of thousands of Americans every year with fentanyl-laced drugs. They helped terrorists and migrants from many adversarial nations get across the border. Rick shuddered to think of their intentions.

He would rather have had the Secretary of State submit the designation to Congress so it had more teeth to it. It was a head-scratcher that this president who wanted to use the military against the cartels did not want to place a mandatory stop to cartel members crossing the border or declare it a felony for people in the United States to act in support of what they were doing.

As they came up to speed on various issues that might be taken up by the Senate, Rick found that he agreed with colleagues on his side of the aisle on most of the issues. However, he was dumbfounded by the way in which they blindly followed President Donaldson on his border policy. He hit it off with a second term senator from West Virginia and felt he could speak openly with him. "I don't understand why no one in our party has doubts about Donaldson's plan to use the military on the border. Am I the only one who believes that we can seal the border without putting our men and women into direct conflict with the cartels?" Rick asked.

"I don't know anyone who expects us to go to war. We will send a really strong message to the cartels and the Mexican government if we give the president the authorization to attack the cartels. That alone will scare the daylights out of them," replied his colleague.

"And if it doesn't?"

"It will. Besides, some of us will be up for election in a couple of years. If we don't support the President in this, we could lose our seats to the other side."

Rick wasn't convinced by this argument. He had heard it before. He was certain that the military shouldn't be brought into the mix unless the government intended to use them. He knew the border could be secured by other means.

A few of the more tenured senators would put a hand on his shoulder and caution, "You really need to rethink your stance on this. It's a viable way to stop the illegal immigration problem. That's what we're after, isn't it?"

Senate Majority Leader Moreno had set up multiple

meetings with Rick to persuade him to change his position. One afternoon, Moreno set the meeting in Rick's office as a gesture of camaraderie. They sat at a small, round conference table in one corner. The meeting followed the same path as it normally did. Moreno gave his team talk, and Rick talked principle. The Leader became frustrated, as always. "Look, Rick, this thing is bigger than you and me, and I would hate for you to end your young political career by fighting it. The voters want it."

"The voters don't understand the alternatives, Frank. If Donaldson wanted to, he could accomplish this without the use of the military. It's not worth risking the lives of our soldiers."

"Look, the US military would make mincemeat out of these cartels. We would have very few casualties."

"One is too many."

"I'll tell you what, if you work with me on this, I'll put together a package to support Minnesota projects that our constituents will love, and I will give you full credit. Your support will be locked in. I'll also promise to give you significant financial support when it comes time for your next election."

"I didn't come here to sell my soul to the highest bidder. There are serious principles here, American principles that I don't want to lose. We are well on our way to losing them now. I want to put a stop to it. I would think you would too."

Moreno's face reddened, and he stood. "Don't you dare lecture me about principles. I am the Senate Majority Leader, and I work with the president to establish principles by which we will live. And don't you forget it!" He stormed out of the office, slamming the door.

21

MAGGIE TAYLOR'S depression continued, even as she focused on her work at the business. She was able to put on a pleasant face for the staff and customers, but at home she felt nothing but lethargic. She didn't play her guitar or piano; she didn't sing. Money continued to roll in from downloads of her song. She authorized all of it to go to Rick's campaign fund for the next election.

She never did go to Washington, D.C. after the swearing-in ceremony. Rick tried to make it home two or three times a month for a few days at a time, but early on he was overwhelmed just getting up to speed. He stayed in Washington most weeks, even when the Senate was not in session.

He continued to ask Maggie what was the matter when they talked by phone. She told him nothing at all. She said she probably was just coming down from the excitement of the early campaign when they were working so hard to introduce Rick to the voters of Minnesota. She missed that. He suggested that she see a counselor. Perhaps it was a chemical issue, he told her. She ignored his advice, saying, "I'm just coming down from all that election activity. This will pass."

In late April, Rick spent five days in Minnesota. He used some time in the office with Jim and hosted one town hall meeting to gather input from his constituents on a few issues. The rest of the time he stayed home with Maggie. She had planned to take some time away from the office with him, but it seemed she had to go into the office every day for one thing or another. He noticed that she was drinking more wine than usual. It was not uncommon for her to have a glass of wine before dinner. Now, the one glass turned to two and sometimes even three.

One afternoon while Maggie was at the office, Rick called Hank Jerod, an old college buddy.

"Hank, this is Rick Taylor. How the heck are you?"

"*The* Rick Taylor, the Senator from the great state of Minnesota?" Hank chided. "It's great to hear your voice! To what do I owe the pleasure?"

"I wish I could say I just called on a whim, but I wanted to tap that incredible reservoir of experience of yours."

"Oh?"

"I hope you don't find this too personal a question, but I heard that you'd had a bout with depression a few years back but were able to lick it. I hope I heard right."

"You did indeed. Are you feeling down yourself?" Hank asked.

"No, it's not me, but my wife, Maggie. I'm sure you're going to say being married to me would send anyone into depression," Rick said, trying to keep it light.

Hank did not keep it light. "It's not a fun thing, Rick. I'm glad you are trying to find some help."

"I guess I'm at a loss, though. I don't even know if it is depression."

Hank explained some symptoms of depression and told Rick that it might appear differently in different people. "The best thing you can do is to help her seek professional help. There are therapists who can help talk people through it. If it seems to be related to a chemical imbalance, a psychiatrist might be helpful. They can diagnose and prescribe medication."

After asking a few more questions, Rick thanked Hank for his openness and willingness to help an old friend. That night, he spoke frankly with Maggie. He told her he noticed her change in demeanor and that he was concerned for her.

"Oh Rick, I'm sorry. Please don't worry about me," she said. "I guess I get lonely for you, but at the same time feel that I'm needed at work right now."

"Well, let's get you to Washington."

"I'll get there soon. In the meantime, don't worry about me. I'll try to put on a happier face," she said with forced cheer. "You've got plenty else to worry about."

"Maybe you should talk with a therapist to help you get things sorted out."

"Really, I'm fine, darling. I'm sorry you've been worried. Trust me, you don't need to be concerned." Rick didn't believe her, but he left it for the time being.

A couple of days later while still at home, he received a morning phone call. "Good morning, Senator Taylor, this is Stan Kauffman. I'm sorry to bother you while you are at home, but the president asked me to give you a call."

"Oh, really?" Rick replied with a bit of a laugh. "I had no idea that I was even on the president's radar."

"You sure are. He continues to be very concerned about the attacks that the Mexican cartels are making against us. I don't have to tell you about the impact they're having on our citizens and migrants alike. In the next few weeks, the president will be requesting Congressional authorization for the use of military force in defense of our country. He wants to make sure you are on board."

"Thank you for your call, Mr. Kauffman, but you will have to tell the president that I am *not* on board. I do not want to send our troops into harm's way when there are other options that will effectively seal the border and all but stop that activity."

"Senator Taylor, the Senate will need sixty votes to bring the motion to the floor for a vote. Yours would be the sixtieth vote. President Donaldson needs your help on this. Perhaps there is a way for us to structure this vote that will make it more palatable to you."

"Nothing will make expending American lives needlessly palatable to me."

"Look, the president understands that you are a principled man and one who is with us on 90% of his agenda. Why don't we set up a process that will allow you to make your voice on this matter very clear to your constituents, one that will enable you to vote to end debate and move the bill to the floor? Of course, at that point you could vote against the bill itself if you felt the need to."

Rick couldn't believe what he was hearing. All the focus was on making it appear that he is principled while allowing him to, in essence, permit something that he strongly opposed. "Mr. Kauffman, perhaps you don't understand me. I am going to do everything in my power to avoid the use of military force on our southern border. Please pass that along to the president."

"Listen to me, Taylor. There are a variety of ways to accomplish what needs to be done if you choose not to support the president on this. There will be hell to pay. Do you understand?"

"No, Mr. Kauffman, I don't. Is that a threat? Perhaps you could clarify that for me."

"You will have total clarity when this is over." The phone went dead.

While Rick hated such confrontation, he was proud that he had stood up to Kauffman. He refused to be intimidated, even by the President of the United States and his cronies.

After the call, Rick called his own chief of staff in Washington. "I think I might have created a problem for myself," he began. "I just told Stan Kauffman to go to hell, in no uncertain terms."

"Rick, what are you talking about? Tell me you haven't made an enemy of the president," Sandra said.

"He threatened me if I didn't vote to allow the authorization for use of force to go to the full Senate for a vote."

"They must believe you are the sixtieth vote. What did he threaten you with?"

"He left that unclear, but I can tell you he was really pissed. He hung up on me."

"Oh, Rick. I wish you had called me. You may have just made yourself one-term senator."

"I don't give a crap about this Senate seat. If I can't follow my conscience, I might as well resign. Now we know that they need my vote. Now I know I have the ability to stop it. And stop it I will."

22

THE NEXT Tuesday, the president gave a prime time address to the nation. He gave his normal rationale before notifying the country that he had asked Congress to authorize the use of force against Mexican cartels and any entity that assisted them in facilitating the illegal entry of people or drugs across the southern border of the United States.

The most extreme voices on the right were ecstatic. The majority of citizens of the United States were encouraged that something was finally being done to seal the border. The news media clamored to interview Rick because they had learned that he was the sixtieth vote needed to move the authorization forward for a final Senate vote. All forty senators on the other side of the aisle were lined up against the president on the issue. Rick's refusal to cooperate would bring the vote against to forty-one, in essence filibustering the bill indefinitely.

The secretary of state submitted an administrative report to Congress officially designating the Mexican cartels and those helping them as foreign terrorist organizations. The week went by with no action by Congress, so the new, stricter designation occurred on its own.

The bill was introduced by Texas Senator Roy Chandler, Chairman of the Senate Foreign Relations Committee. Rick calculated that it would be debated for a few weeks in Chandler's committee before being voted on. He knew that it would get the approval of the committee and would go to the full Senate for debate. In order for debate to end and go to a vote, sixty votes would be needed. That is where Rick's vote would kill it.

Rick worked in Washington for three more days but took the next week off to go home. He needed to at least try to help Maggie get through the difficult time he knew she was having.

He sat in first class for the first time on his flight to Minneapolis/St Paul. Utilizing the on-board wifi, he did some Internet searches on his iPad. He searched for symptoms of depression and read several medical articles that came up. It seemed that Maggie had the classic symptoms. He searched further to explore treatments. By the time he started reading about managed care for people with mental and emotional struggles, he was convinced that he would have to do whatever was necessary to get Maggie to see a therapist or a psychiatrist.

He needed a professional that they could work with on this. He didn't know if it would be better for her to be in Washington with him or to continue living alone and working. He made a commitment that he would not leave Maggie again until she was getting the help she needed, even if that meant resigning from the Senate. He had set up a meeting at the house with Jim the following morning, but other than that his focus would be completely on Maggie.

It was June fifth, and spring was giving way to summer. It was warm and new full leaves on the trees made for a beautiful and picturesque countryside. As he drove to St. Cloud, the new beauty was a welcome relief after the long, cold winter weather. The farm fields no longer appeared as lifeless fields of black dirt, and the small corn stocks were now tall enough to cover the soil with fresh, green life. He was happy to be home and looked forward to a ride on his motorcycle. Maybe Maggie would enjoy that too.

He pulled into the alley and clicked the garage door opener to enter their back garage. The two-car garage that was connected to the house was not long enough to fit his truck, so unless he had a lot of places to go, he typically parked in the back garage. Before he went inside, he stopped and pulled the cover off his Harley. He hadn't ridden in ages. He wondered if it would even start. He threw his leg over the seat, inserted the key, turned it to the 'on' position, and hit the start button. The battery had power. It growled a few times, but the engine cranked up pretty quickly. *Yes!* Rick said to himself. *Maybe we can go for a ride this afternoon.*

He went out the rear door of the garage and walked up to the back door of the house. He tried the door, but it was locked. Retrieving the key from his pocket, he unlocked the door and went inside. "Honey, are you home?" Rick called out. He got no response.

He looked through a stack of mail briefly and walked into the living room. Maggie sat on the couch with wet streaks running down her face. There was a glass of wine in front of her and a bottle next to it. He couldn't tell how much wine was in the darkly tinted bottle. She looked up at him with tears in her eyes.

"Maggie, what's wrong?" Rick rushed to the couch and got down on one knee in front of her. He pulled her close to him and hugged her. "What's the matter, sweetie? What is it?"

Her tears dampened the shoulder of his shirt. Her crying became audible as she sat there limply in his arms with her own arms hanging by her sides. She smelled of alcohol.

He pulled away a bit and looked at her. "What's the matter, Maggie?" he repeated. "Whatever it is, we'll work it out together."

Her face contorted into an unrecognizable form, and she cried out loud. She shook her head no and said in a barely audible voice, "I killed him." She sobbed. "I killed him."

Rick's heart sank. He couldn't understand what she meant. Had she been in an accident? "What are you talking about? What happened? Tell me if you're alright."

Maggie continued to cry like a child who'd fallen. "Jeff Sands. I killed Jeff Sands."

23

"**WHAT ARE** you talking about? No, Jeff Sands had health issues. You saw how badly out of shape he was. He was overweight and had trouble breathing," Rick said, trying to keep the tremble out of his voice. "Why would you blame yourself for something like that?"

She shook her head. "No, that's not why he died. I killed him."

Rick didn't know what to say or do. Now it appeared that Maggie was having some sort of breakdown and was nearly psychotic in her ranting. "No, sweetheart. We were both there, remember?"

Maggie's look changed instantly. "Stop it, Rick. You don't know." Now her tears had been replaced by a forceful glare with fire in her eyes.

He had never seen her this way. He wasn't sure what to do or say to calm her down. "What don't I know?"

"You don't know what I did. I gave Jeff Sands a drug that I thought would make him sick, but it didn't. It killed him."

Rick, still kneeling on the floor in front of her, sat back on his heels on the floral area rug. He was holding her hands now. They were damp and clammy. He didn't know whether that was from tears or perspiration. He had to help her keep talking it out. "I'm sure you're mistaken, Maggie. What could you have possibly done to cause Jeff's death?"

"I gave him a drug, something that would cause acidosis in his system. I thought it would make him sick, that's all. Then I thought he would leave the race for health reasons."

"You never met the man directly, so how could you have given him a drug?" Rick countered. "Sweetheart, you're not thinking clearly."

The look came back; her eyes were blazing. "You're not listening to me," she snapped.

"Okay, when did you give him the drug?"

"I put it in his water at the two joint events," she said, sobbing again. "When I went up to sing both times, I took a bottle of water with me and changed it out with the bottle that was under the podium."

Now Rick felt sick. He didn't know if it was because he believed her or didn't believe her. *Keep her talking,* he thought.

"I don't see how you could do that. He would have realized that his bottle had been opened before. Wouldn't the drug make the water look differently? A different color, or cloudy or something?"

"They were white pills. I crushed them up and put them in the water bottle. The water was in those blue bottles."

"Maggie, you're not making sense. How would you know how to make him sick?"

Her look changed to one of frustration. "Three years of pharmacy school?" she said in a questioning tone, reminding him of her expertise and letting him know she didn't appreciate him not knowing the answer to his own question.

Now fear began to grip Rick. He got up off the floor and paced. "You don't know that what you did killed him. There must be another explanation. It was a coincidence. Maybe there were other bottles under there, and he didn't drink from the one you tampered with," he rationalized. "He would have known if the bottles had been opened."

"I fixed that too. I cut the bottle out from inside an unopened cap from another bottle. Then I removed the cap and cut the little ring off of a full bottle of water. After I put the crushed tablet in the water, I screwed the intact cap onto that bottle so it looked like it had not been opened." She gave a little whimper, looking down at the floor.

Rick's face reddened. His mind was racing. *She did it. She actually killed the guy*, he thought. *If anyone finds out, they will assume I was part of it.*

"Maggie, I can't believe it. You really did this? You murdered Jeff Sands?" His voice was raised now.

She burst into tears again. "I didn't mean to. I just wanted him to get sick. I wanted you to win. The party was ignoring you. I wanted you to win so badly."

"Great, Maggie! So now we're both going to prison for the rest of our lives for conspiracy to commit murder!" He put his face in his hands. "Oh, Maggie, what have you done?"

"No, it was me. You didn't know about it. You had nothing to do with it."

"And who's going to believe that?" Rick barked.

Maggie stood crying and walked to him to put her arms around him. He brushed her arms away and went to the coat closet and pulled out his leather jacket. "I've got to get my mind around this," he said. "Oh my good Lord, forgive her… Oh my good Lord—."

"I'll be back. I need some time to think," he said as he walked out the door, not looking back at her.

He slammed the door behind him and walked across the backyard to the garage. He slapped the garage door opener and the door rolled up slowly, making him impatient. He grabbed his dusty helmet and threw his leg over the Harley. He started the bike, twisting the grip to give it gas. As he did, the rear end of the big cycle spun around. He put both feet on their rests and gunned it, heading down the alley and out to the street.

He barely paid attention to where he was going. He just needed to ride. He needed to figure this out. *It couldn't be as bad as it seemed, could it?* He got onto the freeway and headed toward Minneapolis. He wasn't sure where he was going; he just needed to think. As he drove, he still couldn't comprehend what had just happened. *Could he be headed for prison? Was he going to have to watch his wife be charged and fight to ensure he didn't take her punishment with her? Should he resign from the Senate?* There were too many thoughts racing through his mind to make sense of any of them.

After forty-five minutes he saw the freeway exit ramp for Maple Grove, on the eastern edge of the metropolitan area. He needed to decide where he was going. He needed to think. Suddenly it came to him. One of his favorite places in the world was the Boundary Waters between Minnesota and Ontario, Canada. He had attended camp there in his junior high years and been a camp counselor three summers during high school. He could get away there. Really get away and think.

His mind was drawn back to Maggie. He felt guilty for running out on her the way he did. His emotions were confused. He was so angry at her he could spit, yet his heart reached out to her. He loved her. He pulled off the freeway in Lino Lakes on the northern edge of the city. He stopped at a gas station and filled the tank and moved the bike to the outer edge of the lot. He walked into the convenience store and bought a premade burrito, heated it in a microwave, and tried to eat it. It burned his tongue, and he let out a small grunt before he could stop himself. The clerk glanced at him, and he looked away. When he got back out to the Harley, he laid the burrito, still wrapped, on the seat.

He stood looking around at his surroundings. This was obviously a bedroom community for the Cities. There was a field next to where he stood, but across the field was a residential area with some large homes. The sound of the freeway filled the air, but he was sure that if he went farther into the community, he would find a quiet place. Nice people would live here. These were his constituents. What would they say if they learned that Jeff Sands had died at the hands of Maggie Taylor?

Maggie. He glanced at his watch and realized that he had been gone for over two hours. He needed to call her. He took his phone out of his pocket and auto dialed her.

"Hello," she said meekly.

"Maggie, I'm so sorry. I shouldn't have left you the way I did. Please forgive me."

"I know I shocked you. I'm sorry I was in such a state when you got home. You're headed north, huh?" she said, still quiet.

"How did you know that?"

"You gave me permission to track your phone, remember?"

Rick chuckled. "Yes, I did. I'm glad I did. I want you to always know where I am."

"When are you coming home? Or maybe I should ask, are you coming home?"

"Oh yes, sweetheart. I'll absolutely be home soon, and we will tackle this together. So now I know why you've been struggling with depression."

"Uh-huh. Rick, I can't tell you how the guilt has eaten away at me.

"Rick?" she continued. "I'm going to turn myself in."

Tears began to stream down Rick's face as he listened. "Okay, sweetheart. We can do it together. I'll be with you all the way." His voice cracked.

"I'm sorry, Rick. I'm so sorry. I don't know what I was thinking," she said. "I don't know what I was doing."

It sounded like Maggie was now holding it together more than he was. "We'll handle it together," he sobbed.

"When will you be home?"

"I need time to think. I'm going to ride up to the Boundary Waters and spend a couple of nights there. I'll call you. You can see where I am on your phone."

"Okay," she said. "And Rick?"

"Yes, sweetie?"

"I love you."

"I love you too. I'll see you in a couple of days."

#

As Maggie tapped the red button to end the call, she realized she was standing in a nearly dark house. She turned on the lamp next to the couch. She picked up the wine bottle, poured what was left down the sink, and tossed the bottle in the recycling bin. As she set the wine glass by the sink, the doorbell rang.

She looked at her watch. It was nearly nine-thirty. She couldn't imagine who was ringing the bell so late. Maybe a neighbor.

She walked to the door, wiping her face with her sleeve. She opened the door. A stranger asked, "This is Senator Taylor's house, isn't it?"

"Yes. Why do you ask?" Maggie cleared her throat and did her best not to show that she had been crying.

"I'm so sorry to bother you so late. Is the Senator in, please? Sandra Dellingham has been trying to reach him. It's a matter of national security."

"Oh my," Maggie said as she opened the door and made a motion to come in. "I'm sorry. Rick isn't here. But his phone is working, I just talked to him. He's on his way to the Boundary Waters for a couple of days."

"The Boundary Waters?"

"Yes. Uh, he needed some downtime, so he went up there for a couple of days. As a matter of fact, let's see," Maggie said as she grabbed her phone. She swiped the screen, and it opened by facial recognition. She went to her tracking app. "I track him with my phone," she said, somewhat embarrassed. "Right now he's on I-35 northbound near Forest Lake."

"Thank you, that's very helpful."

24

RICK FELT fatigue setting in as he approached Duluth. He pulled into a small motel that had only a few cars in the lot, paid for a room, and immediately got into bed. He didn't think about Jeff Sands, he didn't think about the Senate, but he did think about Maggie. He hoped she was okay. He was asleep within minutes.

The next morning, he decided to sleep in and let the morning sunshine warm everything up a bit before his ride. He put a 'Do Not Disturb' placard on the outside door handle and went back to bed. He woke up again at eight-thirty, still thinking of Maggie. She had sounded like she was gaining more control when they'd talked again last night. He felt guilty for selfishly taking off for a few days and leaving her alone in that state, but he knew he could be of more help to her if he had some time to think things through. He picked up his phone and called her again. The phone rang four times and went to voicemail. He didn't leave a message but figured he'd try again when he got to Ely.

He dressed and walked over to the office and found a fruit basket. He took an apple and a banana and poured himself a cup of coffee. He wandered back to his room and finished his breakfast. He felt grungy—he had no toothbrush and no change of clothes. He'd pick up a change of clothes in Ely.

A person could get easy access to the Boundary Waters from

116

Grand Marais, east of Duluth along the shore of Lake Superior, but all of the time he had spent here had been in and around Ely. He put five dollars on the little desk in the room for the housekeeper, then left. Getting off the freeway at Duluth, he took the state highway north.

Once away from the city, he was in one of the most remote areas of the state. The area north of Lake Superior was the most beautiful and unusual place Rick had ever experienced. As he rode the two hours north, he was surrounded by gentle hills and towering rock formations as well as streams and lakes. All were interspersed within the million-plus acres of forest. This was what riding a motorcycle was all about.

The air was still cool, but the sun shone brightly and warmed him. He felt hot in his leather jacket, but as soon as he unzipped it he would be cold again from cutting through the chilly air at fifty-five miles per hour. Fortunately, the full-face visor on his helmet protected his face and eyes. He had been pleasantly surprised when he stopped for gas the previous night to find his riding gloves in his coat pockets.

He had set his cruise control to fifty-five miles per hour so he could enjoy the beauty of the area. Cars passed him from time to time, speeding and in a rush to get wherever they were going. That didn't faze him in the least. He just wanted to take it all in. One car remained behind him. It was nice to see others who were not in such a hurry, enjoying the scenery.

Although he always enjoyed riding, his mind kept returning to Maggie and the trouble she was in. He tried to think logically if there was any way to verify what had caused Sands's death. He assumed Maggie knew her stuff regarding drugs and that whatever she had given him would have impacted his health. *But would it kill him?* She thought it would just make him sick. How could he find out what actually killed him? Was there a way to find out? HIPAA laws required that medical information like that not be shared without consent. If the person was deceased, he presumed that Emily Sands would have to provide consent. *How could he possibly approach Sands's wife about the cause of his death?*

Another thought crossed his mind as he rode. There had been no suspicion of foul play in Sands's death. Whether Maggie was responsible or not, nobody suspected anything. *Maybe it was just a matter of helping Maggie learn to live with this.* He'd have knocked himself in the head if he hadn't been riding. How could he think like that? Could he actually go on in life, thinking they had hidden the real cause of a man's death? His murder? *NO! Well, maybe. It was unintentional, and there is nothing that can be done about it now. NO!* he countered in his mind.

He realized as he approached Ely that he couldn't remember the last hour of his ride. He was at his destination but had no recollection of how he had gotten there. He pulled into the lot for the Boundary Connectors Outfitters, where he had rented canoes before. They used to carry cargo pants with zip-off legs, sweatshirts, and t-shirts. If they still did, he could get some comfortable clothes and change before renting a canoe. He could also pick up some water shoes and a toothbrush.

25

SHE SET her cruise control to maintain a quarter-mile distance behind Taylor. She had hoped to catch him at home last night, but this would work out just as well, perhaps better. Once she had located him at the motel, she was able to buy gas at the station next door and get three hours of sleep in the car. She had gone forty-eight hours and more without sleep when she was in training for special ops. Three hours would keep her sharp for what she had to do. She made a phone call to check in.

"It's me."

"How did it go?"

"Unfortunately, he wasn't home. I was able to learn that he took a trip on his motorcycle. It seems he wants to spend some downtime in the Boundary Waters. I was able to take care of things there and locate him where he spent the night. I'm following him now. I actually think this will fit the narrative nicely. Grief-stricken and remorseful, he goes to a remote place and takes his own life."

"I wish it had been cleaner, but it sounds like you've got it under control. Are you sure nobody saw you last night?"

"It was after dark, and their place is surrounded by trees. It was no problem. I parked in the alley. He even left his back garage door open and his truck unlocked for me. Guess what I found?"

"No guessing games, just tell me."

"I found a gun in the console of his truck."

"Oh, that's perfect. You should be careful, though. Once this is done, everything should fall nicely into place." He hung up.

She stayed well behind Taylor, even as they approached Ely. She would have no trouble locating him. She could track where he was going. He pulled into the parking lot of an outfitter and parked his cycle in a designated motorcycle spot. She followed.

Rick swung his leg off the Harley and stood there and stretched a bit as he looked around. There were about thirty vehicles in the lot, but few people. He knew that most of them were out on the water someplace. That's why they'd come. He saw one woman getting out of her car, and out of the corner of his eye he saw another pulling a double-bladed kayak paddle out of hers.

He pulled his phone from his coat pocket and saw that he had missed a call from Jim and another from a number he didn't recognize. He started walking toward the outfitter's store, tapping the screen on his phone to check for messages. Rick jumped when he heard a woman's voice say, "Senator Taylor?"

He hadn't realized anyone was that close to him, although he wasn't surprised that a stranger would talk to him. After his campaign and election, some people around the state recognized him. They would often just say "Hi, Senator Taylor," but some would approach him and want to talk about a particular issue. When he looked up from the phone, he saw a woman with dark hair and complexion just a few yards away approaching him.

"Yes, good morning," Rick responded politely.

She walked up close to him and tipped her open handbag toward him. Inside he saw the woman's right hand with a latex glove on it, holding a gun. It looked similar to the compact 9mm gun that he owned. She gripped the gun tightly. Her finger was not resting on the trigger guard; it was on the trigger. His heart sank to his stomach and began to pound. He looked up at the woman with his mouth half open. He stopped breathing mid-breath.

"Senator Taylor, I would appreciate it if you could walk with me to my car. I have some very important business to discuss with you."

The other woman in the parking lot was walking directly toward the front door of the shop, well away from where Rick and the woman were standing. She glanced at the two of them and did a double-take. A big grin came to her face, and she immediately backtracked and walked toward them.

"Patrick Taylor, is that you?"

Rick was startled. He looked up at her but said nothing.

"Patrick, you really don't remember me? Cindy Potter from Ely Youth Camp."

Rick looked back at the first woman, who wore an alarmed look on her face. She closed the handbag and backed up slightly away from him.

Looking back at Cindy, he smiled and said, "Cindy, it's so great to see you. I can't tell you how many times I have thought about our good times at camp." Now Rick had a decision to make. He closed his eyes briefly. Could this interruption provide an opportunity to move away from the woman with the gun? She could just pull it out and start shooting. She could kill them both. He took the gamble.

"Cindy, you look great. Have you got time for a cup of coffee? I'd love to catch up with you." He looked back at the other woman, who had turned and was walking away. He grabbed Cindy by the arm and said quietly, "Let's get inside. That woman just pointed a gun at me."

Cindy looked up at the woman, who was now getting into a white Honda. His old friend seemed totally flustered, but she walked along with him. They entered the rustic building through the center doors to an open lobby with a concrete floor with access to the camping store and the canoe rental service with restrooms and lockers inside. Once inside, Cindy pulled away from Rick and looked him in the eyes. "What is going on? Do you know her?" She squinted her eyes at him as if she were gathering as much information as possible before deciding how to proceed.

Rick's heart was racing. He looked through the windows of the wooden door they had just come through and saw the woman back out of her parking place. She drove toward the exit slowly and then stopped. He said, "No. I was just heading for the store, and this woman calls me by name and walks up and tips her purse toward me. Inside her purse she has a gun in her hand. She wanted me to follow her to her car."

They both looked outside again. The woman had not left. She had parked her car in another space and was getting out again. Cindy took Rick by the arm and said, "Let's go."

Still stunned by what was happening, Rick followed as Cindy quickly walked him out the back door and onto the gravel shoreline where a kayak and several canoes were staged, half in the water and half on the shore. "Here, let's take this one," she said. She picked up the front of one of the canoes and pushed it fully into the water. "Get in," she barked. Her eyes were riveted on him. Her expression and the tone of her voice left no doubt that this was a command.

He tried to step directly into the canoe from the shore, but the boat rocked side to side from his weight and clumsy movements. He nearly capsized it, but he stepped into the water with his left foot to steady himself in time and got back in, squatting quickly to lower his center of gravity. "Hurry up!" Cindy hollered as she lifted her end of the canoe again, which had bottomed out with Rick's weight. She pushed it deeper into the water.

He sat on the middle bench facing her. Having considerable experience canoeing in his younger days, he realized he should move to the end seat, opposite her. With his hands on the edge of the canoe, he scooted backwards, still facing back toward the shore. Cindy laid the paddle in the boat, grabbed a backpack that was lying on shore, and threw it in as she stepped into the stern and pushed off with her back foot. Her smooth and deliberate action maintained balance in the center, showing she did this a lot. Rick hadn't been in a canoe since his junior year in high school.

Cindy grabbed the paddle and forcefully pushed off the bottom of the lake to move the boat farther into the water. Being a bit of a purist, she would seldomly touch the lake bottom with the paddle, but she wasn't so concerned about form at the moment. She pushed off several times until the lake bed was too deep to reach and started paddling as fast as she could. One side and then the other, she worked the double paddle. She dipped deep into the water and close to the boat in order to get maximum power. Rick sat there, still shell-shocked by what was happening but impressed by this woman's command of the situation and handling of the canoe.

When they were about fifty yards off shore, Rick saw the woman come out of the back door and walk toward the edge of the lake. "There she is." He knew enough about guns to know that she could not hit them from where she was. Her right hand with the glove now held a cell phone, which she seemed to be fixated on.

Cindy turned in time to see the woman back away from the shore and walk into the boat rental section. She continued her quick pace, and the boat moved swiftly through the rippled surface of the water. The only sound Rick heard was the slight splashing of the water being displaced by the bow of the boat as it cut through the lake and the tinkling of drips trickling into the water from each blade after Cindy's powerful strokes.

"Is she renting a boat?" she wondered out loud. They were through the inlet now and about to turn left out of sight when they saw a young man talking with the woman and pointing to the kayak that was still on the bank.

"Shit!" Cindy said. "If she gets a kayak and knows what she's doing, she'll be able to move a lot faster than we can." Already thinking ahead, she recognized that they could portage a canoe much easier than an individual could a kayak. There would be plenty of opportunities to portage from lake to lake to gain some advantage. Cindy stopped paddling and strained to twist the midsection of the double paddle. Nothing happened. She banged the middle part of the paddle on the edge of the boat and twisted again. Finally it broke free, and she was able to unscrew the unit, making two paddles.

"Sorry, but I wasn't planning for this, obviously, so I don't have the handles to screw back into the blades. It will be a challenge to work these with ragged open ends, but we both need to be paddling if we have any chance of staying ahead of her."

"We need to call the police," Rick said as he carefully turned around on his seat so he and Cindy would be facing the same direction when paddling.

"I'd rather we get some distance between us and her first. Hopefully we know this place better than she does."

26

WHEN JIM Gunderson arrived for his meeting with Rick that morning, nobody answered the door. He rang the bell several times, then stood on his toes and peered into the garage door windows. Maggie's car was there, but Rick's truck was not. He walked around to the back to see if Maggie was outside. He had never walked their property before and was not aware that they had a second garage in the back.

He could see no one around, so he walked to the back garage and looked into the window of the back door. The garage door was still open, and Rick's truck was there. He returned to the front and walked around for a few minutes. He tried to call Rick but got no answer. Maggie didn't pick up either. He walked up to the front door again, and this time he pulled open the screen and banged on the door with his fist. Still nothing. He reached down and twisted the doorknob. It was unlocked. He peeked his head around the door and called out, "Rick? Maggie?"

He stepped fully into the house and immediately saw the legs of a woman lying on the floor, the rest of her hidden by the sofa. "Maggie?" She was lying on her back and had a small hole above her right eye. Blood had pooled on the area rug behind her head. Her lifeless eyes were open. Jim covered his mouth with his hands. He was at a loss of what to do. Should he walk through the house and look for Rick? Tears welled up in his eyes. He had never experienced anything like this before.

He decided it would be best if he left the house and called the police. He dialed 911 and was connected with a dispatcher. He told her what he had found and where he was. He heard tapping on a keyboard as the woman calmly asked him questions. Who he was, where he was, did he know the deceased woman, and several other questions that he thought, under the circumstances, could have been handled when the police arrived. The dispatcher kept him on the line for ten minutes until the first police car arrived.

The officer walked through the home. Rick was nowhere to be found. As he waited, wringing his hands, Jim watched as multiple cars were dispatched to Senator Taylor's home. Reporters and others who monitor dispatch frequencies quickly recognized that some sort of story was developing at the senator's home. After a couple of hours, the chief, who had arrived on the scene quickly, made a statement.

"This morning, at approximately nine-thirty, a friend of the family found a body in the Taylor home. We're not able to provide further information at this time."

The reporters shouted questions, "Is it Senator Taylor? Is it Mrs. Taylor? Do you suspect foul play?"

The chief said, "I'm sorry, we have nothing more to add at this time. We will try to update you later in the day if we can."

When the police questioned Jim, they asked him if he knew where Senator Taylor was and if he had seen a gun or Maggie's cell phone when he had been inside. The officer who questioned him acknowledged to Jim that they had not been able to find either. The police went to all of the neighbors' homes. No one they found at home had seen or heard anything.

A different officer approached Jim later and told him that the questioning officer should not have given him that information relating to the gun and cell phone. He was asked not to share it with anyone, or it could hinder the investigation. He was asked not to speak with reporters at all.

Jim couldn't believe he was even thinking this, but he couldn't keep the thought from surfacing. *Could Rick have shot Maggie and run?*

27

THEY PADDLED continuously for twenty minutes. Rick looked down at himself. He was a sight to see. He was still dressed in the slacks and dress shirt he had worn on the plane ride home the previous day. The dress shoe on his left foot was soaked. He was drenched in sweat as he still had on his leather riding jacket. He had left his helmet on the seat of his bike.

The sun was high in the sky now, making it feel warmer than it was. They saw others in canoes and kayaks going in different directions, and they passed a few campsites along the way with tents pitched. He smelled the aroma of campfires from time to time. The sound of people talking and laughing seemed to be amplified by the openness.

Rick was struck by the contradictory nature of it all. They were half panic-stricken, while others were enjoying their campouts. He and Cindy discussed trying to get the attention of someone to tell them what was happening, but they decided it would take too much time. They also didn't want to put anyone else at risk.

As he paddled facing the water, he challenged his mind to remember what he could about Cindy Potter. They had both worked as camp counselors for a couple of years. They had hit it off well, and during the second summer actually had begun spending more time together alone. Sometimes they would go into the woods and talk. They made out on many occasions. Her naturally blond hair reached her mid-back at that time, and he remembered thinking that she was beautiful. The kids had loved her because she could always keep them laughing, even in the midst of a downpour.

Now, sitting four feet away from her, he could barely remember what she looked like now. Everything had happened so quickly. He thought about the way in which she had taken charge and acted so decisively. That was not the Cindy Potter he had known. Back in camp, she had always seemed so carefree and fun-loving. The adult supervisors used to get annoyed at her when she would crack jokes during training sessions.

His phone rang, and he stopped paddling. Without thinking, he fished it out of his jacket pocket and saw that it was Jim Gunderson calling. Only then did he remember that he had asked Jim to come to their home in St. Cloud to meet with him. He swiped the arrow to answer the call. "Jim, I am so sorry. I forgot about our meeting. Something crazy just happened."

"Rick, where are you?" Jim's voice broke up as he spoke, indicating a weak signal.

"I'm up at the Boundary Waters. Somebody just tried to kidnap me with a gun."

Jim seemed to ignore what he had just been told. "Rick, when was the last time you saw Maggie?"

"Last night, why?"

There was a long pause. "Maggie's dead, Rick." .

"What? You're breaking up."

"I said Maggie is dead. She's been shot."

Rick dropped the paddle in the boat. He began panting. "What? Oh God, no! She took her own life because I abandoned her!" He started crying uncontrollably. "Oh God, what have I done?"

"No, Rick. I don't think it was suicide. They haven't found a weapon."

"What? No, that can't be," Rick said between sobs. "Who would hurt her? Nobody would want to hurt Maggie!"

The scratchy sounds that came from the phone were unintelligible.

"What? I didn't get that."

Jim repeated it, and this time Rick heard what he said. "Rick, you need to get home now. The police are calling you a person of interest. They need to talk—"

The call disconnected.

Cindy watched as this man fell apart in front of her. She watched the back of his shoulders quake as he cried. One second it appeared that his face was in his hands, and then it was as if he was trying to stand up. Was he going to jump in and try to swim to shore? She wasn't sure what he was going to do. He couldn't stop crying. "No, no, not my Maggie. I should have been there. Not Maggie. Oh God, not Maggie."

She reached up and took hold of the blade of Rick's paddle. She screwed the ends together again and began paddling again on her own. She didn't know what to say. She had come out for an overnight kayak trip and suddenly found herself in the middle of a tragedy and wondering if her life was in danger. Now, hearing one side of his phone conversation it sounded like his wife had died. Finally she said, "Talk to me, Patrick. What's going on? What's happening?"

Rick turned and looked at her, still weeping loudly. "My wife's dead. Somebody killed my Maggie."

Cindy couldn't believe what she was hearing. Someone had murdered this man's wife, and now this woman was after him ... and her. She had no idea where their pursuer was. She was likely moving more quickly than they were. It seemed that Patrick was going to be of no help at all, and she didn't blame him.

Think! She said to herself. She knew the Boundary Waters. She had begun to learn them when she was at camp as a child. She had also been a camp counselor with Patrick and had the responsibility of getting fifth and sixth graders out to the Waters and back safely. As an adult she had returned, sometimes alone and sometimes with others, to enjoy the solitude and the beauty of the place. Lately, she had continued the trip regularly during the summer months, almost always alone.

Think! Where can we go to get off the water and away from this woman? She figured that they would want to find a place where they could readily hide the canoe and get to higher ground so they could see her if she was near. She thought about where they were now and decided on a plan. She knew that there was a spot ahead where they could jog to the right and get out of the open water. She also remembered a couple of places where they could portage the canoe across some land points to get to narrows where they could row for about another mile west. There was a fairly large section of ground there where they could hide the canoe in the woods and move up. Would other people be there? She decided it was worth a shot.

Rick's crying had quieted down a bit. He just stared into the water, looking as if he was about to throw himself off the boat.

Portaging the canoe across the two sections of land was a challenge. When they got to the first section, she paddled straight into the sandy shoreline and stepped into the water. She walked around to the bow, where Rick sat, and pulled it as far onto the shore as she could, which was not very far with the extra weight. "Okay, let's go," she said. "I have an idea of where, but we will need to portage a couple of times." Rick didn't move. He continued to stare out in front of the boat. "Let's go!" she said again, louder this time.

Rick stood slowly and stepped out of the boat and into the water. Now Cindy was able to pull the canoe entirely out. She had to yell at him again to get his help carrying the canoe. She could have done it herself, but having him help kept him with her. She didn't know where he would wander off to if left to himself.

About twenty minutes after they hit the narrows he said, "It was her, I know it was. She killed Maggie, and now she's here to kill me."

It was difficult to hear what he was saying with him facing away from her. "What? I didn't hear you."

He twisted around and looked at her. "She must be the one who killed Maggie."

"You're probably right," Cindy replied, "but right now speculation doesn't help us much. We've got to get as far away from this woman as fast as we can." Rick didn't look up. It was as if he hadn't even heard her.

They got to the spot Cindy was looking for. There didn't appear to be anyone there.

"Patrick, listen to me. Let's get this out of sight, and then we'll find some higher ground so we can keep an eye out." He looked at her and nodded his head in agreement. "Pick up your side. Let's get moving." He picked up the other end of the boat, and they walked up onto a trail through a wooded area. She led them off the trail near some brush, where they laid the canoe behind some bushes so it couldn't be seen from the trail. Rick took his coat off and started to toss it into the boat.

"I'd hang onto that if I were you. You might wish you had it if we have to spend the night out here," she said as she grabbed her backpack.

They walked about a quarter mile up the trail, passing a couple of vacant campsites along the way and eventually reaching one that had a view of the lake below. Rick pulled out his phone to see if he could call the police. There was one bar, then there were no bars. He thought it might work to text Jim and have him call the police. "Are you getting any cell service?" he asked Cindy.

"My phone is in my car. Cell service out here is almost nonexistent. I come out here to try and get away from all that." She reached into her pack and removed two bottles of water. "I brought six bottles of water that we'll have to share. We should try to stay hydrated," she said, handing one of the bottles to Rick.

"Thank you," Rick said quietly. "I'll see if I can send a

friend a text. Maybe he can call the police for us."

"I'll walk around and see what there is to see," she said as she went north toward a rock outcropping. She walked out to a ledge that had a nearly 180-degree view. It was hard to judge distances, but she thought it was about three-quarters of a mile to the shoreline across the water in front of her. The large lake to their east was surrounded by sections of land, with what appeared to be tributaries of water separating the terrain. Some peninsulas stretched out, encroaching into the water. Much of the shoreline was filled with trees and green brush, with some narrow sandy beaches. It was difficult to tell which were islands and which were not.

In the Boundary Waters, she knew, it was hard to even define what an island was. It was a massive area with lots of land and lots of water in and around it. The land was covered with a vast variety of pines and deciduous trees of all sorts. Other areas were covered primarily with bushes and other foliage. She supposed you could get around any stretch of the land on water if you went far enough.

In the distance, maybe half a mile or so away, she could see someone in a one-person kayak. She jogged back to the camp and got the binoculars out of her backpack. Out on the ledge again, she kneeled next to a large rock formation and looked through the field glasses. The image was still too far away to see clearly, but it looked like a female in the kayak. The woman kept looking at something in her hand as she drifted. Suddenly she looked in Cindy's direction. She immediately turned her kayak and began paddling toward them. *What in the world?* Cindy said to herself. *How could she know to turn this way? There's no way she can see me from that distance.*

She ran back to the campsite. Rick was focused on his phone but looked up when he heard her. "I'm texting with an associate in the Twin Cities. He said whoever killed Maggie seems to have taken the gun with them and may have taken her cell phone as well."

"I may have just found her phone," Cindy said somberly.

Rick looked at her quizzically.

"Can … Could Maggie track you on her phone?" she asked.

"Uh-huh. Why?" he said softly, still in a daze.

"There's a kayak about a half-mile away with a woman in it. She just changed her direction and is headed this way." Cindy put the binoculars in her pack and zipped it up. "Hurry! Turn your phone off. Grab your jacket and let's go. Now!"

Rick stared at her for a few seconds and then held down the power button on his phone. He picked up his jacket, and the two took off running down the trail. They completed the downhill trek much more quickly than it had taken to go up. They got to the canoe, threw their possessions into it, and hoofed it out of the brush and down the trail.

"What are we doing?" Rick whispered, seeming to come out of his funk a little bit.

"She'll approach from the other side of the island, but if we're quick we can be out of sight before she's able to get a view of this side."

They walked as carefully and as quietly as possible into the water, still carrying the canoe, and laid it in the water gently. He got in on one side, and she got in on the other. Water splashed from their feet as they stepped into the canoe, but there was no way to avoid that. Once in the boat, Cindy unscrewed the two halves of the paddle and handed one up to Rick.

"Wait," she said. "Listen."

They both sat there for a few seconds and listened carefully. They heard nothing.

"Let's go," Rick said, and they both began to paddle as quickly and quietly as they could. Cindy was relieved that he seemed to be coherent again. She would never get them out of there in time if he wasn't able to help.

They glided along swiftly. The wind had begun to pick up, as was typical in the afternoon in the Waters. Rick worked as quickly as he could, the technique coming back easily as he practiced. Each paddled without speaking. When a turn needed to be made, Cindy moved the canoe with her paddle by using a J-stroke or a C-stroke, depending on the direction she wanted the bow to turn. The island landing was about a hundred yards from the narrows that had gotten them there. She thought if they could get to the narrows without being seen, they could turn left and continue their travel without detection. Even from the top of the bluff, the narrows were hidden by tall trees on both sides.

Cindy made the turn and looked back at the place where they had portaged up the trail. Nobody was there. Before they moved out of sight, she looked up and down their side of the island and saw nothing, but she knew that didn't necessarily mean the woman hadn't seen them. They paddled for thirty minutes more, continuously, with neither saying a word. They were getting into an area that was unfamiliar to her. She looked for other potential places to put out and take a breather.

"You haven't forgotten everything you knew after all," Cindy finally said, breaking the silence.

"It comes back. Why in the world did you bring double kayak paddles for a canoe?" he asked with a forced chuckle.

"The kayak at the landing was supposed to be mine, but I figured it would be a tight fit putting you and I into a single-person kayak. Aren't you glad my paddles separate?"

"Yes, I'll admit we would have been in a world of hurt with only one paddle. But I am getting blisters on my palm from this grip."

Cindy had on rowing gloves with padding in the palm and open slots for her fingers. "Don't you have any gloves?"

Rick slapped his forehead. "I probably would have paddled all day without thinking of that." He stopped rowing for a minute and fished his riding gloves out from his coat pockets.

"We can also change sides if you want," she added. "But first help me look for another piece of land that might have good lookout points like the last one. And please tell me that your phone is off."

He cringed and took the phone out of his back pocket. He exhaled loudly. "It's off."

They paddled for another forty-five minutes before seeing a location that they thought might work. It took them fifteen minutes to get there. The landing spot was suitable but there wasn't a trailhead, as such. They both got out of the canoe and carried it onto the shore this time. Rick pointed to a spot where they could hide the canoe. They portaged it up and laid it down behind some foliage. They hiked up the wooded hillside until finally cresting it. There were no campsites, but they did find a clearing where they could rest and camp if they needed.

Cindy sat down on a fallen tree to rest and looked up at him. She said, "Patrick, I'm so, so very sorry."

"What are you talking about? You saved my life today, more than once," he said, attempting to dismiss her sympathy. Now he looked at her trying to compare this woman to the Cindy he remembered. She still had the same blond hair, though shorter, but she was bigger and stronger than she was back then. Her muscular arms and chiseled thighs suggested she exercised a lot, maybe lifted weights. Her face looked the same, but there was something in her eyes—a seriousness that seemed to show that this woman had experienced a lot since her days at camp. "Thanks for taking charge when I lost it."

As he thought of that moment tears welled up in his eyes again, and he couldn't stop himself from letting go. She slowly stood up and walked to where he was standing. She embraced him and didn't let go while he cried. She held him without saying a word. *What was there to say?*

28

AT TEN-THIRTY that morning, Stan Kauffman received a call from Cork Thompson, the Attorney General. "Stan, I wanted you and the president to be aware that this morning Senator Rick Taylor's wife was found dead in their home. She had been shot in the head. The police have not found a gun. Her cell phone is also missing. Nobody knows where Rick Taylor is."

Kauffman, who had just come out of a meeting with the president and the treasury secretary, stopped in the hallway and leaned against the wall momentarily. Once he gained his composure, he hurried to his office and closed the door. "Is Taylor in Washington?"

"No, his staff says he took a flight yesterday to Minneapolis. He should have gotten home yesterday afternoon."

"If he's not around, who found the body?"

"Jim Gunderson, Rick's deputy chief of staff. He says he was supposed to have a meeting with him this morning."

"What are you telling me, Cork? Is Taylor a suspect?"

"Well, it's early for that, but it's certainly a possibility."

Kauffman briefed President Donaldson immediately. "Oh, that poor thing," Donaldson said as he stood from behind the desk in the Oval Office. He paced the floor. "Where is Taylor?"

"Nobody knows. His staff says he went home yesterday

afternoon. He hasn't been seen or heard from since."

The president continued to pace. "Is the Senate in session?"

"Senators will be in tomorrow, but they leave for the weekend. Same applies to those in Congress."

"Do I have any time open later today?"

"You're open after six-thirty this evening."

"Set up a meeting with Speaker Hanson and Leader Moreno for seven. This could be our opportunity."

"I beg your pardon?"

"Look, Stan, I fully appreciate the gravity of the situation, and I want only the best for Taylor and his family. But with him gone, we can get a vote on the use of force bill tomorrow. It's a narrow window, but it's a window."

Kauffman nodded. "Okay," he said as he walked to the door. "I'll set it up."

29

THE SALTINESS from Rick's tears seeped into his lips, and he realized that he was also getting Cindy damp. The top of her head touched his cheek, and her short blond hair was moist and sticking to her freckled face. He pulled away from her and said, "I'm sorry. I guess I'm a mess."

"You have every right to be," she said. "Patrick, I'd love to hear about Maggie."

He smiled faintly and looked at the ground. "How much time have you got?"

Rick started to share all of the things he loved about Maggie. "We met at Northwestern, and we just immediately felt comfortable with one another," he said. "I sometimes wondered if it was love because it wasn't fireworks or lust ... it was just comfortable. We started the business together because we trusted one another and wanted to be together.

"When I told her I wanted to run for the Senate seat, she challenged me on it to make sure I had thought it through. We prayed about it, and then she was completely on board. When she wrote that song that became so recognized, I couldn't have been prouder or more grateful."

"I envy you for having found such a partner," Cindy said. "It sounds like you were a lot alike."

"We were alike in terms of our values and our priorities. But we're different too. Sometimes I take things so seriously, and she laughs at me and reminds me how insignificant most things really are." He paused, realizing he spoke of her in the present tense. "There was friction, as there is in any marriage. I could get annoyed at the way she always wanted to have every detail figured out before we could move on something. I'm more of a big picture guy. She would growl at me because my mind was always on something else other than the present. I think she felt that sometimes I didn't give her the full attention she deserved. And she was right. That was the other frustrating thing. She usually was right."

While it didn't take away his grief, it did seem to help to talk about her. He didn't say anything about what had happened with Jeff Sands.

As she listened, Cindy made a *come with me* motion with her right index finger, and they hiked around the top of the island to find a spot where they could see in all directions. He paused a few times as they walked. Cindy said, "Keep talking, I'm listening." And she was listening.

They saw no kayaks. They saw a few canoes, typically with two people in them. This far out, it would be those who loved to canoe and get as far away from civilization as they could.

When Rick finally finished talking, Cindy said, "She was an incredible woman. I can see why you loved her. It sounds like you complemented each other well."

Neither said anything more until they were back at the campsite. Once there, she turned to face him and asked, "Why are you here?"

"What?"

"Why are you here? Ely, the Boundary Waters? Why didn't Maggie come with you?"

Rick walked over and sat down on the tree trunk. "You always were a perceptive one, Cindy Potter."

"Not so perceptive. Just an unabashedly shameless prier into things that are not my business." She grinned, then looked at him seriously. "You don't have to answer if it makes you uncomfortable."

Rick stared at her with his mouth crooked to one side and exhaled deeply. He thought to himself, *Should I burden this poor woman with this?* He looked at the ground and didn't say a word. Cindy turned and started picking up some sticks to clear the area for a campfire. Finally Rick spoke. "What I'm about to tell you is something that only two people in the whole world knew. Maggie and me. I only found out yesterday, and now Maggie is gone." He spoke softly and raised his eyes to see her turn and look at him. There was concern on her face, not like she didn't want to hear what he was about to say, but as if to say, *Poor Rick, as if this isn't enough. There's more you're having to deal with?*

"I'm sure you remember Jeff Sands, my primary opponent who collapsed and died in a Fourth of July parade." She nodded. "Well, after his death, Maggie began to lose interest in the campaign. She seemed to withdraw from everything. After my election, she showed no interest in coming to Washington. She returned to work full time in the business and appeared to be depressed, withdrawing even from me."

He told her all that had happened when he had returned home from Washington the day before. When he got to the part about Maggie's confession, Cindy's hands covered her mouth, and her blue eyes grew larger. "Oh, Maggie!" she said, almost as if she were there with them and they were old friends.

Rick described his reaction—the way he had stormed out of the house and how he decided he needed to get away and think through it all. "I left her in that vulnerable state. I got on my Harley and rode away. I later called and told her I needed to think. That was the last time we spoke." He paused. "That's why I came here." He shook his head and began to tear up again. "I deserted her. If I had been there, I could have protected her."

"Oh no, Patrick. I understand you feeling that way, but if you had stayed, it's very possible that you would be dead too. The person who killed Maggie is out there someplace trying to find us right now, remember?"

Rick said nothing. He leaned over and put his elbows on his knees and his face in his hands. Then his head came up again. "Oh, there's something else. Jim told me the police are looking for me as a person of interest."

"All that means is that they want to talk to you to get more information."

"Think about it. After my wife's death, I disappear and can't be found, even after I become aware of her death. What do you suppose they're thinking?"

She walked over and sat on the log beside him. "Yes, I suppose you are high on their suspect list," she agreed. "They don't know about Jeff Sands's death, right?"

"Nobody knows that."

"Well, that's a positive thing. If they knew that, you would probably be their only suspect. That could be viewed as motive."

Rick looked at her. "Cindy, I promise you that I had nothing to do with her death."

"Save it," she said. "Remember, I've met the murderous wench who is carrying Maggie's phone." She got up and started collecting rocks to make a circular fire pit. "Why don't you go take a look around again to make sure she isn't nearby? You can bring back some firewood as well."

Rick said nothing but stood and did as he was told. He didn't see anybody on the lake. It was early evening and still pretty windy; he figured most sensible people would be setting up camp by now. He gathered some medium-sized branches that could be broken down for the fire. Back at their makeshift campsite, he said, "It looks like we may lose a few pounds on this trek. I'm getting hungry."

Cindy smiled. "You're probably right. I wasn't expecting to feed two. However, ..." She grabbed her backpack and unzipped it. She reached in and pulled out a snack bar and tossed it to him. She took one for herself. "I have a couple cans of SpaghettiOs that we can have later."

She reached in again, put on her most pretentious air and

said, "I also have fishing line and some bait."
Rick smiled slightly. "I'm impressed," he said.

30

THAT NIGHT in the Oval Office, President Donaldson got down to business. The Senate majority leader, the speaker of the House, the secretary of defense, and Stan Kauffman were all present.

Donaldson began, "Thank you for meeting with such short notice. I am shocked and saddened by what we're hearing from Minnesota with regard to the death of Senator Taylor's wife. We hate to think that Senator Taylor may have been involved, but as time passes, it's hard to believe that he isn't.

"You all know that I want to tackle this border issue as quickly as possible but have been stymied by Taylor's lack of cooperation. We now know that he will be unavailable, at least for the foreseeable future. I'd like both houses to take up the bill authorizing the use of military force against the Mexican cartels and any who would support or assist them."

Ken Jensen, the Speaker, spoke first. "Yes sir, I think this is an opportunity we shouldn't pass up to move forward on this front. I can schedule a vote for tomorrow."

"Leader Moreno, how about you? With Senator Taylor, uh, tied up, you should be able to approve the authorization, right?" the president asked.

Moreno spoke haltingly. "Well, Mr. President, to directly answer your question, no, Senator Taylor's absence alone would not change the outcome of the vote."

"What do you mean? The forty-first vote against us would be taken care of. Surely you can make this happen."

"Well, sir, the Senate rules require three-fifths of the Senate to end the current filibuster of the bill. With ninety-nine Senators voting, three-fifths of the Senate would be 59.4 people. Fifty-nine will still be less than three-fifths. With Taylor's absence, you still require sixty votes to clear that threshold."

"Leader Moreno," Donaldson said with contempt. "Do not lecture me on Senate rules. As vice president, I was president of the Senate for eight years. I'm asking you to consider what you might do to have another member of the opposition fail to show up or abstain when the vote is taken."

"Mr. President," Moreno asked, "what would you have me do in the next twenty-four hours to accomplish that? I've worked for over a year to try to make that happen. The opposing party is strongly against it and is sticking together in their opposition."

The secretary of defense jumped into the fray. "Senator Moreno, wouldn't the vice president's vote get us to sixty?"

Donaldson shook his head. "The vice president is not allowed to vote on ending the debate of legislative matters, only to break a tie when voting on legislation."

The secretary tried to be helpful. "Then why couldn't the Senate rules be changed, just for this vote?"

Moreno rolled his eyes. "Mr. Secretary," he said condescendingly, "it would take two-thirds of the Senate to vote to change the rules." He paused and continued, "Yes, there might be ways to shortcut that, but even if it could be done, it would take so much negotiation that we would still be working on it a month from now."

"Is there anything you can think of that could make this happen, Frank?" Stan Kauffman interjected.

"Again, not in a twenty-four hour period. The president knows that I am fully supportive of this effort, but dropping it in my lap eighteen hours before we need to take a vote is totally unreasonable. No, it's impossible."

The president looked disappointed and turned to Jensen. "Ken, why don't you take up the bill tomorrow? Let's get it through the House for now and then work on the Senate."

"We can do that. Both committees have approved it. I'll send out notification tonight that the bill will come before the full House at three tomorrow afternoon."

The president turned to Moreno. "Do what you can, Frank," he insisted.

Moreno was obviously uncomfortable. He didn't know what the president expected him to do, but he said, "Yes, sir."

31

RICK WAS tired. The stress from the day and the unusual physical workout left him exhausted. It was nine o'clock and the sun had just gone down. It would be another forty-five minutes before it would be dark.

Cindy had just made the rounds again to monitor the waters around where they were camping. When she got back, her arms were full of firewood. She dropped the wood a safe distance from the fire. "We probably should eat something. I have some apples, those cans of spaghetti, and more snack bars."

"I'm so tired. I don't feel like eating."

She pulled two apples out of the pack and handed one over. "Here you go; let's have an apple at least. We'll need the energy; plus it might help us sleep better."

He took the apple and crunched on it. It was a sweet honey crisp apple—his favorite.

She finished eating her apple, core and all, and smiled at him. "While I was out, I saw a beautiful blueberry bush. Too bad they aren't ripe yet." She sat down beside him. "Do you remember when we used to pick blueberries when we were camp counselors?" She leaned forward and peered into his eyes.

Rick rolled his eyes. "I seem to remember you wanted to pick blueberries a lot, and half the time we had to scramble to get enough berries together to justify our hike."

She laughed out loud. "Do you think anyone suspected anything?"

"Oh, Cindy," he laughed. "Everybody knew what we were doing out there. The guys were merciless in teasing me when you weren't around."

She covered her face with her hands and giggled. "Really? Oh, how embarrassing."

Rick just smiled. "What about you? You haven't told me what you've been up to for the last twenty years."

She sat back on the log and breathed deeply. The smell of burning pine helped her relax. With the ongoing crises of the day, she had barely noticed all the things she loved so much and came to the Boundary Waters for. Nighttime was always her favorite time. The wind died down, and one could see millions of stars in the sky.

"Well, after high school I went to nursing school at the University of Minnesota. I kind of got caught up with the patriotism thing after 9/11, so when I graduated I joined the Army. I went through training to be a combat medical specialist. I did a couple of tours, one in Iraq and one in Afghanistan."

"I'll bet that was some tough duty."

"It was. Seeing people you work with critically injured or die is the worst. It was satisfying work, though. I think the fact that I was able to help save people's lives was a big factor in getting me through without PTSD. Anyway, I got out after four years and moved back to Duluth. I'm a critical care nurse at Duluth General's Trauma Center."

"I don't see a wedding ring."

"No, you don't." She paused. "I was married for a few years to an x-ray tech at the hospital. It was a dumb thing to do. All the signs of his alcoholism were there before the wedding. Over time he became abusive."

"I'm sorry, Cindy. Nobody should have to go through that."

"You're right. But," she said stoically, "with my military

training, I could defend myself pretty darned well. I got the better of him a few times." She had a touch of amusement in her voice. "I gave him his walking papers and, fortunately, he moved away and has been out of my life for a long time. We didn't have any kids." Suddenly she looked at him and gasped. "Patrick, do you have children?"

"No. Maggie was medically unable to become pregnant. We chose not to adopt."

"As bad as it sounds to say, that's a good thing now."

Rick considered that for a moment. "Maybe, but if we had children I would at least have something, someone, who would always remind me of her. Can I ask you a question?"

"Sure."

He turned and faced her, a slight smile on his lips. "Why do you still call me Patrick?"

Cindy smiled broadly and looked at him with a twinkle in her eyes. "You'll always be Patrick to me. Back in the day, I used to call you that just to get your goat. You never stopped me, so it's your fault." She poked him in the arm.

"Do you know that you're the only person in the world who calls me Patrick?"

"I'm glad," she said with a smile. "It will always be something special between us."

She paused, and a split-second of panic came over her face. "I'm sorry, I didn't mean—"

Rick laughed. "I know what you mean. Friendship is a good thing."

She looked at her watch and frowned. "It's almost ten o'clock. We need to come up with a game plan for tomorrow."

"Yeah, we do," he agreed. "Do you think we could do it in the morning, though? I'm too exhausted to think right now."

"I guess so. I do wish we were able to communicate with the outside world."

"Yes. What do you want to do with this fire?" he asked.

"We did a good job of cleaning up the area around it. I usually just go to sleep with it going and make sure it's completely out in the morning. There's no wind."

"Sounds good," he said as he stood. He looked around for a place to lean against. There was a large rock nearby that would work. He put his coat on and zipped it up, sat down in front of the rock, and leaned back. He put his gloves behind his head to soften the stone pillow.

Cindy sat by the fire for a few minutes more and then opened her pack and took out a small pillow and a lightweight space blanket. She had found that she could sleep anywhere as long as she could stay warm and had a pillow for her head. She turned and looked for a good place to curl up. She saw that Rick had tears streaming down his cheeks again.

"Oh, Patrick. This is too much for any person to deal with. Is there anything I can do to help you?"

"Please don't get the wrong impression, but I wish you would just hold me," he said with a trembling voice.

She went over to him, sat and leaned in, putting her head on his chest. She pulled her blanket over them both and softly held on to his arm. Not a word was spoken. They were asleep within minutes.

#

Rick awoke just after five with Cindy's head still on his lap. He didn't want to disturb her, so he remained still except to lift his hand from her hip and bring it to his side. His mind seemed a bit clearer now. He began to focus on their safest way out of there. They were miles into the waterway, and he had no idea how to get back. He hoped Cindy did, or at least that she had a compass in that pack of hers.

He had no idea if he could get cell phone coverage where they were. He also didn't know how much charge he had left on his phone. Cindy stirred and raised her head off the pillow. "How are you feeling?" she asked as she wiped her eyes.

He looked at her and wondered how he could feel so comfortable around her after only a day. He felt guilty at the thought as his mind went to Maggie. "I'm better, thanks. I've been trying to think through our options for getting out of this predicament. You don't have a portable phone charger in your pack, do you?"

"No. No phone, no need for a charger."

"You know, I suggest you rethink that policy. What if something happened, and you needed to call for help? I can tell you know your way around here, but accidents happen and not everyone is a friend."

"I was thinking the same thing. This whole experience has been an eye-opener." She stood up and stretched. The air was cool, and while the light of dawn was well upon them, the sun was only now beginning to appear over the horizon. She picked up the blanket and wrapped it around her shoulders, then reached into her pack for the roll of toilet paper. "I'll be back," she said with a little smile.

Rick stood and went in the opposite direction to relieve himself. While out, he went to one of the lookout points they had found to see what was there. Nobody was on the water. The air was perfectly still. The water looked like glass, reflecting the sun flawlessly as it rose into the eastern sky.

They met back at the campsite and Cindy asked, "How about that can of SpaghettiOs now?"

"Not my usual choice for breakfast, but I'm starving."

"All I have is that, a couple more snack bars, and one other apple."

"Spaghetti it is," he said.

"I'm afraid I only have one spoon. You can have it. I'll eat with my fingers."

Rick curled his lips in disgust. "Not in front of me, you won't. It's okay; we can share." As they ate, passing the spoon back and forth, Rick broached the subject of getting back to civilization. "This morning I got to thinking how it would be nice to know where this woman is. What if we packed up and got the canoe in the water, then I could come back to the top of the hill and see if I can get a track on Maggie's phone? We would be giving up our position, but we would know where she is to go back in a different direction."

"That makes sense," she said. "Actually, I was thinking the same thing, but there's probably a better than even chance that Maggie's phone is dead by now or turned off or that she's in a place with no reception."

"I guess so. Wouldn't the phone give me her last known location, though?"

"Hmmm. I don't know about that."

"Do you have any other ideas?"

"No. It would be better than just guessing. I really don't want to run into her again."

"We might as well try to avoid that if we can," he agreed.

They finished their breakfast, and Cindy neatly folded her space blanket and stuffed it and the pillow into the pack. She pulled the remaining apple and snack bars out and put them into a smaller, more accessible compartment. She walked through the campsite and saw that only the two open cans and the spoon remained. Then she found a two-foot piece of an oak limb in the stack of firewood and began to poke around in the ashes of the fire. It was still smoldering.

Rick said, "I'll go fill up those cans in the lake so we can dampen those embers."

"It would probably be alright, but better safe than sorry. I'll go check our lookout points and make sure she's not out there."

He took both cans and began the five-minute walk down to the lake. He filled them with lake water and turned to make the trip back up the hill. Once back at the campsite, he poured one can of water into the ashes and stirred them with the branch Cindy had used earlier. Steam rose up from the ash.

Cindy returned from her trip to the lookout points. "Nothing of interest there."

Rick poured the second can of water around the ashes and stirred some more. "Let's get the canoe in the water, and then I can fill the cans again and douse the fire when I come back to turn on my phone's tracking app."

She shrugged her shoulders. "You might as well."

Rick was beginning to sweat. He unzipped his leather jacket, which released hot air from inside. "Oh boy, do I stink! I guess two and a half days in the same clothes and working out like we have is taking its toll."

Cindy scrunched up her nose and lips. "Too bad we don't have a longer canoe," she said with a lopsided smile.

Rick grabbed the pack and cans and said, "Let's get that canoe in the water." They hiked down the side of the hill to the brush where they had left the canoe. He tossed the pack under the center seat and held the two cans together with his thumb and forefinger. "Shall we?" he asked as he picked up his end of the canoe.

They maneuvered their way around a tree and down to the lake. He put his end down in the water and let her push the boat the rest of the way in. *Might as well keep my feet dry if I can.* He leaned down and filled the cans with water and joked, "Okay, if I'm not back in fifteen minutes, call the fire department." He turned and weaved his way back up the hill.

Cindy looked out along the waterway. It dawned on her that she probably should get an idea of where they were and what direction they would need to go to reach the outfitter. She pulled the boat back on shore far enough to reach the pack. She unzipped a flat pocket and pulled out a topographical map and a compass tied to a lanyard. She tried to recreate their trek the day before in her mind.

It dawned on her that if they were able to get a track on this woman, it might be easier if the map was nearby so they could get more detail on the terrain between her and them. She folded the map and put it into the back pocket of her jeans. She pulled the lanyard over her head, letting the compass drop onto her chest, and turned and trudged up the side of the hill again.

As Rick arrived at the campsite, he balanced the cans of water on the downed tree and pulled his phone from his pocket. He pressed and held the button and waited for it to boot up. The security screen appeared, and the face recognition app did its thing and opened the main screen. He swiped once to the left and tapped the tracking app. A map appeared on his screen showing the topography and a circle with the image of a person in it. He hadn't used this app for a while, but he figured that must be him. At the bottom of the screen, he saw Maggie's email address. He tapped on it and the screen zeroed in on the same little circle. It also indicated a little blue dot with a shaded triangle emanating in one direction.

Initially, he was confused. He tapped on Maggie's email address again. Nothing happened. His breathing quickened as he moved his phone around on its axis. The shade moved around the blue dot. That was his phone. Maggie's phone was there, where he was. He felt his heart begin to pound in his chest.

"Looking for someone?" he heard.

Looking up, his eyes widened and his breathing stopped. It was the woman. She stood just below the crest of the hill with Cindy in front of her, holding a gun to her head.

32

AT HIS morning briefing, President Donaldson gathered with Stan Kauffman and the attorney general, CIA director, Secretary of Defense Donna Schmidt, and their aides. They had gone through the typical agenda, and he had his questions answered. He looked at his Attorney General, Cork Thompson, and asked, "What's happening with Rick Taylor? Has he been located?"

"His phone pinged yesterday for a while in the Boundary Waters of northern Minnesota, then it stopped. We presume he turned his phone off."

"Does it look like Taylor killed his wife?" the president asked, incredulous.

"Well, right now, all of the evidence is circumstantial, but I can't think of any other reason he would seemingly be hiding in one of the most remote areas of the country. His deputy chief of staff told police that he had been able to reach Taylor by phone yesterday midday. He told Taylor of his wife's death. He still hasn't been seen."

"What about the murder weapon? Has that been found?"

"No. The medical examiner has removed the bullet and found that it came from a 9mm. A police detective spoke with the manager in charge of Taylor's company. The manager said that he had gone to a shooting range with Taylor once, about a year ago. He said that Taylor was shooting a 9mm but couldn't remember the brand."

"What would possess him to do something like this? Were there problems in the marriage?" Donaldson asked.

"None of the people who have been talked to thus far were aware of any. Some said that they thought she might be going through some kind of depression."

"Keep me up to speed on that," the president said. "Stan, is there some other next of kin that we can reach out to with our sympathy?"

"I'll see what we can find out."

"We can probably help with that," Thompson offered.

"Thank you all," Donaldson said. "I'll see you tomorrow."

"Oh, one more thing you might want to be aware of," offered Thompson as they rose to leave. "Senator Karl Hahn's wife was in a serious car accident in LA last night. She's in critical condition."

Donaldson shifted his gaze to Kauffman, who stood there in disbelief. Hahn was a senator for the opposition party. "Oh, I'm sorry to hear that. Stan, please express our concern and see if there is anything we can do." Stan said nothing. "Stan?"

"Yes, sir."

As everyone started to file out, Donaldson called out, "Stan and Donna, could I speak with you both briefly?"

Schmidt and Kauffman turned and waited until the door was shut.

"If Hahn is in California, that should clear the way for a clean vote for the authorization to use military force. Stan, I would think Moreno is aware, but tell him that I expect a vote today on that bill."

"I'll call him ASAP."

The president looked at his defense secretary. "Donna, is everything ready for the Project 51 rollout?"

"Yes, sir. We've quietly been moving components into Texas, New Mexico, Arizona, and California for the past two months. We can initiate movement of assets within forty-eight hours of your word to go."

Donaldson nodded. "Good. Stan, is everything set with our AI public information campaign?"

"It is. The AI-based news source that we've developed has gained some legitimacy through accurate reporting. There have also been questions raised regarding President Cuevas's commitment to cracking down on cartels. Give us the word, and we will ramp it up quickly."

The president nodded and looked from one to the other. "Very good. We're about to go to war. Let's hope it's over quickly."

33

CINDY'S FACE was ashen. She stood stiffly, and Rick saw what appeared to be a compass protruding from her throat. The woman had the lanyard pulled tightly against her neck. "I'm sorry, Patrick," Cindy said with a quivering voice.

Rick began to stand.

"You stay right there," the woman said, keeping the gun against Cindy's head.

He sat back where he was.

"Those campfires are nice, but they're also telling," the woman said with a smile.

"It was you, wasn't it? You shot Maggie," Rick challenged.

"I did indeed. You were supposed to go at the same time. I don't appreciate you running out on me like that."

"But why? What's this about? What did Maggie do to you?"

"Oh, it's not about Maggie. But with her popularity, we didn't want the governor to put her into your open Senate seat after your untimely death. A murder-suicide seemed to fit the bill nicely. Now it will be a double murder-suicide, but that's workable," she said as she walked Cindy toward him. "The fact that you scurried out here and turned off your phone plays into the narrative nicely. I'm sure the police will be combing the place soon."

"Why? What's this about?" Rick demanded again.

"Senator Taylor, you just couldn't understand that the will

and progress of the United States does not revolve around you. Progress must continue, with or without you."

She continued to push Cindy forward until they stood right in front of him.

"Who are you? Who is doing this?" he insisted.

"I'll just say that we are patriots and will do whatever is necessary to achieve what's best for our country. Now, enough of the questions." The woman was just a foot away from him. She had maneuvered to his right with her gun in her right hand. He noticed that there were latex gloves on both hands now. "If you'll cooperate, I can make this quick and painless for both of you."

"Wait, you don't want to do this," Rick said, holding out his right hand with his palm out.

"Keep your hands down!" she barked.

Rick lowered his hand to the log again. It landed on one of the cans of water he had brought back to douse the fire.

A tear ran down Cindy's cheek, though she said nothing. She mouthed, *I'm sorry,* and shook her head. She needed him to know that she didn't mean to get into this predicament.

"Keep still," the woman told her, tightening the lanyard around her throat.

Rick breathed deeply, trying his best to remain calm. Guilt crept over him as he watched Cindy stiffen again, fear in her huge eyes. *She should not be involved in this.* He had chosen to get her involved. She saved his life and now was going to pay for that with her own. "Please don't hurt her. She has nothing to do with this."

"She does now, thanks to you. You signed her death warrant yesterday when you brought her into it."

He wondered how this would go down. If the woman wanted it to look like a murder-suicide, she would probably want to put the gun to the side of his head and pull the trigger. She stood on his right, gun in her right hand. She would have to change hands to make that happen. He wasn't about to cooperate with his head position. He turned his head slightly to the right.

"Let's take care of you first, Senator Taylor. If you cooperate, maybe I'll let her go," she lied. She loosened her grip and dropped the lanyard. The compass fell back to Cindy's chest, leaving an indentation in her neck where it had pressed into her flesh. The gun came away from Cindy's head and, with the barrel pointed upward, the woman brought her hands together to make the exchange.

Rick raised the can of water as quickly as he could and jerked his wrist, splashing lake water into the woman's eyes. She didn't blink quickly enough, and the water stung her eyes. She took a few lengthy blinks to calm them. While the water flew, Cindy ducked down, exposing the woman's arms.

Rick reached up and grabbed both of her wrists with his hands. The gun was now in her left hand. He was surprised at how powerful the woman was. He moved forward, pushing her back onto her heels. She stepped back with her right foot to catch her balance and pushed back, stepping toward him again. She was too close to him to involve her feet in the fight as she had learned in special ops training, so she thrust her knee into his groin. The pain was more than he could bear. He let go of her wrists and bent over with his arms crossed in front of him. He felt sick to his stomach and ready to collapse.

Released from his grasp, she took a step back and drove up with her left foot, but suddenly the power behind the kick was gone. The force caught Rick in the left shoulder and sent him to the ground, but the woman was also down on one knee, stunned.

Rick looked up to see Cindy grasping the branch they had used for stirring the fire with both hands. The woman still had the gun in her left hand. She dropped to her other knee to stabilize herself and brought her hands together around the grip. Cindy swung the branch again, this time like a baseball bat as hard as she could, into the back of the woman's head. The woman went down and didn't move again.

Rick, wincing, looked at the woman and then at Cindy. "I'm

impressed," he grunted.

Cindy's crying was audible through her closed lips. "Are you alright?"

"I've been better," he said as he slowly crawled to where the gun lay in the dirt. He picked it up, stumbled onto his feet, and stood over the woman. His jaw was clenched in rage and his eyes were damp. He turned and pointed it at her head, his hands trembling as he placed his finger on the trigger.

"Rick, stop," Cindy pleaded. "I absolutely understand your need for revenge. She deserves to pay for what she's done. But don't do this. Let the law handle it. Don't lower yourself to her level."

"What do we do with her? Pack her up and put her under the middle seat in the canoe? She killed Maggie. She needs to die," he said through clenched teeth.

Cindy walked to him and turned his face toward hers. "You're not a killer. You're a US Senator with wonderful values. Don't do this. Don't put me in the position of having to testify about this." She grabbed the lanyard around her neck. "We'll tie her up. We'll get away from here and call the police. They can deal with her." When he didn't answer, she moved in front of him and put her hands on his shoulders. "Please, don't do it. … For my sake."

He exhaled and moved his finger up to the trigger guard, and stepped back. With the gun in his hand, he put his hands on his knees and let his head drop. He grimaced with pain.

Cindy leaned down and felt the woman's neck for a pulse. "It's fairly strong," she said. "How do we cut this lanyard? I have a knife in the pack."

"No time. Come over here," he said as he kneeled in front of the stones Cindy had piled up to make the fire pit. He took the lanyard from Cindy and held it out. "Here, hold one end." He laid down the gun and grabbed a fist-sized rock with his right hand. With his left, he held the other end of the lanyard. "Okay. Lay it across this rock."

They pulled it taut across one of the rocks that had an edge facing up, and Rick pounded on it with the one in his hand. Once, twice, a third time. "Keep it tight," he said. He struck it a fourth time, and it snapped. "Let's roll her onto her stomach." They pulled her hands behind her back. Rick tied them as tightly as he could.

"Be careful not to cut off the circulation," Cindy said.

Rick looked at her, raising his eyebrows, and said, "That's the least of my concerns."

The nylon cord was tight and the knot well away from where the woman's fingers could reach. Rick untied the laces of the woman's sneakers and pulled them from her feet. He worked quickly to unlace the shoes and tie the laces together. He wrapped them as tightly as he could around her ankles. He thought about trying to tie her to a tree, but he didn't have anything to do it with.

"Let's go," he said as he picked up the gun, and then paused. "Wait." He bent down and went through the woman's pockets. He found latex gloves in one and Maggie's cell phone in another. There was nothing else.

"Come on. And bring her shoes," Rick instructed as he turned and ran down the hillside to the canoe. He allowed Cindy to pass him as he turned and looked back at the motionless body in the dirt one last time.

#

They got to the bottom of the hill in less than three minutes, pushed the canoe into the lake, and climbed on board, nearly capsizing in their rush. Once they began rowing, Rick looked up and down the shoreline and saw the tip of a kayak on the edge of the bank, fifty yards to their right. "Look, her kayak," he said, pointing.

They immediately turned the bow of the canoe toward it and paddled as forcefully as they could. When they were ten yards off shore, Rick jumped in. It was waist deep, and the frigid water was a shock. He power walked through the lake until the water level was below his knees, then he made three jump steps to reach the shore and took hold of the kayak. He dragged it into the lake and reached for the canoe that was now in shin-deep water.

There was a rope tied to the front of the kayak. As the canoe made way again, Rick let the rope slip through his hand as Cindy did most of the paddling. Once his hands reached the end of the rope, he tossed it to her. She didn't see anywhere to tie it, so she wrapped it around her waist and sat on it.

After paddling hard for thirty minutes, they decided to take a breather to get oriented and plan a route back to the outfitter's lagoon. They both drank a bottle of water as they rested. Rick pulled the gun from the back waist of his pants, where he had shoved it as they came off the side of the hill. It was still wet from his jump into the water. He laid it in his right palm. It was a Sig Sauer P365, just like the one he kept in the truck. The safety was off. He pushed the lever up to engage it. Then he laid it in his left palm, and his heart began to pound. There was a drop of white paint on the safety lever; this was his gun. He had put a drop of paint there to help him locate it quickly. He stared into the water for a moment, realizing he had left his truck unlocked and the garage door open when he left. *What an idiot!* he thought.

Keeping the gun pointed toward the water, he used his thumb to press the triangular lever at the left base of the trigger guard to release the magazine, which he laid in his lap. When he pulled back the slide, the round in the chamber fell to the bottom of the boat.

"This is my gun," he said to Cindy.

"What?" she said, uncomprehending.

He twisted around to face her. "She stole my gun from my truck. This is my gun." He hesitated. "I'll bet this is what she used." He was drained of the emotion surrounding Maggie's death and spoke calmly. If the murderer had gone to the house to kill them, she surely would have had her own gun. But his carelessness had allowed her to kill his wife with his own gun. A convenient addition to her murder-suicide story.

"Patrick," Cindy said with concern. "How can you be sure?"

He thought for a minute. "This is how." He picked up the magazine and pushed the bullets out, one at a time. He counted eight rounds in the ten-round magazine. The one that had ejected from the chamber was nine. One round was missing.

"Yep. One round is unaccounted for," he said softly but loud enough for her to hear. "And I put this speck of paint here."

Cindy didn't know what to say. She couldn't imagine what he was thinking. She had learned to shoot in the military but had never had to fire a gun in combat. As a nurse, she had seen the devastation guns did to the human body and had no use for them now. Truth be told, they scared her. "Are all of the bullets out of it now?"

Rick nodded.

"Please don't load it again."

"Okay," he agreed. "I'll put them back in the magazine so they aren't laying around loose, but I won't put the magazine in the gun."

"Thank you," she said quietly. After a couple of minutes, she said, "I have a pretty good idea where we are. I think we're two or three hours from the outfitter in Ely."

"I'm glad you're with me," he said sincerely. "If I were alone, I'd probably wind up in Canada someplace."

She smiled. "No, you wouldn't. You've been doing well all this time. I knew it would come back to you. But I'm glad I'm here to help."

Rick turned in his seat again to look at her. "Cindy, I would be dead were it not for you. Several times over."

She just smiled again. "Yeah, I guess you owe me one now." She winced at the thought that he could take her comment the wrong way, then added, "Buy me a hamburger when we get back, and we'll call it even."

34

CLARISA GRADUALLY began to return to consciousness. She remembered someone going through her pockets but didn't know if it was real or not. It took several minutes before she realized where she was and what had happened. Her head was pounding. Her hands were tied behind her. She realized that her shoes were gone and that her ankles appeared to be bound with her own shoelaces. In addition to the headache, she felt another pain on the side of her head.

Cautiously, she was able to maneuver her way into a sitting position and sat there for about five minutes. She felt a tickle on her right cheek and scratched it with the front of her shoulder. The shoulder came back crimson. She sighed and looked around for a time to get her bearings. She saw a can of something sitting on a log in front of her. The same type of can was lying on its side not far away. That must be where the water had come from. She didn't see any kind of sharp tool that could have been used to cut whatever material tied her hands together.

She struggled her way onto her knees and looked behind her. There was the fire pit that had given them away, surrounded by stones, with a stack of kindling nearby. She was able to shuffle on her knees a couple of inches at a time until she was in grasp of the kindling. She sat on her heels with the wood pile to her back and groped for a stick that was small enough and short enough for her to handle. Turning her back to the fire pit, she laid the stick down and began to move rocks out of the way with her foot, one at a time. Finally, she grabbed the stick again, backed up to the ash, and stirred the fire. She twisted her head as best as she could to see what was uncovered.

She sighed again, this time with relief, when she saw that there were still some hot embers within the fire. She worked the stick away and back to draw the embers toward her. Scooting herself backwards toward them, she leaned back, placing her tied wrists onto the hot coal. Tears came to her eyes as her skin burned. *I can do this,* she said to herself. *I'm trained for this.* She whimpered as her skin continued to burn.

Eventually she sat up, pulling her hands apart as hard as she could. When nothing happened, she returned her wrists to the fire. Finally she felt a pop and a give in the binding. She worked her wrists back and forth and in and out, writhing in pain from the fire, until her hands were free.

Clarisa looked at her hands and wrists and was sickened by the redness that surrounded the yellowish layer of skin in the center of the burns. Loose skin fragments surrounded the area where blisters had broken. Sucking in several deep breaths, her head cleared and she turned her attention to the strings on her ankles. She had nothing to cut them with, and her movement had tightened the knot. She reached out her hand and grabbed the can. She used her knee against the ground to bend the can both ways until it was flimsy enough to bend back and forth with her hands. Finally, she was able to break the can in two, and the sharp edge made quick work of freeing her ankles.

Once unbound, she stood and looked around. No shoes. No gun. She felt her pockets from the outside. All she felt was the lumpiness from the latex gloves she had stuffed into a hip pocket. The phone was no longer in her back pocket.

Limping down the rough hillside, she felt every sharp stone and stick that her feet found along the way. She tried to guess the correct path through the trees and brush to the kayak. She couldn't find it. *Had she come down to the wrong spot on the shore?* Continuing to walk painfully, she traveled along the shoreline until she finally found the tracks from the hull of the kayak she had left in the sand. It was gone. She looked out onto the lake and back and forth along the shore. Taylor and the woman were gone and her kayak was too. Clarisa hobbled down to the water and sat down, getting cold relief for her burns.

35

RICK AND Cindy paddled for another thirty minutes before stopping again. The water had become a little rough as the breeze picked up.

"Do you want to drag that kayak all the way back? We could let it go. They'll find it eventually," Rick asked.

"Well," Cindy said, "If we haul it back in, it will raise questions. If we don't take it in, we can just focus on getting help."

"Let it go, then," he said. "But before you do, let's take a look inside to see if she left anything."

Cindy pulled the rope forward until she could grab the front of the kayak. She leaned over and looked into the cockpit. Nothing. "Let me check the hull," she said.

Knees in the canoe and head buried into the cockpit of the kayak, she looked fore and aft. She moved the paddle that had been left so she could see underneath. She looked at Rick and raised her eyebrows. Reaching her right arm into the front of the kayak as far as she could reach, she grabbed hold of something. She leaned back into the canoe and smiled. "Look what I found," she said proudly, holding up another cell phone. She handed the phone forward, threw the rope into the cockpit, and gave the kayak a shove. They watched it drift away. "Ready?" she asked.

They continued for another hour, rowing mindlessly until

168

they heard the quick *wop wop wop* of a helicopter. The small craft flew over the water, back and forth, as if looking for something. They watched it fly away from them and make a turn back. "They're looking for me," he said loudly over the noise.

She looked at him with fear in her eyes.

"They don't expect me to be with someone," he added.

She nodded slightly.

"I've got to let them know I'm here."

"Okay," she said softly, fearful of what might happen next.

They laid their paddles in the boat, and as the helicopter flew toward them again, he put both hands in the air, waving his arms into a crossed pattern and then out again. The aircraft made a tight turn and came around yet again. This time both of them waved their arms. The helicopter hovered for a few seconds above them and then moved forward and began to fly in a circular pattern around them.

They weren't sure what to do. Should they continue to row or just sit and wait? They decided to wait. Neither said a word.

Ten minutes after the helicopter began doing turns around their location, a boat appeared around a patch of land and headed their way. As it came closer, Rick thought he could see a park ranger driving and two others in different uniforms riding in the boat. The boat stopped about seventy-five yards from them.

The ranger reached under the steering console and drew out a powered megaphone. She handed it to what appeared to be a sheriff's deputy. He held the mic next to his mouth and said slowly, "Are you in trouble?"

Both Rick and Cindy nodded their heads *yes*.

"Are you in immediate danger?" he asked.

Rick shook his head *no*. Seeing that Cindy hadn't done so, he said, "Tell them you're not in danger, or they may suspect me of being a threat to you."

Quickly she shook her head *no*. "No," she said softly, as if to herself.

"Do you have a firearm on your craft?"

They both nodded *yes.*

The two men on the power boat exchanged words. One of them bent down and picked up a rifle. He laid on his belly at the bow of the deck, got into firing position and moved the rifle up, pointing about sixty degrees above them.

"I want you both to hold your hands straight up and out, high above your heads."

They did what they were told. Cindy's face was pale, her eyes were wide, and her lips were pursed together. She was trembling all over. *These are the police; they should be here to help us,* she reminded herself.

"This is very important. Stay in that position until we tell you otherwise. Don't move. We don't want to hurt you." The ranger put the boat in gear and motored slowly toward the canoe.

"You're doing great," the deputy said. "Keep your hands high in the air. This will be over soon." He turned to the ranger. "It's him."

Rick stared at the arriving boat. He looked back at Cindy and saw tears rolling down her cheeks. "It'll be alright, Cindy," he assured her. "They have to be careful. They're here to help us."

She nodded but said nothing.

As they got within twenty feet of the canoe, the ranger put the engine in neutral. The deputy put down the megaphone and motioned for the ranger to stop the boat. She slipped it into reverse to stall the forward movement, and they rested about fifteen feet away. The other deputy was still in ready position with his rifle.

"Are you Patrick Taylor?" the man asked.

"Yes," said Rick, nodding his head again.

"What's your name, ma'am?"

"Cynthia Potter," she said through tears.

"Ms. Potter, is this man a threat to you?"

"No, no!" she said, shaking her head vigorously.

"Have you seen Senator Taylor's gun, Ms. Potter?"

She nodded and said, "Yes."

"Do you see it now?"

"Yes," she said, still nodding.

"Where is it?"

"It's behind Patrick, on the floor of the canoe," she said. "There are no bullets," she assured them.

"Uh, there are bullets in the magazine," Rick clarified, "but the magazine is not in the gun. The chamber is empty."

"Is that right, ma'am?"

She nodded again, "Yes."

"Okay," the deputy said as he motioned for the ranger to move closer. "We are going to move up very slightly and tap the side of your canoe. Keep those hands up; you're doing great."

The ranger put the boat in gear for a few seconds and then in neutral again. The boat moved slowly forward and bumped the side of the canoe. Their boat shook slightly. The deputy on his stomach laid his rifle on the deck and checked that the safety was on and that it was pointed away from them. The one who had been talking took the pistol out of his holster and held it with both hands, pointing it above his head.

The deputy on the deck pulled what appeared to be a handkerchief out of his pocket, leaned over the edge of the canoe behind where Rick sat, and took hold of the gun carefully, by the barrel. The ranger took something like a plastic tub and laid it down beside the deputy. He laid the gun into it. Then he reached in, took the clip and did the same. He got up to his knees and handed the tub to the ranger. The one who had been doing the talking remained with his gun in ready position. "You're doing great," he said. "Keep those hands up, just a little bit longer."

Now the ranger was down on her hands and knees holding the canoe next to the bow of the boat. The deputy next to her pulled a pair of handcuffs off the back of his belt. He took hold of Rick's right hand and clapped the cuff around that wrist. "Okay," he said. "Slowly bring this arm down with me." He guided Rick's arm down and held his wrist against his back. "Now bring your other arm down to meet this one. As Rick did so, the deputy grasped his hand quickly and had the other cuff on faster than Rick could believe.

"You're doing great, Ms. Potter," the one with the gun said. "I'm sure your arms are getting sore. This will be over before you know it."

Tears continued to run down her cheeks, but she nodded.

"Ma'am, please lower your left hand and give it to me," the ranger instructed.

Cindy lowered it and allowed the ranger to handcuff her wrist.

"Good," she said assuringly. "Slowly bring your right hand down and clasp your hands together in front of you."

Cindy did as she was told, and the other wrist was cuffed.

The man who was standing put his gun in his holster. "Okay, Ms. Potter, let's get you up into the boat."

The ranger moved to a squatting position, holding the canoe steady against the boat with one hand while guiding and steadying Cindy with the other. Cindy stepped up onto the boat and was frisked and guided to the stern, where she was asked to sit cross-legged on the deck facing forward. They moved Rick to the boat in the same manner, removing his wallet, cell phones, keys, and a comb from his pockets. They sat him on the deck five feet in front of Cindy with his back to her.

"Great job, folks. Let's get you back to where we can get some questions answered."

36

When Frank Moreno learned about Senator Hahn's departure for California to be with his wife, he notified all senators that the vote on the AUMF would be held at 6:30 p.m. The opposition cried foul, and most of the senators from both sides of the aisle grumbled at scheduling a vote so late. They had hoped to finish early to catch their flights home.

At four-thirty, the House of Representatives sent the final version of their authorization to use military force in Mexico to the Senate. Moreno pulled the bill that had passed in Senate committees and substituted the one from the House. At five the Senate took up the bill for consideration. Moreno limited discussion to one hour.

At six a motion was made and seconded to end debate on the resolution. A voice vote was called for. The opposition demanded a roll call vote. The roll call was taken, and the vote was fifty-nine to thirty-nine to end debate. The three-fifths threshold requirement had been met.

A half-hour later, the Senate took a roll call vote to pass the authorization for use of military force in Mexico. The bill passed easily, well beyond the 50% plus one that was required.

37

THE RANGER pulled the remaining items out of the canoe and placed them out of the reach of Rick and Cindy. She tied a rope to drag the boat, and they spent the next forty-five minutes motoring to the ranger station dock.

"There's a woman out there who tried to kill us. We took the gun away from her," Cindy said as they made their way to the station.

"Okay, we're going to get all of the details when we get back. Just relax. I'm sure this has been a difficult couple of days for you."

Cindy raised her voice. "She's out there now! She'll get away if you wait."

"Yes ma'am; we have more people out here. We'll have them keep an eye out for her. Was she in a canoe?"

"No, she was in a kayak, but we took it with us when we got away."

"Where did you take it?"

"We let it drift away about an hour after we left the island."

"It sounds like she won't be going anyplace too fast. We'll get out there and find her after we get some more information," the sheriff said.

Cindy didn't answer, but her piercing eyes and pursed lips did the talking for her.

Rick sat with his eyes closed, trying to tune the

conversation out and wondering how this was going to go. He had been carrying Maggie's cell phone and the gun that likely killed her. He could be in a lot of trouble. *They probably think I shot Maggie and ran*, he thought. *Why wouldn't they? If I'm charged with Maggie's death, I'll have to resign my Senate seat to fight this.* It felt like a nightmare that he couldn't shake.

They didn't take them to the lagoon where the outfitter was located. They ended up at a single-story building about the size of a mid-sized home. Rick guessed it was a mile or so from where they had launched the previous day.

When they got to the dock, the two sheriff's deputies helped them to their feet. The ranger jumped onto the dock and tied up the boat. She helped Cindy out and walked her toward the building while one of the deputies assisted Rick.

"Go ahead and get them in separate rooms," instructed the deputy who had done most of the talking as they walked into the ranger's station. "I'm going to make a call and be right back." Rick found himself in a small conference room where the other deputy repositioned his cuffs to the front. The ranger led Cindy to a small office and removed her handcuffs.

Two investigators were waiting when they arrived. They asked them a series of questions, focusing on their time on the Boundary Waters. They explained that the St. Cloud or state police would be questioning Rick about the crime they were investigating.

The investigators believed what they heard. There were enough small differences in Rick and Cindy's stories to make it obvious that they had not rehearsed what they would say. The officers knew that two people experiencing the same events would always view some things slightly differently. One might pick up on something that the other didn't, for example. Rick and Cindy's descriptions of the woman were similar, and the additional cell phone that they claimed came from the woman's kayak was an unusual twist that gave them added credibility, especially after the investigators found Cindy's cell phone where she said she had left it in her car. The investigators had also been told that St. Cloud police found that someone with Maggie's cell phone had called Rick the night of her death, and it appeared he was enroute to the Boundary Waters at the time.

Cindy was also able to show them on the map where their confrontation with the woman occurred. The helicopter went back out and located the vacant kayak, but the pilot was unable to find anyone in the area. A team of officers and investigators would have to wait until morning to venture out into the area.

Eventually the handcuffs were removed from Rick's wrists, and he and Cindy were put into a break room together and given something to eat and drink. Rick was allowed to make a call to Jim Gunderson.

"Jim, it's Rick."

"Rick, where are you? The police are looking for you."

"Yeah, I'm with them. I saw the woman that killed Maggie," he said, wasting no time. "She tried to kill me too."

"Are you alright? What the hell is happening?" Jim asked in astonishment.

"I'm not sure, but hopefully they're going to catch this woman and find out."

"Are you heading back to St. Cloud?"

"I think so. Probably tomorrow. I should be released after the St. Cloud police talk with me."

"Oh, God Rick, I am sorry about Maggie. What can I do?"

"Thank you, Jim. Can you see about finding an attorney? I don't think I'm in trouble, but just in case."

"I'll get on that now. Rick—why would someone want to kill you and Maggie?"

"I don't know. I just don't know, but … can you be available tomorrow? If I get released, I'd like to meet with you as soon as possible."

"You know I'm here for you. Just call me, and I'll meet you anywhere as soon as I can get there."

"Thanks, Jim. Please let them know in Washington that I'm okay but will be out of touch for a few days."

Arrangements were made to take Rick back to St. Cloud. Technically, he would remain in custody of the police, but he was given the courtesy of being unrestrained. The officers told Cindy they would take her to her car whenever she was ready. She asked for a notepad and pen. She wrote down her phone number and email address on a piece of paper. She sat down across from Rick and said, "I'm confident that they'll release you quickly. I'm here to help, but I'm not sure what I can do."

Rick was filled with mixed emotions. He needed to get back and do what he could to help with the investigation into Maggie's death and to make funeral arrangements. He was also incredibly thankful to Cindy for getting him through these tough days. She was a strong woman, and he was not sure how he could have made it through without her.

"Cindy, I wish …"

Cindy put up her hand. "You have to get back and take care of business, I know. You have family and friends who will support and comfort you. I know you're going to be alright. I'll bet you also have some work to do in Washington, D.C.," she finished with a small smile.

"How can I thank you enough for your help and support? You've been amazing. I thank God that you were there in the parking lot, that you were there for me throughout this ordeal. I hope you know how I feel."

She tucked the piece of paper into his palm and closed his fingers around it. Then she smiled and stood. "I'm glad I was here for you too. I want you to remember, the next time you are in Duluth, you owe me that hamburger."

He smiled and nodded.

Cindy turned and walked out the door, blinking to contain the tears welling up in her eyes.

38

THE FOLLOWING morning, a Saturday, President Donaldson addressed the American people in a nationally televised address.

"My fellow Americans, last night the Congress of the United States sent to me a bill authorizing the use of military force against nine Mexican cartels and those who support or provide assistance to them. This afternoon I will sign that bill into law." As the president spoke from his desk in the Oval Office, his demeanor was resolute and his voice calm and firm.

"Finally, the crisis on the southern border of our great nation will end, and the threat against our country's sovereignty will be met forcefully and effectively. I have asked Secretary of Defense Donna Schmidt to position troops and military assets at our border with Mexico in preparation for Operation Border Guard. I have given her three objectives for this operation.

"The first is to seal the border, making it understood that every man, woman, and child crossing the border will be pushed back into Mexico within twenty-four hours of crossing. The second is to search out and attack cartel members who are enabling these crossings and neutralize them, with deadly force if needed. The third is to stop the flow of drugs, including fentanyl, into the United States from the south. Again, they have been authorized to use deadly force as required.

"The courageous men and women from our Customs and Border Protection Agency will be tasked with assisting in the return of illegal immigrants to Mexico and seeking out those who have come to our country in the past without authorization. They will be removed from the United States. We will use all of our resources to root out the leadership of the drug cartels and destroy the organizations completely."

Donaldson's voice dropped, and his words came more slowly. "Every citizen of the United States and of Mexico is hereby notified that if you engage in helping with the trafficking of illegal immigrants or drugs across our border, you will be at war with the United States of America and will be met with the very same fury and determination as those in the cartels themselves."

The president then turned his focus to the victims of the crisis. "To those people who are on your way to the southern border of the United States, you need to turn around and return home. You are marching into a war zone, and we certainly don't want you to become a casualty of war. If you camp on the Mexico side of the border, the United States will provide no humanitarian aid to you. I can't speak for Mexico, but they may find it difficult to provide you assistance at this time.

"To the people of Mexico, I want you to know that we are doing this for you as well as for ourselves. The corruption brought to your country by the cartels is standing in the way of progress in Mexico. It will be my personal goal to ensure all corruption tied to the cartels is dealt with once and for all and to help you rise to your economic potential while sustaining your unique culture.

"Finally, I want the American people to know that this will be a different sort of war. We will do everything we can to protect our fighting men and women through the use of technology. I ask for your prayers for our nation and its soldiers, and I ask you to support and encourage all who are a part of the armed forces of the United States. May God bless our efforts, and may God bless America."

Most of the American people received the presidential address with enthusiasm. They were glad that something was finally being done to seal the border for good and to curtail the flow of drugs from Mexico. There were others that railed against the Donaldson Administration for stirring up a new war, and one so close to home, no less. Those people were mostly ignored and assumed to be anti-war activists.

39

THE STILL of the moonlit night was broken by the sound of a canoe moving across the water. The swish, swish, swish of the paddle slowed and stopped in the lagoon in front of the Boundary Connector's Outfitters. It was three-thirty in the morning.

Clarisa was satisfied with her progress. She had traveled on land and water about a mile before she saw the youth group setting up camp. She had hidden herself from the circling helicopter and waited patiently nearby. As nighttime fell, sunset and stars helped her to orient herself and determine which direction she would need to travel to get back to civilization.

As the young campers started settling down, she found that one of their canoes was still partially in the water. Carefully she lifted the front until the back end floated and quietly walked it into the lake. She continued to walk until the water was up to her waist, then turned and followed the shoreline, pulling the canoe to a location around a bend from the camp. Once she reached shallow water again, she got into the canoe, reoriented herself by the moon and stars and began paddling. The three-quarter moon brightened up the lake, so she could easily tell water from land, and it took her three hours to get back to the Outfitter's.

Reaching her destination, she stepped out of the canoe in

shallow water and let the boat drift to avoid the bottom scraping along the gravel shore. She walked around the building to the parking lot. The rental car was still there, but if Taylor had talked to the authorities they would know she had come in that car. She walked into the lot, swearing when the pain flared from the gravel against her stocking feet.

Her training had taught her self-sufficiency, including hot-wiring vehicles, but that was not helpful with the most modern cars, where the steering columns locked and electronic security systems were difficult to bypass without the proper tools. She wandered through the parking lot, trying to figure out her best chance of getting as far away as quickly as possible. If she took the rental car, they would notice it gone right away, and an APB would be issued quickly. Finally she came across an old pickup truck, a 1980s model Chevy with a canoe rack on it. If it was a camper's truck, it could be many hours or even days before it would be missed if she could get it started.

She reached into her pocket and took out two of her remaining latex gloves. She checked both doors. They were locked. She walked to the edge of the lot and found a rock that would suffice. She took it back to the truck and broke the passenger side window. She reached inside, unlocked and opened the door, and carefully wiped bits of glass from the running board. She leaned into the truck and whisked bits of glass off the seat. She did the same with the driver's side, and by four in the morning she had hot-wired the truck and was on her way.

40

The St. Cloud police sent a car to pick up Rick. Arrangements were made to trailer his Harley and take it to the police impound lot. He was concerned that his possession of Maggie's cell phone and the gun could still lead to an indictment but was relieved that the investigators had been able to confirm his phone call to Maggie in St. Cloud from Lino Lakes. They could also see that the phones had pinged from different locations in the Boundary Waters. At this point, the evidence was enough to release him while the investigators continued their work.

The police were unable to access Maggie's phone directly. Rick knew her security code, but the police said it didn't work. They suspected that somehow the killer was able to access the phone and change the access code so she could use it at will. They needed more time with it.

The cell phone that they found in the kayak was a throwaway phone that had been purchased in a department store in Virginia with cash. It had made just one phone call to another undocumented number in the Washington, D.C. area, but that phone had also been purchased with cash at the same store. They found Cindy and Rick's fingerprints on the phone. Other prints were there as well, but they were smudged by Rick's handling of it. They were amazed that they could not find any prints on the kayak or the car and presumed that the perpetrator had been wearing gloves.

When the officers got to the campsite that Cindy had identified on the map, there was nobody there. With careful examination, they were able to confirm a few things from Rick and Cindy's story. The two cans, one filled with water on the log and the other lying in the dirt, matched what they had described. The can in the dirt had been torn apart, probably by the woman. They found the oak branch Cindy had used to bludgeon the woman, and there appeared to be blood and skin on one end. There was a piece of thin nylon cord on the ground as well. It had been strung around something and knotted, and in another spot it had been melted and broken. There were some white shoelaces on the ground not far from the cord. They were able to make out a single footprint in the dirt near the edge of the clearing. The size of the print suggested that it was a woman and she had been barefoot, probably wearing socks.

A forensics team was sent to the site to gather more detailed information, but it was clear to the investigators that Rick and Cindy were telling the truth. One question remained. Where had the woman gone?

41

Clarisa called her husband in Washington. "We've got a big, big problem."

"What's wrong?"

"When I confronted him in Ely, some dear old friend showed up at the same time. We were in the parking lot of a canoe place, so I couldn't follow through. I scared him, he got his woman friend involved, and before I knew it I was tracking two people through the Boundary Waters."

"And?"

"And when I found them, I tried to set it up as another murder-suicide, but that complication gave them an opportunity that they took. They overpowered me, and I lost them. They also took the kayak I had used with the throw-away cell in it."

"Well, the AUMF bill passed last night, so that's the main thing."

"The main thing?" she challenged. "There are now two people who have seen me. One is a US Senator, and I haven't got a clue who the other one is or even where she lives. Right now, you can never be seen with your wife again in public. Don't you think that's kind of a main thing too?"

He ignored the question. "I'm glad we scrubbed the Internet and removed everything with your picture in it."

"No, we removed any pictures of you and me together.

They would have to stumble across my picture online, but it's out there."

He said nothing for a while. He had never even considered something like this. "We'll just have to make sure Taylor has an accident."

"You talk as if it's so simple. When we focused on Tom Blado, I was able to draw him in and take care of him in my own good time. I won't be able to get close to Taylor until it goes down. How do you set up an accident if you can't even talk to the guy?" she asked in frustration. "Not to mention the problem of this other woman out there who can identify me."

"Maybe I can help with Taylor. Maybe I can organize a way to lead him to you. Think about that and let me know what you think might work. When I see him, I'll ask him to tell me about his ordeal. Maybe I can find out who the woman is."

"Alright. But what I'd really like to do is just get away and hide somewhere."

"Clarisa, you had some bad luck. We will figure this out. It won't be long before we're in Mexico City. We'll keep you out of the limelight in the meantime."

"Alright. I'll catch a flight tomorrow."

"Wonderful. I'll see you then, love."

42

JIM GUNDERSON had arranged to have Rick's house cleaned as soon as the investigators cleared it. The area rug where Maggie had been found was removed and kept as evidence. Rick called Jim from the police station and asked to meet him at the house as soon as he could.

The police drove past the gaggle of reporters at the end of his driveway and dropped him off at his front door. He got out of the car and heard reporters hollering at him. He walked down the driveway far enough to tell them that he needed his privacy right now and thanked them in advance for respecting that.

He went inside feeling uncomfortable and ill at ease. He walked into the living room and felt the emptiness, not from the missing rug but from the absence of Maggie. He wanted her to walk in from another room and give him a hello kiss like she always had. When she didn't appear, he walked through the bedroom and saw her clothes hanging in the closet. Tears filled his eyes as he came to the renewed realization that she was not here. She would never be here again. He sat on the bed and wept, wiping his tears with the foul-smelling shirt that he had been wearing throughout the ordeal. He didn't know how he could go on without her. She was his everything.

He finally stood and undressed. He walked into the bathroom, shaved, showered, and brushed his teeth. Again he looked around and felt the depth of the emptiness. His heart ached. He forced himself to dress and then went into the kitchen to fix himself a sandwich. He took it along with a bag of chips and a glass of water into the living room and sat on the couch. He stared across the room at the piano and her guitar on the stand where she always kept it. He cried again.

When Jim arrived, Rick thanked him for getting the house cleaned and asked him to explain what had happened on the day he found Maggie. Jim recounted his experience in detail. His voice began to quiver when he described entering the house. "Everything was quiet. I called out several times, but nobody answered," he said as his eyes filled. "And then I saw her feet, right there," he said, pointing to the floor in front of the sofa. "I said her name but she didn't move. I walked toward her and finally saw her face." He faltered for a moment.

Jim spared Rick the details regarding the bullet entry wound and blood pooling beneath her head. Regaining his composure, he said, "I wanted to get down on the ground and hold her, talk to her, but then I thought I should get the police."

Tears trickled down Rick's face. He hadn't even considered what Jim had gone through. "I'm sorry you had to deal with that, my friend. But I'm glad it was you. I'm not sure why, but somehow it's comforting to know that it was someone she knew and trusted that found her."

They both sat quietly for what seemed like a long time, wiping their eyes.

Rick went through the particulars of his experience and explained what he thought his status was with the police. "Were you able to find an attorney that might be of help?" he asked.

"I was," Jim said. I texted you his contact information just before I left the office. "I suggest you give him a call, even if you are off the suspect list. He can probably help in other ways."

Rick nodded. "Thank you. I'll call him this afternoon."

"Have you caught up on the news since you've been back?"

Jim asked him.

"No. I suppose Rick Taylor, wife killer, is all over the media."

"They did have a frenzy when you were listed as a person of interest and couldn't be found, but the police issued an update this morning saying you are now in St. Cloud and cooperating fully," he explained. "What I was referring to were the happenings in Washington."

Rick shook his head.

"Last night the House and Senate passed the bill authorizing the use of military force on the border. This morning, President Donaldson spoke to the nation, basically saying that we are going to war against the drug and human traffickers."

Rick shook his head. That world seemed so far away. "I'm sorry to hear that. It sounds like Moreno took advantage of my absence."

"Yes, and another senator had to leave town because his wife was in an accident."

"How convenient for them," Rick said sarcastically.

Neither said anything for a minute, then Rick spoke again. "Jim, I don't know if there's a connection, but the woman who killed Maggie and pursued us said they were "patriots." That was her word. She said I was getting in the way of "progress." Can you think of anything else I have been involved with that someone was upset about?"

Jim thought for a moment, staring at Rick. His eyes went to the floor as he tried to recollect anything that might cause someone to wish Rick out of the way. "I can't think of a thing," he said finally. "I can't imagine that this AUMF bill could motivate someone to do that. Maybe she was giving you a red herring."

"Maybe, but I don't know why she would. She was about to kill me."

After Jim left, Rick called Sandra Dellingham in Washington to let her know that he was back. He felt little interest in Washington at that moment, but it was his job, and he knew

Maggie would be in his face telling him that they had fought hard to win that election and he needed to pull himself together and focus on his responsibilities. He listened carefully to Sandra's briefing but didn't get angry at the president's maneuvering. He didn't have the strength for that. He simply shook his head. He promised to be back in Washington within a couple of weeks, after he was able to get through Maggie's funeral.

He also called Ben Wolfe to see how the company was handling things. After briefing him, Ben told him that his call was an answer to his prayers. "Rick, you won't believe how things have been around here. Of course the media wanted an interview and suggested that you killed Maggie. Nobody would talk to them. We were all in disbelief. I apologize, but we were starting to wonder what we would do if you really had been responsible for Maggie's death. All the police would say is that you were a person of interest. And you just disappeared!"

"No apology needed. I'm sure I would have reacted the same way. Now I'm back, and I'll be in town for a while until I can make the final arrangements for Maggie. Is there anything you need from me?"

"No, we've got things in hand here. We're just glad you're home and alright. We are all so sorry about Maggie. Why don't I assign someone to help you with the arrangements? I'm sure you are loaded down with stress and grief. I could ask Wanda to meet with you and take some of this off your hands."

"That would be great, Ben. Thank you. I'll call her tomorrow to arrange a meeting. Right now I could use some help just figuring out what's what."

43

THE NEXT week and a half were a whirlwind of activity. In addition to all that was involved with Maggie's arrangements, Rick was still anxious about the investigation. He got upset when he heard that their attacker had not been found. He thought about how Cindy had pressed the deputies to go find her immediately and wished they had listened.

The police told him that he was not a suspect at this time, although they wouldn't share much information with him. He had gotten a couple of calls from a detective who wanted to talk about possible motives that someone might have to harm him or Maggie. He told the detective what the woman had said to him. His attorney recommended that he not speak to the police further without a lawyer present. He promised Rick he would check in with the police chief regularly to learn all he could about the investigation.

Rick's parents and Maggie's family were with him off and on. All were heartbroken and angry that she should be taken so soon. He took heart in their company as they talked about Maggie and laughed and cried together, but he always wanted to be alone at night. When he was with them, he felt horrified that someone had killed her on account of him. Nobody tried to make him feel that way, but questions always arose about why someone who knew him would want to do something like this. The press continued to hover nearby, which reinforced their unease.

A week after he returned home, Sandra urged him to make a statement. She said it needed to be done soon, lest the press began speculating that he was hiding something. He spoke with his attorney, who wanted to be there when he spoke. Rick told him absolutely not. That would make him appear to be lawyering up because he had something to conceal. Rick did run his statement by him, and they talked through what he should and should not say and how to answer potential questions. They also contacted the St. Cloud police chief to see if there was anything he wanted Rick to avoid talking about.

Rather than just wandering down to the end of his driveway, Rick had Jim set up a press conference at his senatorial office in Minneapolis. He hoped that this would get rid of the reporters at his home. On the morning of the conference, Rick walked out of the office building to a podium with multiple microphones. It was a warm and humid day, although the cloud cover removed the direct heat of the sun. They had set up in a remote section of the parking lot as far away from the street traffic as they could. There was still constant traffic noise from the road in front of the building, but it would have to do.

Rick began, "Good morning. First of all, I want to thank you for allowing me privacy over the past week to begin the grieving process following the loss of my wife, Maggie. She is … was the love of my life, and this has shocked my world to the core.

"As you know, my absence following Maggie's death created quite a stir. There are few specifics that I can share with you while the investigation is underway, but I can confirm what you have been told already. It appears that I may have been the target in this shooting, and, in fact, I was pursued myself during my time in the Boundary Waters. As soon as I could, I reached out to the police and have cooperated fully in their investigation ever since."

"I have re-engaged in my responsibilities as your senator. I anticipate returning to Washington next week. My wife will be eulogized on Thursday in a private celebration of life service and will be laid to rest that afternoon. Again, I ask for privacy as I deal with this tremendous loss."

The crowd peppered him with questions about who pursued him, whether it was someone he knew, how he had managed to outrun them, and other details. He referred them to the St. Cloud Police Department for answers to those questions. One reporter asked if the rumor was true that he had been with another woman at the Boundary Waters.

"Let me put it this way. When I arrived there, I ran into a friend from my high school days. It was completely coincidental. Our meeting was not planned. However, she was a huge support for me as I learned of Maggie's death, and I will be forever indebted to her for that."

"What is the woman's name?" a reporter asked.

"That will be kept confidential, I hope. I would hate for her to be thrust into the middle of this media circus." He smiled slightly at them. "She also cooperated with the police when we were able to get back to shore."

"Were you involved with her romantically?"

Rick cringed and sighed. "No, it was just as I explained. She is a friend who I had not seen in over twenty years and randomly bumped into. As luck would have it, she was there to help me through a traumatic time. That is all."

Other than a few other questions relating to how he felt about this or that, the rest pertained to the investigation, and he again referred those to the police. Jim stepped in after ten minutes and drew Rick away from the microphones. Rick went with him but took a step back to the microphone and simply said, "Thank you."

PART 3

DISCERNING THE MISSION

"Language has an ideological agenda that is apt to be hidden from view."
— Neil Postman, *Technopoly: The Surrender of Culture to Technology*

44

Twenty-five thousand troops had amassed at the southern border of the United States. Tent cities sprang up in southern Texas, New Mexico, Arizona, and California. Most of the tents were for the troops to sleep in and dine in, and to engage in recreation when they had time. Some, however, were warehouses for the primary weapon that the military intended to use against the cartels.

Key areas to be defended were identified along the 2,000-mile border. The thirty-foot tall border wall that had been built by a previous administration blocked entry along 700 miles of that stretch, mostly near the more populous areas in California, Arizona, and Texas. The much hyped "wall" actually replaced about 650 miles of old, deteriorating fencing and added only about fifty miles of fencing where there had been none before.

The military was patrolling the border now, and it was estimated that 98% of immigrants crossing the border were captured and returned to Mexico within eighteen hours of their crossing. Immigrants gradually got the message, and most stopped attempting to cross. Instead, they set up encampments eight to ten miles south of the border to see what would happen.

The Mexican president was outraged at what was happening. His country was not able to provide for the hundred thousand or so people already camped out near many small towns south of the border, nor the tens of thousands more that were moving north through his country to get to the US. "The United States has created the conditions that draw migrants to it. *They* can care for those who gather," he said.

Meanwhile, Donna Schmidt, Donaldson's Secretary of Defense, and George Tompkins, Chairman of the Joint Chiefs of Staff, provided a briefing to the president and his cabinet prior to initiating Operation Border Guard. "The beauty of this operation is that the initial incursion into Mexico will be accomplished by an army of unique, independent drones that are totally self-supporting but are also able to interact with one another through artificial intelligence," Schmidt said. "All of these drones will be linked through larger drones that will be flying overhead and scouting the area."

"Please provide us with more detail on those drones," the president said.

"Yes sir," Tompkins replied. He asked his aide to put a picture of the drone on the screen for all to see. It was an odd-looking contraption. It looked something like a child's transformer toy. The bottom part was about four feet square, and the top section looked like it was about ten feet across. The whole thing was probably five feet tall and sat on what looked like tracks, similar to those of a tank. On top were six horizontal propellers like those of a helicopter. The propellers sat about six feet out from the center of the unit, and in the middle was a solar panel that stretched between all of the propellers. The entire machine was painted in desert camouflage except for the solar panel.

"These drones are operated by electricity, and power is maintained through solar-charged batteries. They are designed for short range, relatively quick missions." At Tompkins's nod, the image came to life as a video. The propellers began turning, and the top lifted off of the base unit and became airborne. The propellers gave off a low whirring or buzzing sound, but there was no engine noise. The underside of the unit was sky blue. Once the base was left behind, its flat top automatically unfolded to become a 16x16 foot solar panel.

"While on an airborne mission, the flying drone runs on battery power that is supplemented by incoming power from the on-board solar panel. Meanwhile, the base unit goes into rapid charge mode through the use of an expanded solar panel that deploys once the drone takes off," Tompkins explained as the video revealed the process in real time. "The drone is able to operate for up to forty-five minutes on a typical mission."

The video was paused. "The purpose of the drone is to identify and kill soldiers. It is programmed to differentiate civilians and combatants by recognizing the weapon being carried. Those members of the cartel with weapons carry rifles over their shoulders or handguns in a holster. The drone recognizes those people as a threat. When it recognizes a threat or target, it will maneuver around to be in the most favorable position, considering wind, height, distance, and other factors."

"You will see that there is a barrel protruding from the drone," Tompkins continued, pointing to the pipe that extended out from the drone. "That is a type of gun barrel. The drone is capable of maneuvering itself and the gun into any position it desires. It analyzes the shot based upon distance, wind factors, and the impact of the shot to the drone itself, like the kick of a gun, and hits its target with 97% accuracy."

A picture of a scarecrow with a rifle hanging from its shoulder came into view on the screen. The drone whirled around quickly, flew to a point upwind from the target, and fired a shot that took the head off the scarecrow from about sixty yards away. There was a gasp around the table as the members of Donaldson's cabinet watched the drone's killing capability.

"It carries forty rounds but will likely take only five to ten shots on a given flight mission. At the end of its mission, it will return to its own base unit for recharging and reloading."

Anthony Weller, the Secretary of State, asked, "All this technology to create a flying rifle? It appears to be a pretty expensive piece of equipment for such a simple application."

"It may seem that way," Tompkins agreed. "However, by going after targets one at a time and differentiating between friend and foe, we reduce the risk of collateral damage. Just as importantly, the drones assume the difficult task of picking out and firing on threats from among migrants."

Secretary of Defense Schmidt added, "We will have larger drones airborne twenty-four hours per day, seven days a week, that will identify targets and communicate with multiple small drones, telling them how many will be required and where the threat is. The smaller drones will analyze the situation once on scene using AI and coordinate with one another, communicating through the large drone above. They will actually be able to coordinate which drone will take out which target."

"General Tompkins," asked the vice president, "how long can these small drones function on their own?"

"Technically, they can operate indefinitely over time, but the number of daily missions is limited based upon the length of each mission. They can accomplish ten to twelve missions per day assuming each is about ten minutes long. In the event of frequent or lengthy missions, some may have to forgo shorter assignments to allow the batteries to be recharged.

"The base unit carries 750 rounds of ammunition and automatically reloads the flying unit each time it docks. Operating in this environment, these drones should have a useful life of eighteen to twenty-four months before being renovated or replaced."

"Can't the enemy just take these base units out while the flying drone is gone?" the president asked.

"No sir," replied the general. "Both the base unit and the flying unit have self-preservation software and hardware built in so that if anyone shoots at it or approaches it in a threatening manner, they will be shot. The base unit has its own gun mechanism. Of course, if ten people charge it from ten different directions, a few might get through and damage it, but it would also coordinate with other nearby drones to join the attack on the threat."

"Mr. President," Schmidt said, "these drones will allow us to take out most of the cartel's men with little or no risk to our soldiers. However, I should advise you that the team that has developed this AI capability is uncomfortable with it being utilized without further testing. They have asked for another two weeks for testing and fine tuning."

Donaldson frowned. "No. We will not delay any further. If we are going to reach our ultimate goal, we need to move now. Does anyone have any other questions?"

Nobody had questions.

He looked at Schmidt again. "What role will our soldiers play?"

"The soldiers will enter the theater once it has been cleared of cartel members, gather the immigrants, and move them to safety far into the Mexican interior where they will be encouraged to turn around and return to their home countries," she explained. "So these drones will move southbound, into Mexico, always advancing in front of our troops."

"How will they be dispersed?" the president asked.

"We have 6,500 units that will be deployed, typically in groups of ten, and more in heavy traffic areas. They are already positioned just across the border from their initially-assigned locations. At the 'go' command, we can have all units in place within twelve nighttime hours."

As the questions around the table waned, everyone watched the screen as the flying fighter maneuvered back to its base unit. It hovered momentarily, then turned to align with the awaiting platform and settled down to rest on its pedestal.

45

RICK WENT to the church early on Thursday to meet with his and Maggie's families before the funeral service. As he interacted with those he loved, he could tell that everyone felt the same awkwardness that he did. This wasn't supposed to be happening. He didn't want to say goodbye to Maggie, yet he knew this was part of the process of letting her go. It all seemed so surreal. He couldn't believe that she was gone.

The funeral was well attended by many of their colleagues and friends as well as their families. Frank Moreno and several other senators came, as did Vice President Marjorie Whittington. The Christian service was uplifting and gave Rick a great deal of comfort. He alone knew of Maggie's great sin. Their pastor reminded him that all are sinful and that Jesus' forgiveness was a free gift for all who trust in him. He knew what the Bible said. He knew Maggie's faith and he knew she was in heaven. He was surprised at the number of people who were moved to come forward and eulogize her. He knew that she had many friends, and all of the stories reminded him of the many lives she had touched.

Jim Gunderson talked about Maggie and the campaign. "After years involved with and managing political campaigns, I knew that Rick's campaign for the Senate was a long shot at best. So what does Maggie, our political novice, do? She sings," he said with a funny look on his face. The people laughed. "Maggie was an amazing woman, as tenacious as they come. She inspired both Rick and me to be our best, never wanting to disappoint her."

The closing hymn was what pushed Rick over the edge, the tears flowing to the last verse of "Abide with Me."

> *Hold thou thy cross before my closing eyes,*
> *Shine through the gloom and point me to the skies.*
> *Heaven's morning breaks and earth's vain shadows flee*
> *In life, in death, O Lord, abide with me.*

His mother reached over and took his hand and held it as they cried together.

After receiving all of the guests at the reception, Rick approached the vice president. "Madam Vice President, I want you to know how much I appreciate you taking the time to come to the service today."

"Senator Taylor, under such tragic circumstances there is little or nothing that the most powerful country in the world can do. We can at least grieve with you and celebrate your time with Maggie. She was obviously a wonderful woman and a blessing to you."

"She was indeed." Rick hesitated. "I know this is the wrong time and place for this, but I think Maggie would be shocked at what is happening in the country right now, and I don't know when I will have another opportunity to ask." He hesitated. "What do you think of the latest move to put our soldiers in harm's way on an incursion into Mexico?"

Whittington looked Rick directly in the eye for a moment, then turned to see if anyone was within earshot of their conversation. "I am part of this administration, but the president sets the policy. Personally, I was hoping he would adjust his plans once in office. Well, he has adjusted them, but only to be more aggressive. You should be aware, however, that much of the initial incursion will be done with drones rather than soldiers. The cabinet received a briefing earlier this week."

"Drones? We're sending drones in among the immigrants, hoping they take out the right people?"

"Well, something like that. The drones will be utilizing AI and advanced visual technology to identify armed cartel members. Are you going to join the group of senators going to the border next week for a briefing?"

"Given the timing, I hadn't planned to, but hearing this makes me definitely want to join." Rick shook his head. "I'm sure that you're aware of my feelings about all of this. What you've told me has only served to cause me more concern. Thank you again, Madam Vice President."

She nodded, and Rick walked over to his chief of staff. "Sandra, do you think I can still get into that border briefing that is set up for next Thursday?"

"I thought you didn't want to attend."

"Whittington just told me that they're using drones and AI for the attack. I've got to see what this is about."

"I'll get you in."

Rick thought back to their interview with Lily Gadis, the intern who was an expert in AI. "Do you think there would be any pushback if I took Lily along?"

"There's no way they willl allow an intern into a classified briefing. It simply will not happen."

"I suppose you're right. Even so, I want you to clear her schedule for the entire day next Thursday. I want to be able to talk with her at a moment's notice."

"I'll make sure she's accessible."

"Good. I'd also like to meet with Lily, you, and Jim on Wednesday morning. I need your insights to make sure that I ask the right questions."

"I'll set it up. Can I change the subject for a second?"

"Of course."

"It sounds like there's a woman out there someplace who's trying to take your life. What security precautions have you taken?"

"Well, the police have made my house a regular drive-by

location for one of their patrol cars. I guess that won't help as I begin traveling again. In answer to your question, I've taken no extra precautions. I haven't even had time to think about it, and I wouldn't know where to begin."

"I've spoken with some other staffers of senators who have security details with them. I know where to go to set it up. We'll have to justify using government funding, but I recommend we set it up as soon as possible. Can you afford to cover it until the funding is in place?

"I'm sure I can. Go ahead; just let me know what's needed from me. And, Sandra, thanks for thinking about this. "

"Okay. I'll work on it this afternoon."

#

Early Friday morning, Rick fished through his wallet and found the piece of paper that Cindy had given him in Ely. He called the number and was somewhat surprised when she answered the phone, thinking she would probably be at work.

"Hello?" she said quickly. She almost hadn't answered it because she didn't recognize the number.

"Cindy, this is Rick."

"Patrick," she said with a smile in her voice. Then her tone changed. "How are you getting along?"

"Oh, fine, under the circumstances. I'm fully engaged in Washington, so that keeps me busy."

"I'm sure it does keep you busy," she said. "I just thought you would take some time off after the funeral."

"It's better that I'm working. I need to stay busy. Besides, I'm concerned about some things that are developing, and I need to involve myself. It's something that really can't wait."

"A busy guy. To what do I owe the pleasure of your call?"

"I was reminded yesterday that there is a woman out there whom you and I can identify. I'm setting up security for myself, but I was concerned about you and wanted to check in. Do you have a home security system?"

"I have a sign in my front yard that says I do. So far that has kept the burglars away," she answered flippantly.

"You should have the real thing installed. I don't think there is any way she could know who you are or where you live, but I feel like you should take some precautions anyway."

She paused and thought for a moment. "I thought the same thing, that she wouldn't know who I was or how to find me. But … are you serious? Do you think I should take some extra steps?"

"I am. I still feel guilty for putting you at risk like I did. If you need help financially to accomplish it, I'd be happy to give you a hand."

"That shouldn't be necessary. Thanks for thinking of me. I'll call and arrange it after we hang up."

"How far is your drive to work?"

"It's less than a mile. My commute is just five minutes."

"That's good. Talk to the security people and see what other suggestions they might have. I suggest you avoid going out alone. Stay with other people. Do you carry mace or something?"

"I never have."

"I suggest you get something like that and know how to use it. You might want to seriously consider carrying a gu—"

"You know that's not going to happen," she said, cutting him off.

Rick grimaced and rolled his eyes. "Listen, I have to go, but I just got to thinking about you, and I want you to be careful."

"It's nice to know you care," she said cheerfully.

"Of course I care. I still don't know how I would have dealt with everything without you. Keep your head down, and I'll let you know if and when there is an arrest. Be alert regarding what's going on around you."

"I understand. Thanks for the call, Patrick."

"You bet. Maybe we can talk about something other than danger sometime. Take care of yourself, Cindy."

"I will. You too."

46

RICK TOOK the rest of the weekend to gather his wits about himself and think about getting back to work. He booked a Sunday flight to Washington. When he arrived, he did a little grocery shopping and got situated back in his apartment.

On Monday morning, Sandra, Jim, and Lily came to his office at ten in the morning as he had requested. He waved them in, and they all sat around the six-person table in the conference room next to his office.

"Thanks for setting this up, Sandra," Rick began. "What we are going to discuss here should be treated for the time being as confidential. First of all, the information I received came secondhand from Vice President Whittington. Second, there may be elements that are certified as classified, or higher, by the government. Were it not for the immediacy of my concern, I would not give all of you this information. Please don't repeat or discuss it outside of private discussions with one or more of us who are in this room. Do you understand?"

All nodded that they understood. Nobody spoke, waiting for their boss to proceed.

"I have learned that when the cartels are attacked, it will be done not with our soldiers but with drones. I am also told that their targets will be selected with the use of advanced visual technology and artificial intelligence. This has me very concerned. There are tens of thousands of migrants in northern Mexico right now. Picking targets out of that mass or firing into groups of civilians makes me very uncomfortable."

As he talked, Rick looked each of them in the eye to confirm that they understood. "On Thursday I will be in Texas, and I believe I will receive a more thorough briefing of this information. But, I know so little about AI that I wanted your ideas about what questions I should ask."

"Sir, do you know how they will be using AI with these drones?" Lily asked.

"As of now, I do not," Rick replied. "Why? What are you thinking?"

"Well, AI is an amazing workhorse and can process information more quickly than a person. In this sort of application, if it is feeding that processed information to decision makers, it could give us a great heads-up on the enemy. Likely enemies would be identified quickly so that drones or soldiers can be deployed to deal with them."

Rick, Sandra, and Jim were riveted by Lily's every word. "Okay," Rick said slowly. "Is there a but?"

"There is. If these drones are set up with AI in order to have them operate independently, the system had better be scrubbed and tested every which way it can," Lily explained. "If the AI sees something that it has not been specifically programmed to understand, there is a risk that it will mistakenly view a non-threatening situation as a threat."

Sandra put up her right hand as if to say, *Whoa*. "So it could make incorrect assumptions and act on them, rather than stop and ask questions?"

"It could. This is part of the risk of using AI in this manner. AI actually learns through its experience. If it makes such an assumption and receives no negative feedback, it will tuck that information into itself as new factual information that it should use in selecting future targets."

"Okay, so one of the things I need to ask is where within the targeting process the human element of judgment is considered?" Rick asked.

"Correct. If the system operates totally independent of human judgment, it could get off on the wrong track, and the consequences could be disastrous. For example, what if it saw that all of the threats it looks at are Hispanic? It could come to think that all people of Hispanic origin are threats. I seriously doubt that would happen, but it gives you an idea of the danger."

"Okay, what other things will I want to ask?"

Jim answered the question with another question for Lily. "Let's assume the worst. Something like you just described goes wrong. Can they shut them down from a distance?"

"I hope so, but that would have to be specifically programmed in. I can't imagine that the developers would leave that capability out."

"Another question then," probed Rick.

"Yes, sir."

"What other processes would likely be built into the software?"

"Oh gosh, there are a million things possible," Lily said as she leaned forward with her elbows on the table. "I haven't worked with AI in the context of warfare, so I'm sure there are things that I would never come up with. Maybe one thing would be whether these drones are somehow programmed to defend themselves. If so, who would they be told to defend themselves against? That could become sticky if that self-defense mindset, if you will, became too strong."

Rick let out a long fading whistle. "Now I understand why there is such fear over AI. If it's not operating within safe parameters that match our values, it could even turn on its programmers?"

"It's possible. And if it has the capability of using deadly force, just imagine the havoc it could generate," Lily said.

"Oh Lily, I wish I could take you along to this briefing. Your insights would be valuable. However, I guess I'll have to wing it based on our conversation today. Thank you all. At least I know where to probe during our tour this week."

47

CLARISA MORENO used her connections to request a copy of the police report relating to the arrest of Rick Taylor and the woman he was with. She was disappointed to find that the woman's name had been redacted.

She knew that Taylor's death would now be much more challenging to enact and wanted to take care of the woman quickly to get that out of the way first. She called her husband late Sunday evening and asked for his help in learning the woman's identity. She knew that the Senate majority leader could accomplish things that an ordinary citizen could not, and his motive would never be questioned.

Indeed, on Monday, Leader Moreno was able to contact the Justice Department and ask the favor. He explained that he wanted to send a personal thank you to the woman who had helped Senator Taylor in the recent attempt on his life. That evening Frank called to let Clarisa know what he had learned. "Hello love," he began. "I've got the information you asked for."

"What would I do if my husband wasn't such an important man?" she said, stroking his ego. "It makes me want you just thinking about it."

Moreno wasn't surprised by his wife's erotic comment. It was what he loved best about her. Power gave her passion like he'd never seen. His power or her power, it didn't matter.

"Oh, don't do this to me," he groaned. "I need more than phone sex from you. When are you coming home?"

"Oh," she whispered in a sultry voice. "I want to be there right now. Give me some time to take care of this, and I'll be at your beck and call."

Frank smiled just thinking about it. "Okay love, do you have a piece of paper?"

"Uh-huh," she said slowly with that voice that still teased him.

"Her name is Cindy Potter. She's a nurse at Duluth General. Her home address is 1647 Superior Way. That's all I have. That idiot Taylor. I hate that someone else has become involved. How are you going to handle it?"

"I'm not sure yet. I need to check out her comings and goings first. I'll make sure it doesn't appear to be related to her experience with Taylor."

"Good. You know I don't question your judgment, love. I just appreciate your amazing thought process. I'll look forward to hearing all about it."

Now she smiled and gave a kiss into the phone. "Good night, my love."

On Tuesday morning she rented an economy car under one of the aliases she had established since this project began. She drove to Duluth and checked out various routes between Cindy Potter's home and the hospital where she worked. It was only about a mile. That could make it challenging. However, between Potter's work and home was a block-long park with some nice trees and shrubbery. There was a very small playground area, but it wasn't a sports park and appeared to be more like a green belt that the city required of the developer when the homes were built, fairly recently, Clarisa guessed.

At five that evening she parked near Potter's home and watched. There was no activity at all. Cindy Potter didn't seem to be home. No lights were on except a dim lamp in what she figured was the living room. Clarisa moved the car every hour or so to avoid curious neighbors noticing a strange vehicle in front of their homes. After midnight Cindy finally pulled into her driveway. The garage door opened automatically; she drove in and lowered the door again before getting out of her car.

"Good girl," Clarisa said out loud. "Safety conscious." She was satisfied. Her first day had been productive: She had found the house and seen the gray Volvo that Potter drove. The park was an interesting feature. Perhaps she could work out a way for Cindy to have to walk home through it. She could set it up as a sexual assault and murder. *Yes*, she thought. *If she gets home this late every night, that could work.*

She drove to a remote road outside of Duluth and napped until five that morning. She parked between Cindy's house and the hospital on the street that Cindy was most likely to use when leaving her neighborhood. Again, she moved her car from time to time. It was a long morning with no sign of Cindy Potter. *Patience*, she thought. Patience was something she had been good at on her military assignments. She had learned that moving too quickly caused mistakes. It was possible that Cindy was off today. Clarisa knew that nurses had different kinds of shifts and must be available seven days a week.

At last, at eleven-thirty that morning, she saw the Volvo come out of the neighborhood and turn in the direction of the hospital. She stayed two blocks behind but followed as Cindy drove into the hospital parking lot. So, one possibility was that Cindy Potter worked twelve-hour shifts. She starts at noon and gets off at midnight. Clarisa very much liked the thought of darkness when it was time for the woman to get off work, but it would take a bit more time, perhaps several days or even a week, to lock in her theory. Her thoughts went to her husband who was hungry for her in Washington, D.C. He would have to wait.

48

ON THE Thursday flight to El Paso where the tour and briefing was to take place, Rick spoke with a number of other senators, probing into how the vote to authorize force had gone down and to get their perspectives on the seemingly imminent invasion of Mexico. Opinions on the vote to authorize force were predictable and split down party lines. There seemed to be more discomfort, even from many senators in the president's party, when Rick asked about a potential invasion of Mexico.

They got out of the air-conditioned bus at a temporary military compound at the border. It was a sweltering 107 degrees. Rick remembered hearing people talk about the blistering temperatures in the Southwest, saying, *Oh, but it's a dry heat.* Those people had obviously not experienced it. He felt like he was in an oven. Dry or not, it was miserable. Having extensive experience fighting in the Middle East, he knew that the military knew how to deal with the heat, but he also prepared himself for an uncomfortable experience today.

They were taken to a large tent for the tour and briefing. The shade helped somewhat, but it also blocked the breeze. Inside the tent were hundreds of drones. One had been separated from the rest, and they were able to see a demonstration of how it worked. The drone took off, flew inside the tent, and then docked with the ground unit again. The general doing the briefing acknowledged that the exact flight pattern for this demonstration had been pre-programmed into this unit.

Senator O'Brian from Nebraska asked, "Is there a single point of command where all of the computer software is stored? If so, where is that?"

The general explained, "Well, yes and no. There is a central point where software resides and updates are completed, et cetera. However, each drone has software resident in it that does the analysis for that unit. They interact with that central point, but they also interact with the large drones and other units like themselves. As one develops new information, it's shared with the others. When multiple targets are in range, the units will actually coordinate with one another to determine which unit will focus on which target. That way, we don't have ten drones all going after just two of the ten targets. It is very complex but well thought through."

Rick asked, "These units are selecting targets and distributing them among each other. Where does the element of human judgment factor in?"

"All of that was done in the programming. They are built to make quick decisions and to act on them."

"What if we find there is a glitch somewhere, and these machines make an incorrect decision. How will they be corrected?"

"Well, naturally I'm not an expert in this area, but I'm sure a tweak can be made in the programming and sent to all units."

"General, if you would, I would appreciate it if you could provide more detail in a follow-up report to this delegation."

The general's jaws clenched, but he maintained a neutral expression. "I would be happy to," he answered.

As the morning progressed and more questions were raised, the look on many senators' faces changed from being impressed to having some misgivings. As they wrapped up, Rick asked, "Is there a self-defense mechanism built into these units? If so, is that handled in the central processing center or within each unit?"

"Yes, a self-defense process is built into each unit. When a threat is identified, the units can shoot anyone who is deemed a target, either from the ground position or by going airborne. Again, when the system gains experience, even in self-defense, it is shared with all the drones."

"How will it differentiate between the guy coming to reload ammunition into the base and someone coming to do harm?" Rick asked.

"Again, I'm not a programmer, but I'm sure that has been taken care of."

"Thank you, general. I would appreciate a follow-up on that as well."

"Yes, sir," said the general curtly.

"I have one last question. When the president declares this war with the cartels over, what will cause these drones to stand down?"

"The programming team will have the capability of sending program changes or instructions to all drones at any time. They can send a stand down command to one of them or to all of them at a moment's notice."

Rick looked at the other senators, who were looking at him now. He shook his head. "All of this leaves me very uncomfortable."

"Technology drives change, Senator Taylor, in your world and in mine. We need to embrace that change. It will lead to things that we never dreamed of just a few years ago."

"Yes, and that's what I'm afraid of," Rick remarked to the woman next to him.

49

AFTER TWO days, Clarisa's stakeout confirmed that Cindy worked twelve-hour shifts, noon to midnight, most likely three or four shifts per week. Clarisa didn't know what days she had off, but there was enough information to put a plan in place to make certain that her next shift would be her last.

Clarisa decided she would wait until about ten o'clock at night, well after visiting hours were over, so that there would be fewer people coming and going in the parking lot. She would flatten two tires on the vehicle, using the same technique she had used with Senator Blado's car. A little luck would be needed for this to work. She hoped that with two flat tires and only one spare, Cindy would decide to walk home and deal with it the following morning. An assault in the park would make it a stretch for anyone to link Cindy Potter's death to the Boundary Waters incident.

She threw the items she had used for Tom Blado's death into the car just in case. The bag included a cordless drill, the appropriate-sized drill bit, a box of roofing nails, and a hammer. Thinking about possible techniques for the killing, Clarisa bagged up some other tools, including her gun and a knife.

Now she just had to wait until Potter's next shift.

50

FOLLOWING THE trip to El Paso, Rick had Jim reach out to the big networks and news channels to let them know that he had serious concerns with the president's plan for the border and that he would make himself available on Friday morning for interviews.

Two interviews were conducted from the Capitol. The view was dramatic, with Rick standing against the backdrop of the stately, marble structure. In the first interview the network anchor asked, "How does it feel to be the sole senator from your party that doesn't support the president in his plans for the border?"

"Let me be clear. I support the president's desire to seal the border. However, I disagree with the premise of your question," Rick began. "I may have been the sole dissenter from my party on the authorization to use military force on the border, but I was in the Senate delegation that was recently briefed on the military's battle plan, and, while I can't speak for others, I suspect there are those in both parties who are uncomfortable with the president's plans."

"Can you tell us what you are uncomfortable with specifically?"

"Obviously, I can't divulge any of the confidential information that we received from the briefing. However, I believe that the scope of the operation is far beyond what is needed to secure the border. You can see that the massive military presence on the border has already stopped a significant portion of immigrants from even attempting to cross over. We should take that success and give it time to work. Once people understand that they will not be allowed entry into the country, they will stop coming."

"You're saying that there are additional military phases to this operation that have not yet been implemented?"

"Well," Rick paused to think how he should respond. "Let's just say that the president hasn't really taken on the cartels yet, as he seems anxious to do. From what I heard in the briefing, he has the capability to do that and more. I really don't understand what the president's end game is. Again, I believe the scope of the operation is inappropriate for the goal of sealing the border. I call on President Donaldson to outline for the American people exactly what victory will look like in this military endeavor."

"Are you saying that the president is not being truthful with the American people regarding his intentions or in how he will fight the cartels?" the reporter probed.

"Yes, both. I have no military experience, but I believe the capabilities we have assembled at the border go far beyond the president's stated agenda. Not only that, but there are also elements of the operation that raised red flags in my mind. I hope the president will rethink this approach."

"What other elements are you concerned about, Senator Taylor?"

"I'm not going to reveal details about that. I don't want to project our military's intentions to the enemy."

Clips of the interviews were on most major newscasts that evening. Reporters began following him about, and he soon had more requests for interviews than he had time to give. News agencies also called other senators that were in the El Paso delegation. Senators in the opposing party used the opportunity to bash the president and everyone in his party, while most senators from his party hid from the reporters.

They didn't want to be on record either way. The few that agreed to interviews voiced some level of discomfort with what they had seen, but stated their belief that this was because they hadn't yet received details on the president's strategic plan.

51

BY FRIDAY afternoon, the president had heard about Rick Taylor's interviews, and he was livid. He called his team into a meeting in the Oval Office and demanded that the invasion be initiated that night. "Rick Taylor is going to destroy any element of surprise. His big mouth has reporters digging for details any way they can."

"The troops are ready," Secretary of Defense Schmidt acknowledged. "However, I recommend we give them twenty-four hours' notice to ensure everything comes together flawlessly."

"Denied," responded the president firmly. "We've screwed around enough. Let's get this thing going." They had not seen the president quite this animated before. His face was crimson as he pounded the table in front of him. His glare said, *Get it done, or I'll find someone who will.* There was precious little discussion to be had about it.

Kauffman stayed after the meeting. "What caused this sudden need to move forward immediately?"

"Taylor is out stirring up discontent. If we wait too long, he'll sabotage everything. We have planned too well to allow a freshman senator to stand in our way."

"I understand, but we need to be careful and not rush through this. Everything needs to roll out one step at a time, or we risk losing the final objective."

"Stan, everything is lined out from the start date of the invasion. We won't stray from the plan, but we need it to get moving. Are we ready to initiate the media attack on President Cuevas?"

"Yes. By this time next week, Cuevas will be viewed as a traitor to the country and in the pocket of the cartels."

"Okay. Moreno assures me that he is ready to move when needed to take charge of the provisional government. We have a lot of people in the Mexican Senate who have assured their support, but this will still take some serious diplomacy."

"Yes, sir."

#

President Donaldson reached out to Frank Moreno and asked that he come to the White House that afternoon. When he arrived, President Donaldson said, "Frank, thanks for coming on such short notice. Let's go to the SCIF."

Donaldson had arranged to have the Sensitive Compartmented Information Facility available for his use. It was a room that was built and maintained in such a way that conversations could take place in secret, assuring that nobody outside of that room could hear the conversation inside. The room would be swept for listening devices before each use, and everyone entering the room would be required to leave their phones and other devices in a locker outside.

Once inside, the president turned to Moreno. "What happened to the murder/suicide you promised me?" he asked with a snarl.

"I'm glad I can finally talk with you about it," Moreno said. "There were a lot of things that happened that couldn't have been anticipated." He explained to the president about Taylor not being home when Clarisa got there. He went on to describe what had happened in the Boundary Waters and how another person became involved. "Both Taylor and this woman have seen her. Fortunately, they have no idea who she is or where she is."

Donaldson, still standing, exploded, causing Moreno to take a step back. "Just wonderful! Now we have two people who can identify her!" He waved his arms in front of Moreno. "And now Taylor is still out there pissing on my leg with the press. Get him taken care of, Frank!"

"Yes, sir," Frank said. "Clarisa is in Duluth and will take care of the woman any day now. Then she'll focus on Taylor."

Donaldson closed the gap between them and raised a finger to Moreno's face. "Maybe you didn't understand me. I said get Taylor out of my way, now!"

Moreno took a step back. "It won't be that easy. Now he has an armed guard with him at all times and he's become a media darling. Reporters are constantly clamoring around when he's in public."

"You told me you and Clarisa would do anything in support of our mission. Do it, now! Why are you wasting time on some woman who doesn't know me from Adam when Taylor is out there threatening the success of the whole deal?"

"Well, she can identify Claris—"

"Did you not hear what I just said?" Donaldson screamed.

"Yes, sir, I'll redirect her immediately."

Donaldson took a loud breath. "You're about to be the governor of Mexico. Get this taken care of so we can focus on that."

"Yes. We'll get it figured out," Moreno said.

"Now," Donaldson said with a new, calmer demeanor, "the invasion begins tonight. That means in seven days I'll need you in Mexico City to take the reins. Be prepared and get this unpleasantness with Taylor and the girl behind us. Our strategic vision for the growth of the United States is dependent upon it."

"Yes, sir," Moreno agreed. "I'll be ready."

52

CLARISA WAS gratified when Cindy Potter drove to work as she usually did late Friday morning. The wait was finally over, although it hadn't been so bad. She had spent the days Cindy was at work often relaxing, in her method. She went to a local waterfall just to hear the roar of the water as it dumped into Lake Superior. It wasn't beautiful—the water was rust-colored from the high concentration of iron in the area, but that didn't matter.

She liked this manner of preparation. It cleared her head as she went over the plan again and again in her mind and tried to think of every contingency. She hadn't had that luxury on the Boundary Waters. Now, she was relaxed and could visualize what would take place. She had brought a hunting knife with her. A sexual predator would never use a gun. He would confront his victim and pull her into the place he had picked out in advance. A place hidden from view. A dark place, though not too dark. He would want to see her face as he wielded his power over her. The victim's death was typically planned for later, but if she screamed he might be forced to kill her before he wanted.

Clarisa had eaten a late dinner. Her plan was to leave her car in an out-of-the-way place and make her way to the hospital parking lot at about half past ten. After flattening the tires, she would return to her car and park in a dark corner of the park's lot to avoid being seen. Parking on a residential street ran the risk of an insomniac looking out their window in the middle of the night and seeing her coming and going.

She would don the surgical scrubs she had brought with her and wait at the place she had chosen. A stabbing death was messy, and she couldn't risk leaving a blood trail. After it was over, she would remove the scrubs, double bag them in lawn bags hidden nearby and make sure nothing traceable remained behind.

At seven-thirty Clarisa returned to her room, the third hotel room she had stayed in during her time in Duluth. She had used a different alias for each, and none of her stays were at a national chain. Her cell phone rang. It was Frank.

"Frank, you know better than to call me when I'm working. I need to be focused," she said, irritated.

"Something has come up. I need you in Washington first thing in the morning. I've booked you on a five o'clock flight."

"I can't make that. Tonight is the night."

"Change your plans. Donaldson is pissed. Taylor is stirring up all sorts of trouble. He wants him out of the way now. The woman can wait."

"Bullshit! A lot of planning has gone into this. Let me just take care of it and catch a later flight."

"No, we can't risk that. You need to be at 110% when you're here. We can't risk you being injured or something going wrong there. This is going to be a tough one. Taylor has security around him."

"Oh sure, and let me guess. Donaldson wants me to just waltz in there and have him dead by the end of the day?"

"Nobody expects that, but we need to focus on him so we can have him out of the way as quickly as possible. We'll likely be in Mexico within a week."

"Really?" She became excited at the thought of soon being the First Lady of Mexico. Finally, she would share in Frank's notoriety and respect.

"That's what he said. Now get ready for that early flight and let's begin work on getting rid of Taylor."

53

AT EIGHT Friday night, Secretary of State Anthony Weller called Mexico's President Cuevas to advise him that the US military would be entering their sovereign territory that night. He assured him that they would not be a threat to Mexico's people or its government. Their total focus would be on attacking the cartels. However, he was told, if Mexico's military confronted the US troops, they would be destroyed.

The military had already been in communication with Mexico's generals to ensure they understood what was going to happen and to avoid a skirmish between the nations' troops. The generals had offered their assistance, but they were being kept at arm's length with regard to planning because the CIA knew that half of the top Mexican military officers had been corrupted by the cartels.

A half hour later, the temperature still 97 degrees, military scouts crossed the border to clear the way for the movement of the drones. Hundreds of trucks and barges were used to get them into position along the border. By 3 a.m. the next morning, the drones had been dropped off and were spread out, each to its assigned position, each under its own power.

The transport vehicles had returned to the US side of the border, along with the military scouts by 4:30 a.m. Twenty-seven large drones were up and monitoring activity south of the border, and all of the small drones were fully activated. Within fifteen minutes, the large drones began feeding information to their counterparts below. Concentrations of people throughout the 2,000-mile stretch of border were identified. The small flying drones whirred into action, and by 5:10 a.m., forty-three armed cartel guards were dead.

Panic spread throughout the community of cartel members and migrants alike. They scrambled to hide, but they didn't know where the enemy was. Some migrants turned around and ran south to try and get out of the apparent battlefield. Cartel members who were still alive and unarmed argued with one another about what to do. Most had been asleep during the attacks and had no idea where it had come from or what was happening. The cartel thugs who were guarding the camp had heard the whirring sound of the drones' propellers, but it was not a sound they recognized. Before they were able to explore its source, they were dead. Cartel members assumed that snipers had shot the guards during the night. When those with arms went down, others would pick up the guns to defend themselves. Within an hour, another wave of gunfire took out everyone now carrying weapons.

There was no command and control in place by the cartels. They would assign a team to escort a group of migrants to the border, and there was no further expectation of communication until the team called in to report that their mission had been accomplished. However, each team had a satellite radio in the event something came up that they weren't sure how to handle. Hundreds of calls began pouring into the various cartel headquarters. Most could not get through because of all the traffic. However, those that did get through brought the same story: Armed guards were being taken out everywhere. As soon as dead guards were replaced with new guards, they were killed as well. Amid the panic and confusion, groups of migrants scattered and spread out everywhere.

The small flying drones could be seen by 6:30 in the light of day. The low buzz of the drones could be heard first, then suddenly the rumble would be upon them and anyone with a gun would be shot. The US military was able to monitor the satellite and cell phone calls. They were also able to watch drone attacks through the video feed they sent up to the large circling drones above. Information from every source indicated complete success. The drones were working exactly as planned.

President Donaldson went on national television at 9:00 a.m. to announce that the military had crossed the border into Mexico. He told the American people that the cartels who had for so long been responsible for so much suffering were under attack. "The human trafficking, drug trafficking, and the terror that they have caused migrants will be over soon," he promised. He assured the American people that the attack was going well and proceeding exactly as planned.

<h1 style="text-align:center">54</h1>

RICK TAYLOR learned about the invasion of Mexico in the same manner that most Americans did—he saw it on the Saturday morning news, though the news crews were required to remain on the US side of the border and had little information to share. In the distance the journalists would occasionally hear gunfire, but they only knew what the military communication team told them, which was precious little.

The large drones that looked like those that had monitored the border for years flew east and west at about three-thousand feet above the ground. Occasionally they would bank and turn southward and then north again in unpredictable patterns. As the day progressed, their east/west track moved farther south, stretching deep into the Mexican interior. Most television news coverage was of the large drones or US military personnel moving north of the border in jeeps and humvees.

One cameraman in Arizona captured something different. Above the horizon what looked like a mechanical demon seemed to rise up, hovering for a time. It suddenly moved around to the south and west, paused, and then slowly sank below the horizon again. In the midst of the display two gunshots could be heard, but it wasn't clear where they were coming from.

The unusual sighting stirred things up quickly. The network news crew that captured it on video started playing it on repeat. They called on the experts, former military generals, and colonels to speculate on what they were seeing. Most thought that it might be a secret weapon, but they had to admit that they weren't sure. Reporters speculated that the sighting could be of a drone operated by one of the cartels. It was reported that the cartels made millions of dollars per day in their drug and human trafficking business and had money to spend on high-tech defense systems.

Rick shook his head as he watched the coverage. He knew what they were seeing were the small drones that the Senate delegation had been briefed on, and he prayed that the systems worked as intended. He wondered what communications were taking place between the US and Mexican governments.

He didn't have to wonder for long, because within an hour of the first reports the President of Mexico made a televised national address. He railed against the US over the illegal invasion into his sovereign territory. "I want the United Nations Security Council to address this violation immediately," he demanded. Rick couldn't disagree with him.

He started getting calls from network news producers asking for interviews. He agreed and followed their instructions on setting up his laptop computer with downloadable software to use as a portable camera and audio feed. When asked on air about his opinion, he began with, "I am praying for the safety of our troops and praying that innocent people who are in harm's way are also spared injury or death."

The news anchor responded, "Senator Taylor, are you saying that you do not support the American cause in this military action?"

"I don't understand the motive for this military action," he replied. "The president has said that this is to seal the border. Illegal border crossings are down more than 90%, and those who are crossing are being returned to Mexico. I would like the president to tell us what his purpose is in invading a sovereign nation. Certainly I want our military to be successful in carrying out their orders. However, the president owes it to the people of the United States to tell them what the end game is here."

"You have previously expressed concern over the use of new technology in this fight. Do you still have those concerns?"

"I do. When briefed on this technology, I asked a number of questions and either received weak answers or have not yet received answers. I pray that this technology works properly. We are in the midst of many innocent people stuck in a US-designated battlefield."

#

By midday, a security team for the Vegas cartel had made it north to one of the sites of the unusual shootings. Of the team of seven, six carried AK47 rifles, and one was unarmed. Fifteen minutes after their arrival, they heard a low buzzing sound.

The team looked at the horizon to the east and saw six desert-colored machines rise straight up and begin moving toward them. They spread out and took firing positions. One stopped near the jeep they had arrived in, two moved toward the few migrants that were still there, and three moved into nearby brush, kneeling and pointing their weapons.

The drones remained at about twenty-five feet above the ground and moved toward them quickly. The flying weapons moved almost as though in a choreographed dance, then some rose higher and some lower, but all moved in one direction or another. Suddenly, six shots rang out.

Blood splattered as bullets pierced the skulls of all six members of the security team. Migrants in the area scattered, ducking their heads and running. They stopped, still crouching, and looked at the drones. The unarmed team lead, who had held his ground, watched as the deadly machines hovered. He hollered at a teenage migrant in Spanish, "Pick up that rifle!" and pointed to a gun dropped by one of his armed soldiers. "Pick it up!" he screamed again.

The frightened, intimidated young man who was traveling alone walked over and picked up the rifle. He began to walk toward the team leader to hand it to him, but after only two steps a hollow point bullet took off the bridge of his nose, entering his head and pulverizing his brain. The boy crumpled to the ground.

The leader jumped at the sudden noise of the shot but remained where he was, watching the drones. After about two minutes, all six machines moved back in the direction from which they had come. They paused and hovered briefly, then all six went down behind the horizon. As quickly as it had begun, the buzzing sound stopped.

The leader, wiping his brow with a rag, looked up to see a large drone high above them, circling. He left the guns where they were and got on a satellite phone and called for another team.

Three hundred and sixty-seven miles away in the desert south of El Paso, a mother and her young sons, who had separated from a larger group, came upon a dead cartel soldier. One of the boys ran and picked up the soldier's gun. His mother screamed at him to put the gun down. Her panicked scream at her eleven-year-old son frightened her five-year-old, and he began crying uncontrollably. The mother went down on her knees trying to console him.

Between the crying and the mother's own screams, they never heard the buzz of the single drone, although the mother soon got a glimpse of it out of the corner of her eye as it stopped its movement toward them. In another blink of her eye she saw blood splash from her older son's face and watched him fall to the ground like a limp towel.

This sort of scene repeated itself several times in camera view of the drones.

#

At the border near El Paso, soldiers scurried from tent to tent in the temporary command headquarters for the operation. Inside one of the larger tents American soldiers responsible for monitoring the video watched in horror as innocent people, including children, picked up guns and were quickly gunned down by the drones.

A tall and slender soldier walked into the tent. The insignia on his shoulders indicated that he was a master sergeant. His name tag said Kelly. One of the soldiers said, "Sergeant Kelly," and waved him over. The soldier showed him what they were seeing.

"How many of these have you seen?" the sergeant asked.

"I think we have seen five so far, sir."

"I want all of you to begin taking a count of innocents being killed," Kelly said as he walked out of the tent.

He immediately sent word to his commander, and the grave news moved quickly up the chain of command. Within fifteen minutes, a full bird colonel walked into the tent and looked around. There were seventy-five monitors in racks. Fifteen soldiers were watching five screens each, and each screen was split into four scenes.

Sergeant Kelly walked him over to one of the stations. "Show the colonel a couple of those videos," he directed a soldier softly.

"How many?" the colonel demanded as he watched.

"We count nine so far, sir," the soldier said.

"However," Kelly added, "as these cartel guards go down, the immigrants are frightened and scatter. They don't seem to understand what is happening and apparently feel comfort in finding a gun with which to protect themselves."

The colonel frowned. "This wasn't in the plan." As quickly as he had arrived, he marched out of the tent and called the commanding general of the operation.

55

CLARISA ARRIVED at their Virginia home at one in the afternoon. There was a note on the kitchen island that said Frank was in a meeting but that he would be home by four. She grabbed some crackers from the pantry to ease the hunger pangs, poured herself a glass of merlot, and turned on the television. She was pleased to see the news coverage of the invasion of Mexico. She knew it was going to happen quickly and was thrilled to see things moving forward.

She decided to take a nap. She didn't know what her schedule would be like while pursuing Taylor, so it might be best to get some sleep now. She turned off the news and crawled into bed, but she wasn't able to sleep even though she felt tired. She kept thinking about the change in her life that was about to come. It was actually going to happen. She and Frank were going to Mexico! She longed to live in her native country again. She had only lived there as a young child before her parents had immigrated to the US, and she had always wanted to go back.

Since she and Frank both had Hispanic roots, they were excited to think of Mexico becoming another state in the union. They loved to vacation there, speak the language of their parents, and immerse themselves into the culture, so when Donaldson felt Frank out about his vision for the country Frank bought into it completely. He assured the presidential candidate of his support and that he would do anything to help make the vision a reality. He also made it clear that he would very much like to be the first governor of the state of Mexico.

Clarisa thought back to almost two years before. They had spent the night in a Maryland hotel and talked about Vice President Donaldson's vision for America. Frank admitted that, as perfect as Donaldson's aspiration was, it remained a long shot. While there were a lot of lemmings in Congress who would do whatever their party wanted, there were also people that would do anything to fight Donaldson's imperialistic ideas.

They had made love that night, and the next morning they took a cold January walk on the beach at Sandy Point. Clarisa said that sometimes great strides in achievement require great sacrifice. "At the end of the day, everyone will agree that it was both necessary and worthwhile." She had stopped walking and looked into his eyes. "You happen to be married to someone who has been highly trained by our government to eliminate barriers on the battlefield. I'm sure I could adjust to other theaters of operation as well."

Frank had returned her gaze. He told her that the warmth of her eyes could never reveal what she was suggesting. When asked if there was anyone in particular that might be a problem, Frank predicted that Senator Tom Blado would be. He was the chairman of a committee that could wield a lot of influence. But Frank declined her offer. "I could never ask you to do something like that."

"This is what I trained for in special ops," she had told him. "I can still serve my country with my special skills, and I will be proud to do it."

He had continued to push back a little, but she was very convincing. She made very clear to him that this was something she wanted ... no, something that she needed, to do for her country. He had kissed her there on the beach, and their pact was sealed.

Weeks later, Frank had been less agreeable when she

explained how she thought she should approach eliminating Tom Blado. He wasn't about to share his wife's pleasures with any man, much less Blado. Once again, she was very convincing. It was the safest way for her to get close to him so that she could be in control of when and how to do it. Frank had actually cried a little. It wasn't just the infidelity that his wife was suggesting; it was mostly over the sacrifice she was willing to make and the risk she was willing to take.

Now, as she lay in their bed, she continued to be self-assured in all that had happened and all that was to come. As she thought of the dream becoming reality, her breathing slowed and sleep finally came.

56

By THREE in the afternoon on Saturday, Stan Kauffman and the president had left the situation room and were in the Oval Office study just off the Oval Office, where Donaldson did most of his work.

They were watching the news coverage. "In about an hour, the Defense Department will begin a briefing that explains our attack, including the use of the new drones," Kauffman said.

"When the public sees what we are able to do without putting our soldiers at risk," President Donaldson smiled, "they're going to trust us to accomplish anything."

"Everything is falling into place, just the way you predicted," Kauffman said admiringly.

"When will the Cuevas revelation be made public?"

"Tomorrow morning. Our AI team has done brilliant work. They have video of Cuevas talking with his interior minister and the president of their Senate at a recent gala. In the video, they are off in a corner having a conversation. Our AI people were able to generate an audible conversation that will incriminate them. Cuevas reminds the others in it that they have each accepted tens of millions of US dollars from the cartels, and for that to continue, they would need to get this crisis addressed quickly."

"You're sure the quality of the audio is good?"

"You bet. People in those positions speak publicly often. We have hundreds of hours of their voices on tape. AI has learned the voice patterns of each and now can have any one of them say anything we want," Kauffman assured him. "The video was a gift," he mused. "We were going to set it up as a phone conversation, but when the video was in the news last week we were able to make it appear that we had eavesdropping equipment in place."

Donaldson nodded. "Good. I've told Moreno to be ready to step in as provisional president next week. After we stage some concerned dialogue, I'll tell the Mexican people that their government is filled with corruption, and we are going to help them with free and fair elections."

Kauffman shook his head and smiled in adulation. "Within six months, Mexico will be well on the way to becoming the fifty-first state of the union. Congratulations, Gerry."

Donaldson walked over to a small buffet and poured them both a small glass of scotch, something that they had drunk together for many years. As he handed Stan a glass, Donaldson's administrative assistant tapped on the door. "Mr. President, the defense secretary would like to see you. She says it's urgent."

Donaldson closed his eyes briefly and looked at Kauffman. "Bring her into the Oval Office."

"Yes, sir."

Donaldson and Kauffman put down their glasses and walked into the Oval Office. Donna Schmidt was escorted in.

"Donna, it sounds like everything is coming together."

"Yes, sir," She said. "However, we have something taking place that we weren't expecting."

"What's that?" he asked as he gestured for her to sit on one of the couches. Kauffman sat on the opposite couch. The president sat in his favorite chair and faced them.

"It seems that migrants don't really understand what is happening when our drones attack the armed cartel members. They're picking up the guns and, as a result, are being killed by the drones."

"The drones are attacking migrants?" Donaldson asked in surprise.

"When they pick up the guns, yes, sir."

"How many?"

"The initial count I have been given is nine, sir. Including some children."

"We're able to see this happening?"

"Yes, each drone's video images are being monitored."

Donaldson stared at Secretary Schmidt as if her incompetence was showing. "Haven't those responsible called the drones off when there is such an obvious problem?"

"I'm afraid it isn't that easy. The drones operate independently. They are not set up to take instructions during operations."

"Well, reprogram them to recognize when they're dealing with children, at least," he said, raising his voice.

"Reprogramming something like this isn't easy. Every situation is different. I'm told there is no simple solution to rewriting the software."

"Donna, I'm sure you came in here to give me a recommended solution."

"Yes. The only thing that we have come up with thus far is to drop leaflets to advise immigrants, but it will also let the cartels know how they are being targeted."

Donaldson stood and shouted, "How many days do you think it's going to take the cartels to figure that out anyway? I'll bet they know it already! Just drop the flyers."

Donna Schmidt stood. "Yes, sir," she said and walked out of the room.

Donaldson turned to Kauffman. "We've got to keep this from getting out, Stan."

"I'll get on it," Kauffman said and followed Schmidt out the door.

57

AFTER RICK heard of the invasion, he asked his assistant if she would mind coming to the office on a Saturday. He got to the office at 11 a.m., and Carla was already there. As soon as she saw him, she held up a phone message slip and said, "Senator Taylor, Deputy Chief Kirk Banfield from Del Rio, Texas has called several times and would like you to call him."

"Thank you, Carla. Would you please try to reach him for me?" Rick walked into his office and closed the door.

Almost instantly he heard, "He's on your line" over the intercom.

He punched the speaker button. "Kirk, I'm glad to hear from you. I hope you're keeping your head down."

"Thanks for taking my call, Senator Taylor. There are some things going on down here that I'm really concerned about. I hoped you might give me an ear."

"You bet. Have you run this up your chain, or does it concern them?"

"Yes, I've sent it up my chain of command. They say they've notified the military but have been told not to worry, that they have things well in hand. It's hard for me to believe that's the case."

Rick hung up his suit coat and sat down. "Okay, what's happening?"

"The number of immigrants getting through has slowed

significantly, but the ones who have made it through this afternoon have some frightening stories. They're all scared to death. Several have told my people that there are multiple accounts of immigrants picking up guns from the cartel people who were killed in drone attacks. As soon as they did so, the drones attacked them as well. I'm told migrants are dying all over the place. One of my counterparts in Lukeville, Arizona tells me children are being shot by drones."

Rick set his jaw. He felt sick. "How confident are you that this is accurate information?"

"I've only spoken to one immigrant myself, but he was very convincing. The thing is, I'm getting similar stories from my counterparts up and down the border."

"Okay, let me see if I can run this down. Is there anything in particular you want me to do besides raise the red flag?"

"First of all, I'd like the military to let us know what's happening. They are being totally tight-lipped. I am concerned for my agents. It doesn't seem like these drones are operating as intended, unless the planners were totally incompetent. I don't want to lose any agents."

"I can't imagine why they wouldn't be communicating. What else?"

"Well, I was hoping you could find a way to stop the government from shooting migrants," he said wryly.

Rick nodded. "Yes. Thanks, Kirk. I'm on it." He sat in his chair for a minute, wondering what to do. He called Carla in and gave her a list of people to call, starting with the Majority Leader, Frank Moreno.

Carla's voice came over the intercom. "Leader Moreno's answering service says he has left specific instructions not to be disturbed. I have Senator Franklin on the line."

Jeff Franklin was the head of the Senate Armed Services Committee. "Jeff, thank you for taking my call," Rick said. In his first seven months in the Senate, Rick had only spoken to him once before, but Senate collegiality allowed for the use of first names.

"Good afternoon, Rick, what can I do for you?"

"I just got a call from a very responsible contact on the border. I'm told that these new drone fighters are killing migrants right and left."

"I find that hard to believe. I was told they only go after armed personnel."

"That was the intent, but the problem is that once cartel guards go down, so do their weapons. Migrants are picking up the guns for their own protection and getting killed. In some cases even children are being shot."

"Oh, my God. I hope your source is incorrect, but I'll go ahead and give a call to the Pentagon to see what I can find out."

"Thanks, Jeff."

Five minutes later Carla was able to reach Roy Chandler, the Chairman of the Senate Foreign Relations Committee.

"Roy, thanks for taking my call."

"Any time."

"The reason I'm calling is that the military's new fighting drones are killing migrants south of the border. I thought you would want to know in the event you haven't heard."

As with Franklin, Rick explained what he'd been told. Chandler had heard nothing about it. He recognized the international stir this was about to cause and promised to call the State Department to see what was being done.

Rick sat alone in his office, feeling helpless. He couldn't think of anyone else to reach out to. Since Moreno had assigned him to the Senate Library Committee, his position provided him access to almost nobody in the military or Executive Branch.

"Senator Taylor," Carla said through the intercom. "A news producer is on the line asking for an interview."

He paused for a moment and then picked up the phone.

58

BY FIVE-THIRTY that evening, more cartel muscle arrived where the last ones had met their demise. All eight had been cautioned not to carry guns. They were told they could put a couple of AK47s in the jeep, hidden, but nobody who wanted to survive should carry a gun.

The original team leader described for them what had occurred when he arrived with his last team. Their eyes and expressions grew dour. It felt to them like their leader was telling them a ghost story.

"So, what now?" one of the new soldiers asked.

"We're going on a scouting mission. Everyone stay close and follow me."

The leader began walking in the direction from which the killing machines had come. He didn't walk with confidence. He walked slowly, even gingerly, as if he needed to avoid land mines along the way. His trepidation rubbed off on the others as they followed. They looked carefully around, although they were not sure what they were looking for. They eventually approached a short rise in the terrain. The leader peeked over, stopped, and put his left hand out behind him, causing the others to freeze. He moved slowly up the grade until he could see the entire machine.

He recognized the top of it. It was what had flown into the clearing and mowed down his men where they stood. It sat quietly now, as if it were asleep. He motioned for the others to come. Slowly they joined him. The machine remained docile. He turned and whispered to them, "Spread out and find a big rock, no bigger than you can carry in one hand." They did what they were told and returned. He spoke more loudly this time. "Let's wait a minute," he said as he panned the sky for the large, high flying drone. He saw one, but it was flying away from them.

"Do you see those flat panels on top of the machine?" he asked. They nodded as they stared at the lifeless beast. "We are going to walk over to it very slowly. When we get to it, I want you to surround it, and when I tell you, use your rock to break that panel. Break it into as many pieces as you can."

"Are you sure?" one asked.

"You're joking, right?" said another.

"No," he said, pointing at the thing. "It's not afraid of us because we don't have guns. See?"

They all stared at him, and he motioned with his head. "Now go," he said loudly. The eight men walked over the shallow hill and down the other side. Off in the distance they saw another one of those things. One turned to their boss and pointed, "Look."

The leader shook his head and repeated, "Go, now."

They approached the thing slowly and surrounded it. They could feel the heat that emanated from it atop the solar panel. One raised his free hand over it. "Hot," he said.

"Hit it, now!" their leader cried.

They all started banging on the solar panel with the rocks they had brought. The glass coating over the panel shattered, but it was thick and did not fall to pieces. A white shattered circle was left behind when the rocks struck. Cracks spread out from the circle, turning into tiny chunks that clung together. It looked like a car windshield that had been hit by a rock while driving at a high speed.

They screamed as they bashed the thing. Only the leader noticed six other machines coming to life and lifting above the horizon. Finally the machine they were pounding on began to stir. The propellers moved and roared to a high speed, and the drone lifted off the base. The men around it were startled and began to run in different directions. By this time they could hear the loud, low buzzing of all of the coming drones.

Within twenty seconds all of the men who had attacked the creature were dead. The drones remained hovering in place for a minute. The leader remained perfectly still. He had challenged this thing before, and he would do it again. He turned his head slowly and looked up at the sky far above him. He noticed that the large drone had returned and was now circling at about two thousand feet above where he was. The flying killing machines continued to hover about ten feet off the ground..

He looked around the horizon in every direction to see if anyone else might be nearby. He saw nothing but sand, brush, and cactus. He was alone. He returned his focus to the machines. That bothersome buzzing sound continued as the drones all seemed to be watching him. Simultaneously, all of the machines that had come to this one's aid began to move. Each flew back to its base. They hovered and then dropped, almost as if being directed by a maestro's baton.

The machine in front of him remained hovering. The burly cartel man stared at it. It was doing nothing. It was almost like it was thinking and trying to decide on something. The barrel of its flying gun was pointed at him. He knew he couldn't outrun it. He saw what had happened to the others. He had survived before by remaining where he was and standing up to it without backing down.

The loud *pop* was all he heard, and then nothing. He dropped to the ground in a bloody heap. The damaged machine turned slightly, then settled back down onto its base.

59

LEADER MORENO'S answering service let him know that Senator Taylor had been trying to reach him. Moreno wasn't about to call him back. He was enjoying time with his wife.

Clarisa and Frank walked out of the bedroom together at six that evening, holding hands. He was in pants and a t-shirt, and she was wearing his dress shirt with the sleeves rolled up. "I wonder what we have to eat in the kitchen," she said, pulling away from him to investigate.

"We may have to order something out. I haven't been cooking since you've been gone," Frank responded as he turned on the news channel.

When he saw Rick Taylor front and center on the screen, being interviewed, he yelled, "You son-of-a-bitch! What is your problem?" He picked up a box of coasters from an end table and threw it at the TV, coasters flying everywhere.

#

"Senator Taylor, allow me to play a clip from an earlier interview with you."

A video clip showed Rick saying, *"There were also elements of the operation that raised red flags in my mind. I hope the president will rethink this approach."*

The reporter stopped the clip and asked, *"We have heard*

stories from migrants who have been turned around and returned to Mexico. They have said that migrants are being killed in the desert by this special weapon. Were the red flags that you referred to related to what is happening out in the desert now?"

"I can't provide any detail as to what is happening in the military operation. That is for them to communicate at an appropriate time. However, based upon the briefing I received previously, any problems that are being experienced should have been anticipated. We are talking about a computerized weapon. Any bugs in such a weapon should obviously be tested extensively before deploying it in such a role."

"Are you saying that the new weapon is malfunctioning?"

"If it is true that migrants are being killed by the weapon, then I would say that, yes, that is a major malfunction, and a tragic one. We'll have to see. But if things are happening as you say, someone will have to be held accountable for authorizing its use without adequate testing."

#

"That man is going to drive me insane," Frank barked as Clarisa approached to watch with him.

"I hope you realize that it will be nearly impossible to eliminate him with all of the media hovering around him and his bodyguard with him all the time," she said.

"There's got to be some way."

"Well, it's not going to happen in the Capitol building or at his house. I can't follow him without being detected. He's not going to meet you for coffee anytime soon, and besides, you don't want him to die with you around."

"Wait a minute," Frank said, staring at the TV. "Taylor has been trying to reach me. I'm sure he's hyped up about the invasion. What if I set up a meeting away from the Capital and then not show up?"

"Tonight?"

"Why not?"

"A lack of planning will get us both caught or killed, that's why not," Clarisa said impatiently.

"Okay. Maybe I could set something up for tomorrow."

"Let's talk it through tonight. If we develop a plan, I can scout out the location before we commit," she suggested.

"Why don't you call and have something delivered for dinner while I find out what is happening at the border? Then we can think this through together."

60

AT SEVEN Master Sergeant Kelly stood over the shoulders of his video monitors. Major Jenkins stood beside him. They watched the playback again from the perspective of the drones that had been involved. The eight cartel members approached the drone and started destroying the solar panel on its top side. Other drones had come to its aid, as they had been programmed to do. All eight men were killed.

The drone they damaged could still fly, but with that panel damaged, it would ultimately run out of power and be out of the fight. That part was to be expected. The enemy was seeking to understand what they were up against and trying to learn how they could kill these machines. The surprise was at the end. The damaged drone hovered, with its camera and gun pointed at an unarmed man, presumably a cartel member, and then fired on him.

The news reached the Pentagon quickly. The system's developers were unsure why the machine would have done that. The drone shouldn't have recognized that person as a threat. From its perspective, he should have been viewed as an innocent bystander.

Within thirty minutes, all hell broke loose. In seven different locations, migrants walking north came across the drones that were idle in the desert. It appeared that their curiosity was piqued, and they wandered over to get a closer look.

In each case, as they approached a drone, a loud, deep buzzing sound could be heard, and as they looked around they saw the machines come to life, rise up, and hover over their bases. It was an eerie sight. It was as if the machines were watching them. Several actually moved closer to the migrants, surrounding them. Some of the migrants watched in horror as many of their fellow travelers were cut down in their tracks. Their nightmare only lasted a few seconds, because just as quickly the flying monsters turned their attention to them, and they too were eliminated.

#

The entire focus of the military turned to fixing the drones. Helicopters were dispatched to fly into the desert in an attempt to tell migrants to turn back, but that effort was futile. The migrants thought it was an attempt to round them up, so they scattered and ran northward in an attempt to reach the border. Some ran into what appeared to be the drone's personal space and were gunned down.

President Donaldson, Kauffman, Secretary Schmidt, and a myriad of military staffers met in the War Room at the White House. "What's happening? Why is it going after migrants?" the president demanded.

"We don't know," Schmidt replied. "The programmers who developed the system are at the Pentagon trying to figure it out."

All Donaldson could think of was how this would impact their plan. It appeared that while news agencies had heard rumors, they had not been able to confirm them, but it wouldn't be long before this became a public relations nightmare. He needed to redirect the media's attention.

He pulled Stan Kauffman aside and said, "Release the video of Cuevas."

"Are you sure?" Kauffman asked. "This is a full day before we had agreed that it would happen."

"Release it! We need the distraction."

#

At nine o'clock, a team of developers and project managers involved in programming the AI application used in the drones came out of the conference room where they were troubleshooting the problem.

The manager of the team approached General Wagner. "It is our conclusion that the drones' self-defense system has learned, obviously incorrectly, that any person within about fifty yards of a drone is a threat and must be taken out."

"Well, that makes sense based on what we're seeing. How do we fix it?"

"We are going to try and update the system by providing more specific direction in these situations. We plan to focus on two things: the size of the individual as well as unarmed people approaching the drone."

"The size?"

"Yes, sir. That would establish an exception that should protect children, even if they are carrying a weapon. Of course, the other will protect unarmed individuals who may be in the area. It could leave drones open to receiving damage, like the one we saw today, but we will make physical damage to the drone the threshold that will generate an attack rather than someone being in the vicinity."

"How long will this take?" the general asked.

"Well, we should have something ready to download by early morning."

"Good, do it."

61

THAT EVENING Rick was still getting requests for interviews. He cursed himself for having given out his private number to a few favored news producers. He declined them. He didn't have a lot of public information to go by and was reluctant to speak openly with secondhand information.

At a quarter to ten he received a call from Kirk Banfield on his cell phone.

"Hello, Kirk. I've tried to get this word out at several levels, but I'm not able to connect with the military at this time."

"Oh, I'm in touch with the military," Banfield said provocatively. "Senator Taylor, we have a massacre on our hands. Now the drones are attacking anyone who comes close. As migrants move northward and approach them, they are slaughtered by the damn things."

"What is the military doing about it?" Rick asked, shaking his head in disbelief.

"I'm told they are going to drop leaflets south of their location, warning migrants not to pick up guns that may be on the ground and not to proceed further north. The flyers will tell them that if they do, they may be attacked and killed."

Rick couldn't believe what he was hearing. "They can't do anything more than that?"

"Well, it's going to be dark soon. There should be little to no migrant movement until it's light again," Banfield said. "I'm told the Pentagon programmers are working on software fixes."

"How many casualties are we talking about?"

"I'm told the fatalities of innocents are in the thousands."

Rick dropped onto the couch. "Those poor people. The previous president invited them in, and cartels led them right into a slaughterhouse. God help them.

"Thank you for the update, Kirk," was all he could say before ending the call.

He wished Moreno would call him back, but that hadn't happened yet. He just didn't know what to do. On a whim, he pulled out his briefcase and called the White House security line. He was pleasantly surprised to get an answer. The agent came on after the first ring. "White House Security."

"Yes, this is Senator Rick Taylor. I would like to talk with Vice President Whittington, please."

"Good evening, Senator Taylor. I'm afraid I can't put you through to the vice president. Would you like me to let her know that you're trying to reach her?"

Rick breathed. "That would be great," he said.

The agent confirmed that the number he was calling from was the right callback number. "I'll see what I can do, Senator, but I can't guarantee a return call."

"I understand. Thank you for trying," he said and hung up.

The next few minutes dragged by. Rick paced the floor trying to think of anyone else he could call. He wished Moreno would return his call. He tried to call him again but got no answer.

Finally, twenty minutes later, his phone rang. "Rick Taylor," he answered quickly.

"Senator Taylor, this is Marjory Whittington, returning your call."

"Madam Vice President, thank you so much for the call back," he said. "I apologize for bothering you on the weekend. It's kind of you to return my call."

"We don't work a nine to five weekday job, do we, Senator

Taylor? What is it that you're so disturbed about at this hour?"

"Ma'am, are you aware of the rising death toll of migrants south of the border?"

There was a pause on the line. "Well, to be frank with you, the president seems determined to keep me in the dark regarding the military operation. Tell me what you are hearing and from whom."

Rick explained what he had heard from Kirk Banfield and said, "Someone needs to make the call to shut down these machines."

"Ohh," she groaned.

Rick could tell she had not been in the loop. "I presume this is the first you've heard of it?"

"I'm getting my information from the media right now."

Rick couldn't believe that Donaldson was keeping his own VP in the dark in the midst of this war. Suddenly a breaking news banner came across on his television. "Ma'am, there is some sort of breaking news about the invasion coming on the TV. Do you mind if I see what this is about?"

"No, of course not; turn it up so I can hear it," she asked.

The news anchor came on the screen and announced that US Intelligence operatives had irrefutable evidence that President Cuevas of Mexico and at least two others in high office in Mexico were being paid by one or more of the Mexican cartels.

"Oh, no." the vice president said aloud.

"What? What does this mean?" Rick asked.

"The president has told me that if he found government corruption in Mexico, he would take control of the Capitol until regime change could be accomplished." She paused. "I probably shouldn't have told you that."

"You're saying that the president would take control of a foreign nation? That can't be legal," said Rick, not believing his ears.

"We did it in Iraq, and, some would argue, Afghanistan."

"But Mexico?" he said.

"I understand your concern. I wish I could voice mine, but that wouldn't be appropriate, would it? I appreciate your call, Senator Taylor. I'll get on this right away."

"Yes, ma'am. Anything you can do to save lives."

"Senator Taylor … may I call you Rick?"

"Yes, ma'am."

"Rick, between you and me, this stinks to high heaven, and I will interject myself into it as far as I possibly can to see what is happening. I'm sure you understand that I am part of the administration, but I am not the president. I appreciate you sharing what you know. I would very much like for us to stay in touch and exchange information when it makes sense."

"Thank you. Yes, I would appreciate having someone to communicate with on this. I will use discretion in contacting you."

"That would be great," the vice president said before ending the call.

62

Clarisa ran through the airport terminal at Dulles International. Her flight was scheduled for an 11:30 p.m. departure. On one level, she was panicked because she didn't want to miss the flight. On another level, she was pissed that Frank had disrupted what she had been hours away from completing in Duluth in order to get her to Washington and was now sending her back to Minneapolis only twelve hours after she had arrived. If she missed the flight, it was his problem.

They had put their heads together and come to the conclusion that D.C. was the worst place to deal with Taylor. It would take so much manipulation to get him somewhere she could deal with him that they were almost surely to be found out. Instead, Frank remembered that he had been asked to speak at a plant opening in Loretto, Minnesota on Tuesday. He had planned to cancel because he would be preparing to leave for Mexico. He asked Clarisa if she thought sending Taylor in his place might provide a better opportunity for her than trying to do something near Washington.

She was absolutely on board with it but needed to scout things out in advance. He gave her the details of the planned event, and they agreed that she should get back to the Twin Cities to begin working on it. He would fly into Minneapolis that day to begin organizing for their departure for Mexico.

She wondered if two days would be enough. She doubted it.

The challenge would be the bodyguard. She was in all new territory with that. She hated the thought of killing a bodyguard too, but it might be the only way. The challenge would be moving in and out of a location with so many cameras around. Loretto, on the other hand, was west of the Cities and fairly remote. Maybe they didn't have cameras in place. Cameras or not, it might not be possible to get there without being detected.

Just twenty-four hours ago, Cindy Potter was about to be taken care of easily. Now her plan was being complicated by panicked, knee-jerk decisions.

Clarisa did catch her flight, and by the time she was seated, she was exhausted. She was asleep before the flight left the ground.

63

By **EARLY** Sunday morning, the AI-enhanced video clips were being shown on all the news channels. Rick recorded the program and studied them over and over again. It was of President Cuevas at a large party of some sort. He was off in a corner talking with two people, reportedly his interior secretary and the president of the Mexican Senate. There was a lot of background noise, and the voices were a bit garbled.

Listening carefully, Rick was able to make out what seemed to be Spanish dialogue. There was closed captioning provided at the bottom of the television. He presumed that it had been provided by the intelligence agency that gave the video to the media. It had to be accurate. It would be called out by any Spanish speaker if it weren't, wouldn't it?

President Cuevas made a speech to the Mexican people very quickly after the video was released. He adamantly denied the allegations, even telling the people that in the conversation the three were actually condemning the US invasion and trying to come up with options for stopping it. The video looked legitimate to Rick, however, so he called Lily at home.

"Lily, this is Rick Taylor. I'm sorry to bother you at home on a Sunday morning."

"Uh, Senator Taylor, it's not a problem. Do you need me to come into the office?"

"No, thank you, Lily, but I wonder if you have seen the

video being played on TV this morning."

"No, sir. I haven't had the TV on at all."

"I'd like you to do me a favor. When you can, take a look at the video that news channels are playing. It seems to show Mexico's president and two others saying something that incriminates them and demonstrating ties to the drug cartels. It seems legit to me, but you are the AI guru. I'd like your opinion as to whether this could have been generated through AI."

"Well, a guru I'm not, but I can take a look. If it's AI-generated, I'm sure the FBI has the capability to recognize that pretty easily."

"I suppose you're right. The government has allowed it to be given to the media. I presume they would have checked it out before they did that." Rick paused. "I'd still appreciate it if you could have a look and let me know your thoughts."

"Sure. Let me take a look at it. I'll give you an initial impression right away, and then I'll do some more careful analysis of it."

"Great. Text me anything you have."

"I can do that, but I don't have your cell phone number, sir."

"Oh, sorry." Rick laughed a little and gave her his number.

64

AT SIX-THIRTY on Sunday morning at the Pentagon, the AI software team reported to General Wagner that they had developed a patch that should fix the two areas of concern. They were ready to download it to the drones when the general gave the go-ahead. He was cautioned, however, that the drones would need to be down for about thirty minutes.

Wagner wondered if it wouldn't be best to take them down and leave them down. He communicated with Colonel Simms on the ground. Within ten minutes, he was given the OK to take the drones down for the software repair. The patch was sent to the large drones flying overhead, which uploaded it to the small drones closest to them. All indications were that they received the changes. The development manager had told the general that installing the software, once downloaded, would only take about ten minutes.

General Wagner set up a conference call between the development team and Colonel Simms and his key staff in position at the border. "How do we test this rewrite, or whatever you want to call it?"

The development manager was a civilian and had never had to test something like this in a real-time environment. "Well, today we will be testing it on a drone we have here. That should give us the information we need."

"Whatever happens with the model drone here will be what

we should expect from the ones in the field?" Simms asked.

"Well, the drones in the field are in a learning mode, so it's almost as if the base software there has changed through its operational experience."

"Ohhkay," Simms said slowly. "Now, let me repeat the question. How do we test this thing?"

"Unfortunately, sir, it's live. We can only wait and see what happens when someone approaches it."

"General Wagner," Simms said. "Surely we can do better than that, sir."

Wagner gave the development manager a disappointed look. "That's the best you can do?" he asked the developer.

"I'm afraid so, sir, unless we take it down for several days or a week. We might be able to program a disarmament."

"How would we test that?" the general asked.

"Uh, the same way, I guess."

"We'll figure it out," said Simms in disgust. "Thanks for the call, sir. I'll let you know what we come up with here." He ended the call abruptly, hoping the general wasn't offended. Then, he left the room and commandeered a jeep.

"Colonel!" hollered a first lieutenant as Simms got into the driver's side. "I'll test it out, sir. You shouldn't be the one to do that."

"I'm not going to ask anyone else to do it," he said. "But come on, you may need to drive the jeep back."

The young officer jumped into the passenger seat, and they took off across the border. They drove for about four miles. When they got within about two hundred yards of one of the drones, Simms stopped the jeep, put it in park, and climbed out. He looked at the lieutenant and said, "This is a hell of a way to run an army. You stay here, no matter what happens."

He turned and began walking toward the drone. When he was about a hundred yards out, he slowed his pace. He stared at it as he walked slowly toward it. He stopped and looked around at the desert surrounding him. He could see two other drones within his field of view. They sat idle, as did the one he was approaching. He jumped at a movement on his right. It was a roadrunner, walking between the sharp spikes of several yucca plants in a loose cluster.

Simms took a deep breath, turned back to the drone and began moving forward again, one small step at a time. He became aware of a humming sound that grew steadily louder. He stopped. Squinting his eyes to try and see the thing more clearly, he couldn't tell if the propellers were rotating or not. He turned back and looked at the jeep. *I can't believe I'm doing this,* he thought. He took a deep breath, and facing the drone again, he moved forward, ever so slowly. The loud hum became a louder buzzing sound. As he continued to move forward, he saw the machine suddenly rise up, only about two feet above the base.

Simms stopped in his tracks. In the distance, he saw one of the other drones rise up as well. It remained hovering where it was. Both drones slowly spun in place until the barrels of their weapons were on him. Concluding that the software patch hadn't fixed the problem, he began stepping backwards away from these flying devils. He backed up about ten feet. Both drones continued to hover.

Hoping they could recognize that he was leaving, he turned around and began jogging toward the jeep. When he had gotten halfway there, he heard the pop behind him. He was prepared for it and dove for the ground, but his reflexes weren't quick enough. The round took off the top of his head before he hit the desert sand.

The lieutenant stared in disbelief before starting to hyperventilate. He caught himself and slowed his breathing. As quickly as he could, he shuffled over to the driver's seat, started the jeep, and put it in reverse. He stomped on the gas and stopped about fifty yards from where the jeep had been parked. He watched as the distant drone slowly lowered itself to its base unit. The close one continued to hover. He slammed it into first gear and spun around. He kept his head down, punched the clutch, shifted to second, and took off as quickly as he could given the terrain.

He made it back to their starting point in half the time it had taken them to go the other way. Once he reached the base, he stopped the jeep and sat for a full minute with his head forward, leaning on the steering wheel.

Other soldiers jogged over to the jeep. "Where's Colonel Simms?" one asked.

The junior officer pulled back from the wheel and his eyes met the others. "He's dead," he said. "The drone killed him."

#

In the midst of the drone crisis, the Pentagon war room technicians created a station where they could also monitor the video feeds from all of the drones. General Wagner had received word that Colonel Simms was going out to a local group of drones near his border location. He stayed in the war room to look over the shoulders of the personnel who were monitoring the drone feeds. When Simm's jeep was within about fifty yards of one of the drones, the Pentagon's video feed from that drone came alive. It was as if the machine had awakened. They watched closely as Simms slowly approached the drone.

They were horrified to see two other nearby drones wake up and go into hover mode. That meant they were in search of threats. "Get him out of there," one of the developers yelled. An aide picked up the phone and called the command center where Simms was operating from. By the time someone answered, Simms was already backpedaling. The aide on the phone could say nothing. The colonel had already taken off running and was dead within seconds.

Communications exploded up and down the chain of command. General Wagner knew that he would need to brief some higher-ups immediately. He stood and turned to face the members of the development team in the room. "What just happened?"

"The patch wasn't installed," the manager replied.

"What are the possible reasons for that?"

The developers looked at one another but remained silent.

"I said, what are the possible reasons for that?" he said again, more loudly this time.

Three of the developers whispered to one another, trying to organize an answer. The manager looked at the general and said, "There are two possibilities. Either an error was made in the programming of the patch, or ..." He hesitated and looked at his developers. One of them nodded. "Or the drones have developed some full defensive posture on their own. They may now view new downloads as a threat. AI can do that. It learns from experience and adjusts."

"Are you telling me that those things may have stopped listening to us?"

"Yes, that is possible, sir," the manager said softly.

Wagner's face reddened, but he said nothing for several seconds. Then in a voice much more controlled than the fury in his eyes would suggest, the General said firmly, "I want all of them shut down, now!"

"Yes, sir," the team manager said. He nodded at the developers, who all scrambled out the door. "However, there's a chance," the manager said with a quiver in his voice, "... a chance that it will not follow a shutdown order either."

"What?" the general said in disbelief.

"Well, if it really has determined that it is at risk of attack from every angle, including from software direction that would change its status, it could decide not to follow shut down orders."

"You sold us a system that can't be controlled?"

"Sir, we should know its response to the shutdown order in about ten minutes."

"How are we going to know that? Do you want me to send another of my officers to test it out? Are you going to send one of your people to check to see if it has followed shut down instructions?"

"No, sir."

"Who signed off on this piece of crap system of yours? Did you tell them this was a possibility?"

"Um, in the last briefing we told our military contacts and the secretary of defense that we felt more testing was needed before taking it live."

"And?"

"The following day, Secretary Schmidt advised that the president would not wait. He wanted to begin the invasion immediately."

The general closed his eyes and rubbed his temples. "I want your assessment in ten minutes." He left the room and made a call to the commanding general of the operation. He explained their plan and commanded all to stay away from the drones.

The commanding general told him that by their count about 75% of the groups of drones had already been encroached on by migrants or cartel members, and all of them had been killed. "I don't anticipate a lot of people walking into a field where there are already dozens of dead scattered throughout," the commander said.

"Great, only 170 more to go," Wagner said sarcastically. "I hope migrants have enough sense not to proceed out of curiosity." He paused. "Or stumble onto these things from a different direction from those who were killed."

Minutes after Wagner finished his call, the development manager approached him. "Sir, we have confirmed that the patch we sent to the drones was fine. There's no reason it shouldn't have worked. We have sent minor instructions to several units. None have replied to us."

"What about shutting it down?"

"The shutdown instruction was sent five minutes ago. Shutdown will be complete within ten minutes, if it works."

Wagner shook his head. *If it works,* he thought. He turned to his aide and said, "Colonel, I want a full command briefing set up on the hour. I've got to give the bad news to Chairman Tompkins and Secretary Schmidt."

65

RICK DECIDED it would do no good to go into the office on a Sunday, so he monitored the situation from his apartment. He received a text from Lily just before ten in the morning. "It looks legit to me," she wrote, "but there's a good bit of background noise. It will take me some time to analyze it more carefully."

Later, just after noon, President Donaldson addressed the nation.

"Fellow Americans, as we fight to secure our southern border and preserve our national sovereignty, I received, with great disappointment, the word that the Mexican cartels are being helped and supported by none other than the top people inside the government of Mexico.

"I made it clear when we started this campaign that we would perceive everyone helping the cartels as enemies and no different than the cartels themselves. We are working to confirm by alternative means what we saw in the video made public this morning. If we do, we will take action to remove those individuals from their offices, along with anyone else who conspires with our enemy.

"I want to make one thing very clear. The United States is not at war with the people of Mexico. We are not at war with the Mexican government. However, those within the government who have been corrupted by the cartels will be held accountable for their corruption.

"Again, I want everyone to understand. The American people are not at war with Mexican citizens. They are the victims of these ruthless and corrupt groups just as we have been. To the Mexican military I say this: We respect you and support you and your role in defending your nation. We want you to continue to do that, and we want your help in rooting out and cleaning up corruption in Mexico. We will work together to help Mexico grow in stature. Our goal is for Mexico to be viewed with as much respect as the United States.

"You may have heard that some migrants have died during our skirmish south of the border. We regret that, but they were where they should not have been, and unfortunately war by its very nature will always carry with it some collateral damage. If any migrants are able to hear my words, I tell you now, turn around, go south and go home, wherever your home is. If you continue northward, you will be in serious danger. If you get to our border, you will not be allowed to stay.

"Citizens of the United States, please pray for our men and women who are conducting this operation. And pray that God will bless the United States of America."

Rick was livid. This man was acting as if there was nothing wrong at all. He was also signaling his intent to take over the government of Mexico. *He is single-handedly destroying the credibility of the United States throughout the world*, he thought.

66

Secretary Schmidt and Chairman Thompkins concurred with Wagner's recommendation to take down the system any way that they could. However, Schmidt advised that they must brief the president and determine if he had any further directions.

President Donaldson was beyond irate. His face reddened as he heard the assessment. "Shut it down," he shouted. He pointed his finger in the chairman's face. "But the operation goes on. I don't care what you have to do; get our troops beyond the drones and keep them moving south."

"Yes, sir," the chairman said as they stood and left the room.

\#

At the same time the president heard the bad news, Wagner held a teleconference with the commanding general of the operation and a few other key officers.

"Are you telling me that these things have turned into indiscriminate killers of anyone nearby?" the commanding general asked.

"Yes, sir. That is our current assumption."

While the teleconference was still in progress, word came from the monitoring station that two more groups of migrants had been attacked. "That confirms our assumption that the drones have not followed the shutdown order," General Wagner said.

"We need a strategy on how we kill these things," he said, looking at the colonel to his right. "Let's get a plan in place to get our troops through the line of drones without being attacked."

The development manager raised his hand and was acknowledged by Wagner. "Sir, we need to move the large drones out of the theater as soon as possible. That will do two things for us. It will take away the ability for drones to communicate with one another or learn from one another. More importantly, if they remain, it will be impossible to stay out of sight of the drones because the large drones do the long distance sighting for the smaller ones."

"Did you hear that? Get those drones out of the theater," Wagner commanded.

"Yes, sir."

"One last thing: You are authorized to use helicopters to destroy the drones if need be. If someone finds an efficient way of disabling those things, let us know so we can share that information."

67

On Monday morning Rick received an early call from Moreno. He expressed his concerns to the leader in as diplomatic a fashion as he could, and made it clear that he thought this action needed to end immediately.

"Yes, we've got a mess on our hands," Moreno replied. "But war is always messy and unpredictable. Our troops will get this figured out."

"This has been my whole point all along, Leader Moreno. We did not need a war to seal the border."

"I understand where you're coming from, Rick. But at this point, the best we can do is let the military handle it," Moreno said. "So let's move on to the reason I called. Several months ago I agreed to speak at the opening of that big technology center in Loretto, Minnesota tomorrow. With all this going down, I just can't be there. I would really appreciate it if you could attend in my place."

That wasn't what Rick wanted to hear, but he hated for the constituents to suffer because of this border problem. He grudgingly agreed to cover for Frank the next day.

After he ended the call, he stood from his office chair and walked to the doorway. "Carla, it looks like I have to go to Minneapolis this afternoon. Could you please book me on a flight?"

"Yes, sir," she said as she pulled up her scheduling screen.

"What time would you like to arrive?"

He looked over her shoulder. "Let's try to get on that twelve-thirty Delta flight if it's available. If not, anytime after that is fine. I'll be attending an event in Loretto tomorrow at 10 a.m."

"When would you like to return?"

"Wednesday afternoon, anytime."

At that moment Lily tapped on the door to his outer office. "Excuse me, Senator Taylor. I have some more information on that video clip you asked me to look into. Is this a good time?"

"You bet. Come in, Lily." Rick turned to Carla again and asked her to call and have Sandra join them. When his chief of staff arrived, he closed the door and they sat around the small round table in his office. "What have you got, Lily?" Rick asked.

Lily shifted in her seat and straightened her back. Rick smiled to himself at her effort to increase the stature of her five foot, two inch frame. She was a bright young lady, but her long, blond hair and cheeky smile did sometimes make it challenging for Rick to take her seriously.

"After I texted you my initial impression of the audio tied to the video clip released yesterday, I contacted one of my professors and asked if he would take a look. I hope you don't mind."

"Not at all," Rick encouraged. "It's public information that was all over the media."

"Dr. Nelson called me this morning and advised me that while the audio was well done, it is definitely a product of AI."

Sandra looked at Rick and then Lily. "How can he be so sure?"

"Well, when a person speaks, they use muscles and tissue from their lips, tongue, and other mechanisms. They also take breaths as they speak. Speech, regardless of the language spoken, is a series of air movements, audio tones, and inflections being controlled by various muscles."

"Okay," Rick acknowledged. "I've never thought about speech in those terms before, but I think I understand what you're saying."

"Good. Early AI voicing was fairly easy to recognize because it sounded a bit monotonous and often used words that, while grammatically correct, were seldom used in normal dialogue. However, advanced AI has gotten so good that almost nobody can differentiate an AI voice from a human voice simply by listening carefully."

"So what causes Dr. Nelson to be so sure this is AI-generated?" Sandra asked again.

"Back to the way we form words in normal speech. Since human beings form words in the manner I described, there is a physical limitation as to how quickly someone can move from one type of sound to another. This isn't anything that we think about because we're used to hearing speech at the pace human beings speak it. AI voicing doesn't have such limitations.

"Dr. Nelson is sure that the voices are AI-generated because some of the movement from one sound to another is faster than is humanly possible. It's nothing that people would notice, but it would be physically impossible for a human being to accomplish. Not only that, but none of the voices in the audio even take a breath while speaking."

Rick sat there staring at Lily for a moment. Sandra began to speak, but he put up his hand. Both women stared at Rick without saying a word.

Finally, Rick asked, "Lily, I don't know if you would know the answer to this or not, but wouldn't the FBI have the capability to make this determination?"

"I have no idea of the FBI's capabilities, but I can tell you that Dr. Nelson told me that doing this sort of analysis is not difficult. Most universities have the ability to do it."

Rick looked at Sandra. "This could mean that the FBI doesn't want the truth to be made public." He stared at the table in front of him. "Everything seems to indicate that our government is setting the stage to take over Mexico," he said as if to himself. "I can't believe this is happening."

He looked up at Lily and said, "Ma'am, you may have just uncovered a conspiracy of enormous proportions. I need Dr. Nelson's phone number."

"What are you going to do with this?" Sandra asked.

"Nothing until I can get some independent corroboration. Let's keep this between us for now. Okay?" he said, looking at each of them.

They both nodded. Sandra said, "Please discuss this with me before you decide to move on it. We can't be making unsubstantiated accusations regarding who is behind it."

Rick smiled unhappily. "Understood. Thanks for keeping a grip on the reins."

68

THIS IS ridiculous, Clarisa said to herself. She drove a second time around the industrial site where the new plant was about to open. It was eight on Monday morning, and she had already driven the road between Taylor's place in St. Cloud and the event location for the following day. She could see that it was going to be a large site when completed, but at present there was only one enormous, warehouse-like building standing by itself. The building was several city blocks long and about one block wide, but the size wasn't so much the problem as was what was in its proximity: nothing.

It appeared that groundwork was being done, such as grading and trenching for sewer, water, and gas. A couple of concrete slabs had been poured but not above ground level. There was a contractor's trailer there with some activity around it. A few people were coming and going, and there was one backhoe digging a deep trench with workers in the ditch and standing nearby. She assumed they were trying to set a correct depth for the bottom of the ditch. She maintained her speed as she drove in order to avoid drawing attention to herself.

Beyond the new industrial site there were cornfields in every direction. The corn was only waist high, so even that was not an effective way to get in and out without being detected. She stopped the car for a moment and looked at the building through her binoculars. Under the eaves of the monstrosity, cameras watched silently all the way around. Clarisa shook her head and drove away.

69

President Donaldson did not wait for the corroboration that he promised to the people. On Monday afternoon he called a meeting of his National Security Council. They met in the White House Situation Room. Most of the members of the council were familiar with the president's plan and had attained their positions precisely for this purpose. The vice president and the secretary of energy were the only exceptions.

"I believe it is time to finally address the corruption south of the American border," the president began. "My heart goes out to the people of Mexico who have lived with this corruption for generations. We have looked the other way and dealt with the effects of it for much too long. The migration issue is a symptom of a much deeper problem. We have tried to bandage it with border fences and attacking the cartels, but we're still not getting to the root of the problem. It's time we rip the bandage off and rescue the Mexican people from their immoral government."

Most heads around the table were nodding their approval, though not all. "Mr. President, can you please outline exactly what you mean by ripping the bandage off this situation?" Vice President Whittington asked.

"It's time we remove Jose Cuevas and the other corrupt leaders of Mexico and put a provisional government in place until honest elections can be held."

Secretary of State Anthony Weller responded first. "Mr. President, I agree with your assessment, but this will be a shock to leaders in every part of the world, both adversaries and allies. As we've discussed before, you should expect a flurry of hyperbole making charges of US imperialism and everything else. This will be compared to Russia's invasion of Ukraine."

"Anthony, we've discussed this, and you have assured me that we are prepared to handle it diplomatically. Are you getting cold feet?"

"No, sir. I am simply raising this point for everyone to be aware of. It will be important to have messaging prepared for the American people to understand it. They will hear it all."

"That will all be arranged," the president affirmed.

"Mr. President, how long have you been planning for this?" the vice president asked. "From everything I'm hearing thus far, it sounds like there's no difference between what you're suggesting and Russia's invasion of Ukraine."

"Marjorie, your lack of understanding of foreign policy is exactly why you've been kept at arm's length in this endeavor. We have been under attack for years. We are finally fighting back. Fortunately, due to the overwhelming might of the United States of America, this should move quickly and with little bloodshed."

"That's exactly what Vladamir Putin said," Whittington responded. Then she looked at the Counsel to the president and the legal advisor to the NSA. "Can you sit there and affirm that this is a legal action?"

"Well, ma'am, if the president declares a state of emergency, then the law gives him considerable latitude to do what he feels is necessary in defense of the nation."

"From what we're seeing with regard to the beginning of this 'endeavor,' the idea of 'little bloodshed' is already out the window. We're watching innocents gunned down by the thousands due to your drone warfare," she said, looking at Defense Secretary Schmidt.

Schmidt exhaled and looked down, then at the president. Before she could respond, the president interjected, "Marjorie, this action is in following the policy of this administration. You need to get on board," he said, tapping his finger on the table in front of him as he spoke.

He then turned back to Weller. "When will the delegation leave for Mexico City?"

"They leave first thing in the morning. We have a noon meeting scheduled with President Cuevas."

"Alright, and our show of force?" he asked, looking at Schmidt.

"At 10 a.m. local time tomorrow morning," she said. "We'll take control of their air traffic control system and ground all aircraft other than our own. We have people inside and special forces ready to ensure there is no resistance. We will have twenty-one transport aircraft with military personnel and equipment on the ground at two Mexico City airports by 11 a.m. Our fighters will be prepared to deal with any Mexican military aircraft that are dispatched."

"Good. Our offer of immunity and a comfortable retirement for Cuevas in the United States should be ample incentive for him to leave peacefully." He looked around the room. "I want everyone back here at eleven tomorrow morning. That will be nine in Mexico City. I will be available if Cuevas wants to talk with me."

As the meeting broke up, Whittington approached Donaldson. "Sir, I cannot in good conscience approve of this action."

"Marjorie, I did not ask for your approval. You have two choices: either get on board or resign. Do I make myself clear?"

"Yes, sir," she said coldly, her eyes flashing.

#

When she returned to her office, the vice president put in a call to Senator Rick Taylor. Carla told her that he was enroute to Minnesota to give a speech in Loretto the next day, but she was able to get through to him on the road later that evening.

"Senator Taylor, thank you for taking my call."

"Yes, ma'am. Any time."

"Once again, we're in an awkward situation. I am calling to give you some information. I believe we can trust one another."

"Yes, ma'am, I agree. I may also have some information that you will be interested in," Rick said.

Whittington proceeded to tell Rick all that had transpired in the NSC meeting that day. She also mentioned that she was considering offering her resignation in order to fight the administration.

Rick, driving west on I-94 between the Twin Cities and St. Cloud, listened carefully. This confirmed his own suspicions. When the vice president finished, Rick chose his words deliberately. "Ma'am, first of all, I strongly recommend that you not resign. It sounds as if the attorney general and most of the Cabinet have been involved in this from the beginning. That means nobody is going to challenge the legality of the president's directive. If I'm right in that, political accountability is the only resource at our disposal."

"Impeachment?" Whittington asked.

"Yes. Right now, I have no idea what people in the House or Senate know about this, but I'm thinking that there are quite a few who would not go along with it. For the sake of the country, we need you in your position to take the reins in the event of Donaldson's impeachment or resignation," Rick said.

"As I said," he continued, "I also have some information for you. I have confirmed through two independent sources that the audio portion of the video clip that was released Sunday morning was AI-generated. I can't fathom that the FBI wouldn't have the capability to make the same determination. What you've just told me confirms that not only is this a conspiracy, but that those involved have set up the rationale for removing Cuevas."

"Oh, good Lord," the vice president responded. "But, then, knowing what I do now, if I don't resign it will appear that I'm part of this conspiracy."

"Good point," Rick acknowledged. "You need to push back in a very calculated way. What if you go to the attorney general and tell him your suspicions?" He paused. "No, beyond that, what if you tell him that you know the video is a fraud and are prepared to go public with the whole thing? That demonstrates your pushback going through appropriate channels. Hopefully, it also scares the hell out of Attorney General Thompson. If they're smart, this should cause them to at least pause long enough to figure out how they want to handle it."

"I've already made my misgivings known to the president. I suppose this would be my logical next step."

"So here is my question for you," Rick said. "Shall I go public with the information on the fake video, or would you rather I wait?"

"Please wait. As long as I'm on the team, I need to give them an opportunity to fix this in the event the president isn't aware of it."

"Okay, I'll give it a day. However, on Wednesday morning, I am going public with this. Good luck, ma'am."

70

CINDY FINISHED her shift and walked out the door at half past midnight on Tuesday. As usual, she was the last person on her shift to leave. She was tired, but it felt good. It had been a busy night in the ER, and they had done some good work. She enjoyed the sense of accomplishment she got from being part of a team that was saving lives.

Her feeling of satisfaction deflated as soon as she got to her car. It looked like it was leaning to the right as it sat in the parking space. She walked to the right side of the car and groaned out loud when she saw that she didn't have just one flat tire: Both tires on that side of the car were flat.

She looked around the parking lot. It was empty of people. The others on her shift had been gone for at least fifteen minutes. She bent down and turned her phone light on, looking closely at the back tire. At first she didn't see anything. She ran her hand over the tread from the back of the tire, over the top and to the front. She could smell the rubber as she hugged the tire, searching for something that might have punctured it. There it was. She felt it just above the ground on the front part of the tire, a nail head. She moved forward and shined her light on the spot and saw the embedded nail.

Oh great, she thought. She must have driven through a field of nails to flatten two tires at once. She looked at her watch, as if hoping it would tell her it wasn't as late as it was. She could think of no way to get two tires fixed at this time of night. She leaned against the right rear fender and thought about walking in and asking for a ride home. She talked herself out of that because she knew hospital staff were still busy caring for several people who had been brought in from a car accident.

She let out a huff of breath and said out loud, "If I'm walking home, I'm not carrying this thing." She walked to the driver's side door and threw her purse onto the floor where it would be somewhat out of view. As an afterthought, she pulled it back onto the seat, reached in, and grabbed her wallet and put it into the left hip pocket of her scrubs. She put her phone in the right pocket. Remembering Patrick's phone call cautioning her to be careful, she also pulled the whistle out of her purse.

It was an old whistle that she had gotten when she was a camp counselor so many years earlier. She had found it in an old box. It was even on the same woven plastic lanyard she had made on a craft day at camp. It was bulky, made by weaving three wide, plastic strips together, resulting in an inflexible plastic cord. She remembered that the cord had always chafed her neck. She had kept it for the memories, she supposed. She put the wide loop over her head and let the whistle dangle.

Finally, she reached in and grabbed something else that she had bought for self-protection after Patrick's call. She dropped the bag to the floor again and closed and locked the car door. She walked through the parking lot and onto the sidewalk at a brisk pace. She had walked to work many times before but not since her experience in the Boundary Waters. She knew that her walk would leave her exposed, but in her mind she scolded herself for making too big a deal of the possible danger. She knew she would be home in ten minutes. This self-defense stuff was scaring her more than it was giving her any sense of comfort.

\#

Clarisa waited behind a large oak in the park. The tree was in a cluster at the edge, next to the sidewalk. It was halfway up the block, so the light from the corner streetlights was faint. The moon was new, and the shade of the trees darkened the night further. She wore dark-colored scrubs, a surgical head covering, and safety glasses to avoid getting blood in her eyes. Her right hand firmly grasped the hunting knife.

The streetlight provided a clear view, and she watched Cindy Potter cross the street half a block away. She was also dressed in scrubs, as was expected. Cindy walked with both hands cupped in front of her chest, one hand holding a whistle connected to a lanyard. Clarisa would need to deal with that immediately.

She stepped behind the tree so Cindy would walk past her without seeing her. She had made sure there were no leaves or sticks on the ground that would make noise when she stepped out from the tree and onto the sidewalk.

\#

As she crossed the street, Cindy looked into the darkness of the park in front of her. She dismissed her trepidation as paranoia but still picked up her pace to get beyond it quickly. She hoped by holding her whistle in front of her that anyone seeing her coming might be reluctant to try anything. She wished she had bought a knife with a blade longer than two inches. If attacked, what could she really do with the tiny thing she held in her right hand? The streetlight at the next corner, just a half block in front of her, gave her some solace.

After passing the light, Cindy abruptly felt a blow to the back of her head and neck. Before she could turn, the plastic lanyard and whistle were tight against the front of her neck, choking her. She tried to scream but couldn't get any sound out. There was an arm across her back forcing her forward while the hand on her lanyard pulled back hard, keeping it tight. She was pushed into the darkness of the trees and heard a voice. It was a whisper, but it was a voice she would never forget. "So, Cindy Potter, did you really think I wouldn't come for you?"

Fear gripped Cindy. Her hands were still cupped in front of her, and the whistle was still tight against her throat. She tried to say something, but the only thing that came out was a gurgling sound. A wheezing, almost snoring sound came from her throat as she struggled to breathe. The arm was no longer across her back. The hand holding the lanyard was twisting it to keep it taut. Then Cindy felt a blade across her throat.

"Well, isn't this déjá vu? The last time we met like this you left me with an awful headache," Clarisa whispered into Cindy's right ear. "It's such a pity that you fell victim to an unfinished sex crime. Now, I can make this go quickly, or I can make you suffer like you can't imagine. You help me, and I'll make this easy on you. Do you understand?"

Cindy nodded her head.

"Good," Clarisa said, comfortingly. "I want you to pull down the bottom of your scrubs, your panties, and all. Go ahead," she said, increasing the pressure of the knife.

Not happening, Cindy thought. Shaking, she swung her right hand down to her hip and plunged the knife into the top of her nemesis' leg. When she felt her fist touch the skin, she pushed down and across toward the woman's inner thigh.

Even as she wounded the woman, she felt the slicing of the sharp blade through her skin as it came across her neck. She lunged forward, nearly falling, and felt the lanyard go limp as the woman lost her grip. She caught her balance and ran. When she looked back, she saw the woman walk out of the shadows and onto the sidewalk in the faint light. Even Cindy was shocked by the effectiveness of her counterattack. There was a huge gash in her assailant's right thigh, and blood was spurting out two feet in front of her.

The woman's eyes were bulging; her mouth was contorted into a grotesque frown. Her hands and arms were covered in blood. She looked directly at Cindy, and then her eyes moved down to her wound. Blood continued to pulse from her leg and started to pool on the sidewalk around her. "What did you do?" she whispered.

Cindy felt her own neck. Blood was running down onto her chest in a slow, steady stream. She cleared her throat, and the sound was normal, and somehow, it seemed that she was not cut badly. She became aware of the dampness on the back of her scrubs and realized her back was drenched in the woman's blood.

She pulled out her phone and dialed 911. She quickly gave the information to the operator and then laid the phone down without ending the call. The woman in front of her was leaning against the tree now. She still had the knife in her hand.

Cindy took a few steps forward. "I can help you," she told the woman. "You'll have to put down the knife."

The woman raised her hand and pointed the knife in her direction. She said weakly, "Don't come near me."

"Your femoral artery is cut. You'll die if I don't help you."

The woman dropped her hand. She slid down the tree into a sitting position. Cindy heard sirens in the background but knew that this woman had only minutes to live. She walked forward carefully and stretched out her hand. The woman didn't move. Her eyelids were drooping. Cindy took hold of the knife-wielding hand and removed the knife from it. She tossed it a few feet away, then sprung up and grabbed the woman's arm, pulling her away from the tree and laying her on her back. Using both hands, she checked the slash wound and was able to feel the artery. She pressed hard with her fingers against the bone, closing it off and stopping the blood flow.

The woman was barely conscious. With slurred words she said, "I'm sorry, Frank. Frank, I'm—" Her words trailed off.

Cindy thought the woman was still alive but couldn't remove a hand to check her pulse. When the police and EMTs arrived, she identified herself as a critical care nurse. "Get this woman to the hospital now. She has lost a lot of blood. Her femoral artery has been severed."

The police officers weren't used to arriving at a crime scene and being told what to do. "Who are you?" asked one of the officers whose name tag said CHANDLER.

"My name is Cindy Potter. This woman attacked me as I walked home from the hospital."

Officer Chandler looked at one of the EMTs and said, "Can you take it from here?"

"We need to get her to the hospital. She's dying," the technician said as he pulled the stretcher from the van. At that point the EMTs and Cindy worked together in professional unison, getting the woman onto the stretcher and into the van.

The officer turned to Cindy, and she spoke before he could. "We'll need to continue this at the hospital," she insisted as the EMTs closed one door of the van with her inside, then the other. Inside the ambulance she maintained pressure on the artery, and they drove the short distance to the hospital. One of the officers stayed at the scene and began to secure it for investigation. Chandler followed the ambulance to the hospital.

71

AT THE hospital, Cindy briefed the trauma team, and they took the woman into surgery. One of the nurses put her arm around Cindy and said, "Come on, we need to check out that neck injury." With Cindy's permission, they allowed the police officer to follow them into the procedure room. A doctor looked at her wound and shook his head. "I don't understand what happened. Part of this cut is fairly deep, but the closer it got to your jugular, the more superficial it became. There is one point where the knife didn't even break the skin."

Cindy shrugged. "Could she have been that good? Just wanted to scare me?" she said in an effort at humor. Then it dawned on her. She was lying down with her head tilted back. "Check the lanyard," she said.

The nurse who was assisting picked up the whistle and lanyard. "There it is," she said as she pointed to the lanyard. There was a cut diagonally across the plastic lanyard. "If the knife did that to that chunk of plastic, it would have done a number on your throat."

The doctor finished taping the wound closed and said, "You were incredibly lucky." They took Cindy to get a shower and some clean scrubs.

Later, after asking some questions, Chandler brought Cindy back to the scene. She told the officers what had happened, walking through it as best she could in the early dawn light.

She explained that this woman was the same one who had attacked Senator Taylor and her in the Boundary Waters. Then the police officer dropped her off at home, and she promised to be available for further questioning.

As soon as she was home, Cindy called Rick. "Patrick, I just met your gal again." She told him what had happened and assured him that she was okay. Rick called the office and told them to notify the company where he was supposed to speak that morning. He would be canceling due to a personal emergency.

He and his bodyguard were at Cindy's house by noon. He knocked on the door and waited. When there was no answer, he rang the doorbell and pounded harder. A minute later Cindy opened the door. She was wearing shorts and a t-shirt, her hair was tangled, and she squinted as her eyes adjusted to the light, having just been awakened.

Rick gasped when he saw the gauze taped around her neck. "What happened? You didn't tell me you were hurt."

She grimaced and said, "I thought it could wait. I didn't want you to worry."

"Worry? Are you kidding? I'm devastated. What happened to your neck?"

She invited him in, apologizing for the clutter. "I wasn't expecting company."

After having him sit in her most comfortable living room chair, she sat on the sofa and curled her bare legs under her. Then she proceeded to tell him all the details of the attack, including the attempt to cut her throat.

As she described the incident, a wave of guilt came over him. "Oh, God forgive me for getting you involved. I'm so sorry, Cindy. You should have never had to deal with this."

With that, her tears finally came. "Oh, Patrick, I was so scared. That woman is evil. I thought I was going to die."

He stood up and moved to the sofa. He tried to embrace her, but the way she was seated made it awkward. She rose to her knees, put both arms around him and her head on his shoulder, and cried.

"Cindy, I can't believe how brave you are. You did it. You defeated her."

Her head didn't move. "If this is bravery, I don't want to be brave," she said.

He held her and hugged her. He thought about Maggie's death and now this, all because of him. He quietly wept, embracing her and silently thanking God for protecting her.

PART 4

REDEPLOYING THEIR TACTICS

"Be patient; the tables will turn. (And if they won't, make them turn.)"
– Anonymous

72

AT ELEVEN o'clock, Vice President Whittington entered the situation room. She had spoken with Attorney General Cork Thompson earlier that morning. He was visibly uncomfortable during the discussion but assured her that he would check with the FBI to ensure that they had confirmed the authenticity of the audio.

President Donaldson, who had arrived before she did, seemed perturbed about something. He was pacing the floor with a notepad in his hand and then tossed it onto the table in front of his chair as he sat. She didn't know if Thompson had talked with him yet.

"Update me on the border action, General Tomkins," he said loudly. The buzz in the room quieted immediately, and the chairman of the joint chiefs began his briefing.

"Sir, our troops are approximately fifty miles into Mexico at this time. They have received little resistance from the Mexican military, although there was one skirmish just north of Nueva Rosita. A platoon attempted to ambush the unit moving into the area. We lost two soldiers. The Mexican military had twenty-seven casualties, and we took sixteen prisoners. Preliminary information from interviews suggests that the platoon leader was connected to one of the cartels in some way.

"We have seen little in the way of northbound migrants. It

appears that the word is out that it is dangerous to approach the border, and that those who have gotten through will be immediately deported. Media reports show migrants moving south with the intention of returning home. We anticipate Mexico City's airport will be filled with people from other countries wanting to fly home or someplace else, assuming they have the funds to do so.

"We have conducted thirty-two attacks on known cartel facilities. In each case we have met resistance, and a firefight has resulted. We have some wounded, but fortunately no one has been killed so far. We have a list of seventy-four more cartel points that we will deal with as we reach them. We are sure there are more than that. Army intelligence continues to work this and will add locations to the list as they gather information.

"Our troop and equipment transports are an hour out of Mexico City at this time. Thirteen aircraft will fly into Mexico City International and eight into Toluca. We have plans for moving various-sized units into the city as the need presents itself. Mexico's military leadership is in disarray, getting mixed messages from the Cuevas administration. They don't want to confront us militarily but are preparing to do so."

"Thank you, General Tomkins. Does anyone have questions for the general?" the president asked. Vice President Whittington stared at the attorney general across the table, waiting for him to say something. He avoided eye contact and kept quiet.

One of the Council members asked Tomkins about the drone issue, and he assured them that the drones were being systematically shut down. He said that in several cases, the drones had awakened and mobilized toward the troops. In those cases, the drones were incapacitated by grenades that exploded on impact.

"General, isn't that allowing the drones to get close enough for a grenade to be thrown at them?" asked Secretary of State Weller.

"No, sir," the general replied patiently. "These grenades are launched from grenade launchers. They arm themselves by the grenades' rotation while in flight. You might think of them more like small missiles that can be aimed at a piece of equipment."

Asked about fatalities surrounding the drones, he told them that about 2,700 people had been killed, about three-quarters of them migrants. This resulted in a quiet murmur throughout the room.

Finally, the vice president spoke. "Mr. President, this morning I advised the attorney general that I have received, from multiple, highly regarded sources, that the video that triggered this action contained audio that was generated using artificial intelligence. I hope you have been made aware of this and are taking it into consideration as we follow through on this plan."

There was complete silence in the room as Council members glanced at one another with looks on their faces that said, *How did she know that?*

Donaldson glared at his chief of staff. He had been assured that the audio would be so good that nobody would question it. Turning his attention to Whittington he said, "Marjorie, I find that hard to believe. If that were the case, I'm sure our FBI would have advised me. Isn't that right, Cork?"

The attorney general shifted in his seat and finally looked at the president and said, "Well, Mr. President, when the vice president brought me this information, I contacted FBI Director Gregory to confirm that they had put the video to the test. I was told that their experts had given a preliminary affirmation of its authenticity. He also said that they had not done the kind of testing that Vice President Whittington has said revealed the … uh … concern."

The president wiped perspiration from his forehead with a napkin and looked at some others around the room. The others stared back calmly, revealing little of the panic that all involved were feeling. "Vice President Whittington," he said, "may I ask who your reliable sources of this information are?"

"Yes, sir," she responded. "Two top universities that do extensive research in AI have both confirmed that the audio is fraudulently presented. I provided the attorney general with names of the professors that analyzed the video."

The room was silent again. President Donaldson studied the table in front of him. He finally looked at his secretary of state. "Secretary Weller, has our delegation met with Cuevas yet?"

"No, sir," the secretary said, looking at his watch. "Their meeting is scheduled for twenty minutes from now."

"Bring them up to speed. Let's downplay the video and bluff a little. Tell him that we have other information linking him to the cartels and showing that his actions have served to enrich him at the expense of the citizens."

"Yes, sir. I hope I can reach them in time," Weller said as he pushed back from the table and stood up.

"Delay the meeting if you have to, but this change needs to be made," the president said. "I'm sure Cuevas is corrupt. Everyone down there is."

Anthony Weller nodded and left the room.

"Mr. President," Whittington said, continuing her pushback. "You have addressed the citizens of our country, giving them the video as your rationale for potentially involving ourselves in Mexico's government. You have a small army preparing to land in Mexico to remove their president. Not only will our citizens rise up, but leaders throughout the world will challenge you when they learn the video is a fake."

Donaldson's face reddened as he stood. Pointing his finger at her, he said, "Marjorie, you are not to make a public statement relating to this, do I make myself clear?"

"Perfectly, sir," she said, directly looking him in the eye in a way that said, *You don't intimidate me.* "You may also want to know that others outside of the administration are aware of this issue. You should expect that this will hit the media within days."

"Damn it!" the president shouted, throwing his pen across the room. He glared at Whittington again and looked around the room. Almost all of the looks he got back were noncommittal. Stan Kauffman frowned, made eye contact with Donaldson, and shook his head ever so slightly.

"General Tomkins, have the military aircraft return to their base," Donaldson snapped. "Keep them on a short leash." He slammed the chair he had been sitting in forward into the table and walked out the door. Kauffman was close behind.

73

CINDY FINALLY lifted her head off Rick's shoulder. "Look at me," she said, laughing through her tears. "What kind of host am I? Can I get you something? It's lunchtime; you're probably starving."

"Oh, don't worry about me. I'm sorry I woke you. Do you want to go back to bed? I can go out and get something to eat and bring it back in a couple of hours."

Cindy's phone rang. She cleared her throat and said, "Hello."

Rick watched her as she nodded. "Sure, I'm here. I'll see you soon."

She ended the call. "That was an officer from the Minnesota Bureau of Criminal Apprehension. He's coming over to ask me some questions."

"Now?"

She nodded. "Please stay. I want you to be here."

Rick stood and embraced her again. "I'm here as long as you need."

While they were waiting, Rick got a phone call from his chief of staff. "I thought I should let you know that a large contingent of transport aircraft departed two hours ago for Mexico City."

"What are they carrying?"

"I have no details, but it looks to me like something is about to happen there. I just thought you should know."

"He's going after Cuevas. I know it," Rick said. "Sandra, I'm tied up right now. I promised Vice President Whittington that I wouldn't go public about the audio until tomorrow. I'm going to have to trust that she knows what is happening and is doing something about it."

"Is there anything you would like for me, Lily, or anyone else to do?"

"No. Thanks for the update. I'll give you a call later to check in."

Not long after, there was a knock at the door. Cindy opened it for two men who came in and introduced themselves.

"Ms. Potter, I'm Detective Lawrence Wilson from the Minnesota BCA. This is Detective John Bode. We have statewide jurisdiction in investigating crimes. We're very sorry about the attack on you this morning. It sounds like you handled yourself quite well in a life-threatening situation."

Cindy greeted them and shook their hands. "This is Senator Patrick Taylor. I've asked that he be here when we talk."

The detectives glanced at each other. "That's fine, Ms. Potter. In fact, we would like for the senator to be part of this conversation."

Rick shook their hands. "You can dispense with the senator title. Rick is fine."

Cindy and Rick sat on the sofa, and the detectives on chairs. Cindy suddenly realized how dark it was in the living room and jumped up and opened the blinds, letting the sunlight stream in.

"Ms. Potter, Senator Taylor, we just came from the hospital. I should let you know that the woman who attacked you died not long after she was brought in," Wilson began. "I understand you used all of your skills to try and save her. That was an admirable and brave thing to do."

Cindy and Rick looked at each other and she rolled her eyes. He winked.

"Detective Wilson, don't interpret our glance as any sense of satisfaction in the woman's death," Rick explained. "I had just been praising Cindy for her bravery myself. I guess you'll need us to identify her as the person who attacked us at the Boundary Waters."

"It was her," Cindy said.

"No, sir. That won't be necessary. We have DNA from the branch that was used to strike her in the head. If Ms. Potter is correct, there will be a match."

"I don't know much about detective work; how long will it take to identify her?"

Wilson looked at his partner and nodded.

"Senator Taylor, we already believe we know who she is," Detective Bode said.

"Who—"

"Who is she?" Cindy said, cutting Rick off.

"Um, while we have no documentary evidence, I would say that we're 95% confident that we know who she is. We need to do a few things to confirm it. In addition, it may be best for the investigation if we keep it vague for a while. We'd like the opportunity to see who else might be involved in this. We'll just call her Jane Doe for now."

Rick and Cindy looked at each other. "Did the police recognize her?"

"I believe I have met her before," Detective Bode said tentatively. "If she is who I believe she is, this could develop into a ... uh ... high profile case. It's important that we be 100% right about this."

"Are we out of danger now?" Cindy asked.

Wilson pursed his lips. "We can't say for sure."

"Look," Rick pushed back. "You need to be more open with us if there's a chance that we're still at risk."

"Senator Taylor," Wilson said, changing the subject, "in your role as a senator, have you had any run-ins with others that might give them a motive to want you out of the way?"

Rick leaned back on the sofa. He looked at Cindy and then at the officers. "Ever since my wife Maggie's death, I have thought about that every single day. I've been a thorn in the president's side regarding his border policy ever since my campaign took hold. But I can't imagine someone would go on a killing spree in an effort to take me out, if that's what you mean."

"Did you speak to the president about it?" Wilson asked.

"No," Rick said. "Kauffman, his chief of staff, has called me about it. He offered me a lot of incentives to get on board with the president's policy, but when I refused he got really pissed. He said some things that I took as a threat, but I figured he was just talking politics. I never thought he actually intended to harm me."

"Do you remember his exact words?"

"He said something about me having hell to pay. I asked if he was threatening me. He said something about me understanding his meaning soon enough," Rick recalled.

"Is there anyone else in Washington who you have had similar run-ins with?" Wilson asked.

Rick sat with his elbows on his knees, rubbing his temples with both hands. "I had similar conversations with Senator Moreno, less the threat. He offered to do good things for me if I would get on board. He was clear on what he wanted from me and wasn't happy about my response."

The officers looked at each other and then back at Rick. "Senator Taylor, you're probably not aware of this, but the FBI recently became involved in your case. DNA has tied the person who made an attempt on your lives with that of someone who may be connected to the death of Senator Tom Blado last Christmas."

Cindy's eyes widened. She knew nothing of Rick's job or Washington, but the thought of attempts being made on two senators' lives sounded audacious. "Are you suggesting that this woman killed Senator Blado, Maggie Taylor, and intended to kill Patrick?"

"And presumably you, since you could identify her," Wilson agreed.

"Who is she?" Rick demanded.

"I promise you that when we know for sure, you will be advised. In fact, as big as this thing could get, we may need to talk with you a lot more about this."

Rick was frustrated by the detectives' lack of transparency but wasn't going to argue with them. Maggie's killer was dead, and he was just fine with that. His real concern was for Cindy. "Detective Wilson, from what you have just told us, others may be involved with this, and who knows who else they might hire to come after Cindy or me. You probably saw my bodyguard outside. I'm not worried for myself, but you need to provide Cindy protection as well."

Wilson glanced at his partner. "I'll have to check into that and get back to you. We're understaffed, as are most police departments these days. I don't think we're equipped to provide twenty-four hour protection right now. However, there's a security company that we work with sometimes. I'll see if we can't get them over here to see how to better secure Ms. Potter's home."

Wilson turned and looked at Cindy. "It might be a good idea for you to have and learn how to use a gun. Next time you may not be close enough to defend yourself so successfully."

"That's not going to happen," Cindy said stubbornly, closing the subject.

#

After the detectives left, Rick apologized again to Cindy, taking full responsibility for the attack she had suffered. He hated himself for what he was about to do.

"Cindy, I hate to leave you, but I have a hundred things going on right now and some could relate to all this. I'm going to need to take care of them."

She smiled faintly and nodded her head. "I understand. Go, I'm fine."

"I'm going to get a hotel room here for the night, so I'll be close by. Let me know what the security company suggests. I'll cover any costs you incur. Do it right."

She rolled her eyes and said, "Yes, sir, Senator Taylor." She smiled again. "That's all well and good, but I haven't forgotten about that hamburger you owe me."

He kissed her on the forehead and turned to leave. As he walked out the door she said, "Patrick, you be careful."

He nodded and walked to his car. He apologized to his bodyguard but asked him to take a minute right then and find a hotel where they could stay the night. "Set it up any way you feel comfortable with, security-wise. And we need to check in right away. I need someplace to work from while we're here."

Rick called his chief of staff. "Hi, Sandra. Anything new?"

"Not much," Dellingham replied. "Unless you wanted to be aware that the vice president called for you. She said she sent you a text and would like you to call her back."

"Just a minute." He looked at his text messages and there was one from an unknown number. He clicked on it and read,

Please call. I need to update you. MW

"Okay, Sandra, I got it. Anything more on the border?"

"No, I've been monitoring news channels and haven't seen anything new."

After ending his call with Sandra, Rick asked if his guard would step out of the car. His next call would be confidential. When he was alone, he dialed the number he had been given. "Whittington."

He was caught off guard. The Vice President of the United States answering her own phone?

Then he heard, "Taylor? Sorry, I didn't look at my caller ID."

"Uh, yes ma'am. Is this your personal cell phone?"

"Yes. It's primarily for family calls, but I thought it would be best to use it for our conversations. I wanted to update you on my morning."

"Yes, ma'am," Rick said.

"I talked to the attorney general this morning. He played dumb but didn't seem too happy with what I told him. He said he'd have to check with the FBI."

Rick shook his head. "You caught him with his pants down."

"Absolutely. Either that, or he's totally incompetent."

She proceeded to brief him on what had happened in the NSC meeting that morning. Then she added, "Senator Taylor, your country owes you a debt of gratitude. Your information may have prevented a war, or at the very least a very embarrassing situation."

"Well it sounds like, if anything, it may have only postponed things. The president seems hell-bent on taking over the Mexican government."

"Yes, well, I'm sure we have more work to do in that regard. I suggest you follow through on going public with this in the morning. That should create enough of a stir to slow the progress."

"Alright, I'll do that. Is there anything you want me to leave out or position in a certain way?"

"No, you just do your thing. However, at this point I think it best that our work together be kept quiet. I suggest we discontinue our dialogue until further notice."

"Yes, ma'am. Thank you for all you've done," he said.

74

IT WAS after four that afternoon when Rick got to his hotel room. He showered and was toweling dry when he got a call from an unknown number.

"Hello," Rick said apprehensively.

"Senator Taylor, my name is Stuart Kramer." The voice on the other end of the line had a southern accent. Perhaps Texas, Rick thought. "I'm a special agent with the FBI."

"Yes, sir. What can I do for you?" he replied politely.

"I wonder if I could meet with you so we can discuss Ms. Potter's attacker. Sooner would be best."

"I'm in Duluth. I just checked into a hotel here. Would you like to come here, or would you like to meet me someplace else?"

"I'll come there. Thanks."

Rick gave him the name of his hotel and the room number and hung up the phone. He immediately called Jim Gunderson to let him know things seemed to be coming together quickly and asked him to call Washington to tell the staff that he might be delayed getting back by a few days.

Kramer was there within fifteen minutes. They exchanged pleasantries, and Rick looked over the agent's credentials. He offered the only chair in the room to the agent and remained standing.

"Special Agent Kramer, do we have a positive ID on the woman?" Rick asked.

"We do. It has created quite a stir, so we are going to be very careful in how we handle this."

"Okay," Rick said slowly.

The agent took a deep breath. "Senator Taylor, the attacker's name is Clarisa Moreno. From what I understand, you've never met her, but you work with her husband."

Rick felt a wave of something come over him. His jaw dropped, and he felt a tingling sensation in his head. He sat down on the edge of the bed. "Are you telling me she was Frank Moreno's wife?"

"Yes, sir," the agent said. He awaited Rick's response.

Rick's mind was racing. He couldn't fathom being attacked by a senator's wife. *Why? He didn't know anything about her. What possible motive would she have?*

"Are you sure?" was all he could muster.

"Yes, sir," Kramer repeated and waited again.

"Was Frank involved?"

"We don't know that. At the current time, we have not contacted him about his wife's death. We thought it might be helpful to speak to you before we proceed to that."

"Wait a minute. Detective Wilson told me you have connected her to Tom Blado's death as well?"

"We know that she was with him the night he died. We don't know more than that. Would you know if she would have any reason to kill Tom Blado?"

"Wait. You're asking me questions about people I don't know."

"Maybe I should rephrase my question. Are you aware of any reason she or her husband might want Tom Blado dead?"

Rick paused, stood up, and began to pace. "Well, like I said, I never met Tom Blado." He took a deep breath. "But, since being in Washington I have heard some scuttlebutt about Blado being opposed to Donaldson's proposed border policy. I've been opposed to that policy. Blado was the chairman of a powerful committee and likely had the wherewithal to fight it." He continued to pace. Something was coming together in his mind, but the scope of this thing didn't make sense. "Who would murder a United States senator over a political or policy difference?"

"Senator Taylor, I realize that this is all shocking to you, and I'll admit that it is a little hard to get your head around. However, I'd like you to think through your own experiences and what you've heard in Washington and paint me a picture of what may have happened here."

Rick stared at him. "How did you connect this woman to Blado?"

"Her DNA. He'd had sex with her the night he died."

"So you don't know that she was definitely connected to his death."

"Well, this is what we do know. She checked into the hotel about an hour before he did, using an assumed name. She was careful to cover her face when she went to and from her room. She left the room at 1:45 a.m., about five minutes after he did. Early indications of bruising on his hip suggests that he was violently pushed over the rail when he fell to his death."

"All you really know then, is that she had an affair with Tom Blado and was careful not to be found out."

Kramer nodded. "But now we know that she was involved in an attack on another senator who wasn't on board with the administration. By the way, we also know that she was trained in the United States Army Special Operations in the mid 1990s. She knew how to kill."

Rick shook his head. "Well, she certainly knew what she was doing and pursued us with skill and confidence." After a pause he went on. "Okay, I know that Frank Moreno was absolutely on board with Donaldson. He called me and came to see me multiple times to pressure me to change my position regarding Donaldson's border policy. I guess he could have been overzealous and, with his wife's background, they could have decided to remove any obstacles in the way of getting it done. But why? What would be in it for them? I mean, loyalty is one thing, but to kill? It doesn't make sense."

"Senator Taylor, I can assure you that most crimes committed in our country make very little sense to normal folks."

Rick sat back down on the bed and stared at the agent. "What about the president? What if they were doing this at the behest of the president?"

Kramer shook his head. "I can assure you, Senator Taylor, the higher-ups at the FBI have no desire to delve into such a question unless there is strong evidence of the president's involvement."

"Why's that? Is the President outside the jurisdiction of the FBI?"

Kramer didn't respond to his question. "Senator Taylor, we'd like to speak with Frank Moreno at a time and place that works for our investigation. Do you think you could find out where Senator Moreno is, and, if he is not in Minnesota, when he plans to be here? We'd prefer he not know that we're interested in talking with him."

#

Rick called Moreno's office on Wednesday morning. His assistant put him through to the majority leader.

"Frank, this is Rick Taylor. I just wanted to apologize for not being able to speak at the event you'd asked me to cover. I had a personal emergency arise and just couldn't be there at that time. I'm very sorry."

"Thank you, Rick. I appreciate your call. I understand that sometimes things come up. Is everything alright there now?" he asked, wondering if Taylor had become aware that he was in danger.

"It's fine, thank you for asking. A friend was going through a difficult time and needed me," Rick explained. "While I've got you, I wanted to see if you could help me understand what the heck's going on in Mexico. It seems like the border crisis is over, and yet everything I'm hearing suggests that Donaldson is continuing to push into Mexico with the military. When is he going to pull back?"

"Look, I know where you stand on all of this, but you might as well hear it from me. There is so much corruption in the Mexican government that Donaldson is going to step in and clean house. In fact, it will be announced soon that I will be the provisional governor of Mexico until things can be sorted out. I'll be heading to Minneapolis tomorrow morning so my wife and I can begin packing for the move."

"The move? Provisional governor?" Rick asked incredulously. "Exactly what are the president's plans?"

"Well, I think it's best I leave that to Donaldson to say. By the way, are you still maintaining extra security around you? It seems like everything has settled down."

Rick felt the hair on his neck rise with his anger. "Yep, sure do. The police still haven't made any arrests. Why do you ask?"

"Ah, we'll be needing security while in Mexico, and I just wanted to know how difficult it is to get, you know, alone time. Does your detail ever leave you alone?"

"No, Frank. Never. You'll just have to adjust to it. Does that answer your question?"

The line was quiet for a few seconds, then Moreno said, "Okay, well I guess we will, like you say, adjust."

"Have a good trip, Frank," Rick said as he hung up.

He immediately called the number that Special Agent Kramer had given him.

On the other end of the line he heard the drawl, "Kramer."

"Special Agent Kramer, this is Rick Taylor. I may have just found a hint of a motive for Frank and his wife, what did you say her name was?"

"Clarisa. What did you find out?"

"Frank Moreno is in Washington right now and will be traveling to Minneapolis tomorrow morning. He said he and his wife would be packing for a move to Mexico City, where he will be appointed the provisional governor of Mexico by the Donaldson Administration."

Kramer let out a long, low whistle. "Why would a provisional governor be needed in Mexico?"

"Because our president is about to take over their government."

Kramer was quiet for a moment, then said, "Well, let's take first things first. We'll go to his home once he's there and interview him. I'm not sure we have enough to arrest him just now, but we will need to tell him of his wife's death and what we know regarding her comings and goings."

"You can't take him into custody?" Rick asked. "I know you said you're not able to be much help on this right away, but I think we should probe into the possible involvement of Stan Kauffman and Gerald Donaldson before they learn what's going down."

"I told you, Senator Taylor, there is no way I will get permission to escalate this investigation to a higher level until I have a lot more evidence."

"I know, I know. Let me ask you a question, though. If someone came to you with a recording of a confession and told you they had gotten it by talking with the person with a recording device present, what would you do with that?"

After drawing a deep breath and exhaling again, Kramer said, "Well, it would depend on where it happened. In many states it's illegal to record someone without their knowledge. In those cases, the information would be used as a resource as we gather legal evidence, but it could not be used as evidence in a trial."

"Is it legal to record a conversation in Washington, D.C.?"

Kramer said nothing for what seemed to be a full minute. "It is legal if one person involved in the conversation agrees to it *and* if the conversation takes place in an environment where there should be no expectation of privacy."

"Gotcha," Rick said. "Would you do me a favor and keep

me in the loop when you meet with Moreno?"

"Sure," Kramer agreed. "Don't do anything stupid, Senator Taylor," he added.

"Of course not," Rick assured him. "Good luck, Special Agent Kramer."

75

After he finished with Kramer, Rick placed a call to Jim Gunderson.

"Good morning, Jim."

"Hi, Rick. How long do you think you'll be in Duluth?"

"I plan to head home later today. However, I need to make a public statement. Can you reach out to your media contacts and tell them that I have some game-changing information relating to the Cuevas video that has caused such a stir?"

"Sure, what do you have?"

"I'm going to announce that the audio on that clip was AI-generated."

"Whoa!" Jim exclaimed. "I'm sure I can make that happen. When do you want to do it, and how much time do you have available?"

"Well," Rick paused to consider the questions. He didn't want to take up the whole day with this. "Let's say I'd like to do it sometime this morning. If you can get some interviews with national outlets, let's limit it to one or two."

"Okay. I'll get back to you as soon as something is arranged."

Rick made a phone call to check on Cindy. She seemed her normal self, downplaying her injury with some feistiness returning. She told him that she was off work for three more days but would return to her normal schedule after that.

"I'm glad you're feeling better. I wish I had time to stop in before I leave, but things are moving fast and furious. I'd better get home."

"I understand. Thank you so much for coming to see me. It helped a lot."

"I'm glad I was close by and could get here quickly. I wish I could stay. By the way, you may be able to catch me in the news today. I'm about to stir up a hornet's nest."

"Oh my," she said. "You're such a rabble rouser! I'll turn on the TV."

"Talk to you soon," Rick said.

Rick had decided not to share the information about Clarisa Moreno. Cindy certainly had a right to know, but it was important to avoid any possibility of the information becoming public.

Jim got back to him about an hour later. One of the national networks wanted the story but asked if he could do it live during their twelve o-clock news hour. He agreed. They asked if he could go to the local TV station in Duluth. They would use their national news anchor for the interview but wanted him on camera. On his way to the station, Rick called Sandra to discuss the interview. He told her what he intended to say and asked for her input.

"Oh boy, this will really stir things up," she said. "Just make sure you don't make specific charges. We don't know who did it. You don't want to be sued for libel."

"Okay, mom," he said and laughed. "You're exactly right. Thank you."

A little after eleven he sat in a chair behind a desk in the studio. It was somewhat of a makeshift setup because the local news was being broadcast at the same time. With the camera pointed at him, a producer gave him a countdown from five until his picture and audio went live.

The national news anchor began. "This afternoon we have Senator Rick Taylor from Minnesota with us. Thank you for joining us, Senator Taylor. You have been vocal in your opposition to the president's military action in Mexico. You must admit that it has stopped the migration of people to our southern border, though with a cost."

"Yes, that's quite clear. However, my concern with the president's policy has always been his aggressiveness in dealing with the problem. We have lost at least two soldiers, and more have been injured, all needlessly in the midst of this action. More than a thousand innocent migrants have been killed. Granted, that also involves military tactics, and war is ugly and brutal. But the president started this war."

"You say soldiers are being killed? We've not heard that before. Can you provide more specifics?"

Rick tried to maintain his composure but he was kicking himself for getting ahead of the Defense Department in sharing such news. "That information will best be provided by the Defense Department," he said. "My point is that the flow of migrants had all but stopped before the president even started his invasion. Why would we sacrifice innocent lives? Why would we put civilians and even one soldier at risk?"

"Do you feel the president's focus on Mexico's government leaders is too aggressive as well?"

"I do. In fact, we asked a number of experts to analyze the video clip that the president has used to prove the corruption of President Cuevas. Multiple, independent analyses of that clip have confirmed that the audio tied to it was not real. It was generated by artificial intelligence."

"Senator Taylor, are you saying that the president has offered false evidence of corruption?"

"I don't know who offered up that video to the media. However, I am surprised that the talented members of the Donaldson Administration seemingly forgot to check the authenticity of the video. Based upon the president's track record, I must conclude that they latched onto the video because it fit into the president's narrative and his goal of directly interfering with Mexico's government."

"That is quite a charge, Senator Taylor."

"I hope someone can prove me wrong. However, I can think of no other reason for the administration to use this video without authenticating it first." He hesitated. "I am so worried for this nation. Under President Donaldson, this is not the United States that I love. Who could ever imagine the US invading a sovereign nation and attempting to force a regime change with as little justification as this?"

That afternoon the media became a frenzy of talk relating to the news that the military was taking losses in the war as well as Taylor's charges of the use of AI. He had hoped his statement might cause them to ask some key questions. They had accurately reported that migrants had stopped moving north and were in fact leaving Mexico. They also had reported that American troops continued to head south, attacking the cartels at every opportunity. Why did nobody ask the administration why the United States' invasion of Mexico even continued?

The media attacked the Defense Department with a full court press to get details of the information Rick had released. The DOD grudgingly added that information to their regular media briefings that had begun with the military invasion. They elected not to announce that one fatality had been from a US drone attack on an officer.

Members of the media caught up with other members of Congress to get their perspective on the invasion. Many chose not to comment. A few supported the mission and the casualties as a natural result of war. Most, however, expressed shock and concern expressing their desire for the president to be more transparent in both his objective for the invasion and operational reports.

While unhappy to have her hand forced in this way, Schmidt ultimately authorized the embedding of war correspondents with the troops as they moved south through Mexico.

Donaldson was furious when he was shown Taylor's interview. The White House spokesperson hurriedly held a press conference and reminded reporters that despite the new information about the video, the Mexican government was corrupt in many ways. He also advised that US diplomats continued to be engaged in dialogue with President Cuevas and other senior officials.

Behind the scenes, the diplomats' offer of asylum and cash to the top five people in the Mexican government had risen to double of the initial plan. At this point, they were trying to buy the government of Mexico.

The president continued with his plan despite Taylor's interview and the uproar it caused, deciding to move as quickly as he could to try and push through the controversy. He had Senator Moreno contacted and told to be ready to get on a military business jet to Mexico City at a moment's notice.

#

Rick had one more call to make to his chief of staff on his way home. An idea had come to him.

"Sandra, this is Rick. I need to talk with you and Lily just as fast as you can make that happen."

"How about now?" she asked. "She's at her desk. I can have her in here in a minute."

"Let's do it," he said.

In less than a minute, Sandra was back on the line. "I'm here, and so is Lily."

"Hello, Senator Taylor," Lily said.

"Hi, Lily. Sandra, is your door closed?"

"Yep."

"Okay, Lily, can you tell me how long it would take to have AI generate a replica of a voice? And not just that, I would want it to respond to anticipated questions."

Lily thought for a moment and said, "Well, if you can get the person to read some text into the system, it could pick up the voice fairly quickly. Let's say twenty to thirty minutes. To develop a dialogue capability would take longer. I guess it depends on how complex the back and forth would be."

He nodded as she spoke. "Good. As far as getting the voice

right, could that be done by using a recording of the voice?"

"Yes."

"Do you have the capability to do this yourself?"

"Sure. I have the basic software on my laptop. If we want to do something really well though, I would have to get permission to use the university's system."

"Of course. Alright, Sandra and Lily, this is what I need you to do. You probably have less than twenty-four hours to complete it," he began.

"Sandra, I want you to fish up any recordings that you can find of Majority Leader Moreno's voice. Try to find a variety of samples. His speeches, regular conversations, stuff like that. If you can find anything where he is stressed or excited, that would be great."

He stopped and thought for a moment. "Once more, what I'm about to ask from you is absolutely confidential. I need you both to swear to me that you will not say a word to anyone about what you are working on. It is going to seem far-fetched and crazy. I am not exaggerating when I say that the future of our country rests on this." He paused. "Sandra, do you swear to me?"

After a half second of silence he heard her chuckle, "No pressure, Rick. ... I swear."

He laughed at himself. He guessed he was being a bit dramatic, but the situation certainly merited it.

"Lily?"

"I swear," she said nervously.

"I get it," he said. "I'm asking a lot. But here is what I want you to do. ..."

76

FRANK MORENO arranged to have the aircraft take him to Flying Cloud Airport in Eden Prairie, Minnesota, on Thursday morning. He wanted to pack some things at home before getting the word to go. He tried to call Clarisa but got no answer at home or on her cell. In fact, the phone appeared to be turned off, as each time he called it went immediately to voicemail. He became angry at her unavailability. He needed to talk with her about Rick Taylor's security detail, although he was sure she had already figured that out. More importantly, he needed to tell her that they were about to leave. They would have to take care of Taylor and Cindy Potter later.

The next morning, the FBI was staking out Moreno's home when a hired limousine service dropped him off at a quarter past eleven in the morning. Two agents watched as the driver helped him move six boxes and three pieces of luggage into the house.

The agents contacted Kramer, who was not far away. At his request, they also called Senator Taylor in St. Cloud. Kramer arrived at eleven forty-five. He instructed the other agents that they were to keep all vehicles except his away from the front of Moreno's house, unless absolutely needed to move people or equipment in or out. "I don't want to attract attention to ourselves."

Kramer and another agent knocked on Moreno's door. Two other agents were on both sides of the front door, out of sight.

Their guns were drawn but kept out of view of the neighborhood.

Moreno answered. He looked haggard, as though he hadn't gotten much sleep. He was in blue jeans and a t-shirt, and his hair was uncombed. "Yes," he said quickly when he opened the door.

"Hello Senator Moreno, my name is Stuart Kramer. I am a special agent with the FBI. May we come in?"

"Agent Kramer, this isn't a good time. I'm preparing to leave for Mexico at any moment. The president has asked me to go down to assist."

Kramer calmly said, "I understand, Senator Moreno, but this is about your wife."

Moreno gasped. Stepping forward, he placed a hand on the agent's shoulder. "What? Clarisa? Is she alright?"

"May we come in, sir?"

"Uh, yes, certainly," he said as he backed into the house, leaving the door open for the two agents to enter.

The large, attractive house was clean but cluttered. There were several open boxes on the hearth and on the kitchen table. "Now, what is this about Clarisa?"

"Is there someplace we can sit?" Kramer asked.

Moreno nervously led them to the living room and gestured to a chair and sofa. He sat down on an ottoman in front of his favorite chair.

"Thank you. Senator Moreno, we have difficult news for you. Your wife is dead."

Moreno's face gradually turned ashen as he processed the news. "Oh my God, no," he said as tears filled his eyes. "What … What happened? Was it an accident?"

"No, sir. Your wife was killed while in the process of committing a crime."

Suddenly the senator's look changed to fear. "No, that can't be possible. My wife would never intentionally break the law."

"Senator Moreno, we believe that your wife was involved in the murder of two people and the attempted murder of two others. She was killed by her victim in Duluth in her most recent effort."

Moreno became agitated. "No, you must be mistaken. Clarisa is no killer. You're at the wrong house." He stood and said, "This is ridiculous." He looked at Kramer, the door, and then to the kitchen as if he didn't know what to do.

"Senator Moreno, please sit down," Kramer instructed. "We also have a warrant to search your property."

The other agent opened the front door and waved in a cadre of agents, all wearing sterile suits and latex gloves and carrying empty black bags and a few empty boxes.

"What for? No. Do you know who I am? I'm the Senate Majority Leader of the United States, and soon to be Governor of Mexico." His voice got progressively louder as he spoke. "The president has given me an important assignment. You get out of here, now. All of you!" he screamed.

Kramer ignored the outburst and handed Moreno a copy of the search warrant.

"We're doing our jobs, sir. I would also like to ask you a few questions, if I may."

"No, you may not. I want to call my attorney."

"I understand, sir. I was just hoping we could do this here and avoid creating a lot of publicity."

One of the agents walked up to Kramer and showed him a cheap flip phone like the kind a person could buy at a department store. "This was on the island in the kitchen," he said and waited.

"Thanks, Ken. Let's get it printed as soon as possible."

He turned to Moreno. "Senator, is that your phone?"

"Uh, yes. ... Well, no, I mean, it could be my wife's."

"Well, that's interesting. Your wife had one just like that. It was found in her kayak when she made an attempt on Senator Rick Taylor's life."

Moreno seemed to be hyperventilating. He sat shaking his head and wiping sweat from his forehead and then wiping it on his jeans.

"I don't know about any of this. I want to call my lawyer."

"Yes, sir. If you would, just sit here for a few minutes." Then Kramer stood and said, "Actually, sir, if you don't mind, I need you to stand for a minute."

Moreno stood up. Kramer approached him and patted down his clothing to ensure he had no weapons on him. "Thank you, sir," he said.

Moreno sat again and nothing was said until fifteen minutes later when the agent returned with the phone. "We've got the prints off of it. Its number is the same one she dialed from her throwaway phone while enroute to Ely."

Kramer nodded. He turned to the Senator. "Senator Moreno, you're under arrest for conspiracy to commit murder in the deaths of Thomas Blado and Margaret Taylor."

"No!" Moreno cried. "There is some mistake. If my wife was involved in something like that, I had no knowledge of it. I did nothing wrong."

Another agent came and cuffed Moreno's hands behind his back. Kramer pulled the agent to the side and whispered into his ear, "Keep him under wraps. No calls in or out until I tell you. I've got a few things to take care of, but I should be back within a couple of hours." The agent nodded. Others outside had pulled a Suburban up the driveway and into the garage. The agent led the senator through the door into the garage and helped him into the back of the black SUV. He read Moreno his Miranda rights, closed the door, and got into the front right seat. "Okay, let's go," he said to the driver.

#

When he was ten minutes out from Moreno's home, Rick called Kramer. Kramer told him that he couldn't meet Rick at Moreno's home but had arranged the use of an interview room at a police precinct nearby.

Before he got to the police station, Rick called Jim and told him to be ready at a moment's notice. They had set out a tentative plan, but he wouldn't know whether it might work until he talked with Kramer.

Kramer recapped what had just happened at Moreno's home. He told Rick that they had arrested him. He said that Moreno had been taken quietly but that it would likely not be quiet for long.

"You arrested him? How did that happen so quickly?"

"It was a fluke, really," Kramer mused. "There was a throwaway phone on the kitchen island. There was no security on it, so we were able to check it out right there. It was the number his wife called from her identical throwaway phone when she was on her way to the Boundary Waters."

Rick almost felt nauseous. The majority leader of the US Senate and his wife had killed Maggie and tried to kill Cindy and him. "This is so surreal," he said.

Kramer took the phone out of his suit coat pocket, holding it with his handkerchief. "I thought you might want to see it."

"It looks just like the one I found in her kayak."

"They were from the same store, probably bought at the same time," Kramer affirmed. He looked at Rick and said nothing for a few seconds. He stared blankly at the wall behind Taylor as if trying to figure something out. Finally he said, "There are two numbers in the phone's memory. One is for Clarisa's throwaway phone. The other doesn't have a name. Just the initials GD."

"Gerald Donaldson?" Rick asked.

Kramer shrugged. "I need to take this back and put it into the evidence locker."

The agent reached into his other pocket and pulled out two latex gloves, a pen, and a piece of paper and laid them by the phone and stood up. "Give me a minute, I need to take a leak first," he said.

Rick stared at him as he walked out the door, leaving Rick alone with the phone. He quickly put the gloves on and picked up the phone. He knew that his only hope was to act before Moreno's arrest was made public. He flipped open the phone.

Where is the phone directory? he asked himself. He was so tense that he was having trouble focusing. *Breathe.* He took two deep breaths and looked at the face of the phone again. He saw a picture of a directory with the word 'contacts' underneath it. He tapped on the screen; nothing happened.

"The gloves," he said out loud to himself. He took another deep breath and pulled the glove off of his left hand. He tapped the image with his knuckle, and the screen changed. Rick saw the two numbers. One had no name connected to it. The other, "GD." He pulled out his own phone and found his address directory.

"Don't you dare put that number in your phone," Kramer said firmly.

Rick looked up and watched Kramer walking in the door. He froze. His breathing stopped. He was half panicked. Isn't this what Kramer had left him to do?

"Write it on the piece of paper and burn it when you're finished."

Rick smiled faintly and began breathing again. He took the paper and pen and wrote down the number. He also turned the phone over again, keeping his ungloved left hand well clear, and jotted down the type of phone it was.

"Thank you, Agent Kramer," he said, looking up at him.

"I never saw that." The agent stood up and put the phone back in his pocket. "Keep in mind that the phone that calls that number will ultimately be identified, and the location from which the call was made will also be known."

"Yes, sir."

"And burn that piece of paper," Kramer called back as he walked out the door.

Rick stuffed the paper into his pocket and hurried out of the precinct. As soon as he was in the car, he called Jim. "I've got what we need. Do you have access to the AI stuff Lily put together?"

"I've got it. I think I know how to use them. Lily walked me through it."

"Good. Meet me in the office in half an hour," Rick said. He told his bodyguard where they were going and asked him to step on it.

77

JUST BEFORE five o'clock that evening, Stan Kauffman's assistant received a call. "Stan Kauffman's office," she answered.

Jim clicked on the play button on the AI software. "This is Frank Moreno. I need to talk with Stan right away."

"Let me see if he can take your call, Senator Moreno."

"What's up, Frank?" Kauffman finally answered.

"Clarisa's been arrested. They know everything. They've connected her to Blado and Taylor. They're coming to talk to me!" Moreno said without a breath.

"What are you talking about, Frank?"

"They've got Clarisa. They know everything!"

"Frank, who's Clarisa? What do they know? Who is 'they?' Are you sure you're up to this Mexico thing?"

The phone went dead.

"Frank? Frank?" Kauffman looked at the phone and then returned it to the cradle. Moreno sounded like he had lost it. He would have to discuss this with the president at their dinner meeting. Moreno sounded in no shape to take over Mexico.

#

Jim looked at Rick. "Did we capture that?" Rick clicked the file on the phone app that should have recorded the call. The playback was perfect. Both sides of the call came through loud and clear.

#

The phone in the president's desk drawer rang at 5:12 p.m. It took him a few seconds to realize where the sound was coming from. He seldom got calls on it, and only one person knew the number. *Moreno must be looking for an update on Mexico,* he thought.

He fished it out of the drawer. "Hello."

"Mr. President, Clarisa's been arrested. They know everything. They've connected her to Blado and Taylor. They're coming to talk to me!"

"Frank, who's arrested her? You've got to make sure she keeps me out of this," Donaldson commanded.

"They've got Clarisa. They know everything! They've tied us to Tom Blado and Rick Taylor."

Donaldson was on his feet now. "You listen to me, Frank. You assured me that Clarisa could handle this. A 'murder-suicide,' you said. Well, it's her incompetence that screwed this thing up. You and she are going to have to own this, Frank. Don't you dare mention my name." Quickly he added, "I'll pardon you both. You take the hit, and I'll pardon you both."

Frank said nothing.

"Frank, did you hear me? You keep me out of this. I will pardon you."

There was only silence on the line.

78

AT HALF past five, Rick Taylor placed a call to the president's chief of staff's office. His assistant put him on hold and returned to say that Kauffman was not available at the moment.

"Ma'am, I understand Stan Kauffman's loathing of me. However, right now I'm trying to save his ass. Please tell him that he *must* talk to me."

"Just a moment, please."

A minute later Kauffman came on the line. "Make it quick, Taylor. You probably have an interview to do tonight."

Rick spoke as calmly as he was able. "Stan, thank you for taking my call. I have something that you will want to hear. Please tell me you'll give me two minutes. That's all I ask. Two minutes."

"I'm listening," Kauffman said coldly.

Rick played the recording of the call to the president. When it was over, he said, "Did you hear that, Stan?"

"Where did you get that? I got the same call today. It was some AI prank."

"Yes, you got the call," Rick said slowly. "And it was clear by your response that you were not involved in Moreno's conspiracy. Let me give you some more information. When I give you some context of the call, you will understand."

"Sure, give me your context, Taylor," he said dismissively.

"The call that was made to the president was not made through the switchboard like yours was. It was made to a cell phone that the president keeps for direct calls. I got the number from a burner phone that is connected to the murders of Tom Blado, my wife Maggie, and the attempt on my life and Cindy Potter's life," Rick explained. "Are you with me so far?"

"Yes."

"Two days ago, Frank Moreno's wife was killed when she attempted to kill Cindy Potter, the woman who happened to be there in the Boundary Waters when I was attacked. The FBI has connected Clarisa Moreno to these murders and attempted murders. Then today Frank Moreno was arrested for conspiracy to commit murder. Now, I'm going to play this for you again."

Rick played the recording again.

Kauffman felt numb. He couldn't believe that his longtime buddy, his boss, his president, could be involved with murder.

"Stan?" Rick said, back on the phone.

"What?" was all Kauffman could say.

"Do you understand now?"

Kauffman didn't know what to think. "How can this be confirmed?"

"You can place a call to FBI Special Agent Stuart Kramer. I'll let you go through your sources so you can be sure who you are talking to. You can also call the Duluth, Minnesota police department. With your connections, they will tell you that Clarisa Moreno died when she attacked Cindy Potter two days ago."

"Okay, Taylor," he said softly. "I'll do that."

#

Kauffman walked into the president's office at 5:50 p.m.

Donaldson wasn't in the study; he was sitting at his desk in the Oval Office, his hands in his lap, staring at the presidential seal on the carpet in front of him.

"Mr. President, I listened to the recording of your conversation with Frank Moreno a few minutes ago."

The president looked at him and nodded. He took a deep breath and said, "Well, Stan, it's just another bump in the road. We'll get through this."

"No Ger, it's not just another bump in the road. It's murder."

Donaldson looked at him and stood. "Look, in order to accomplish great things, sometimes you need to use extraordinary means," he said. "But that's behind us now. Moreno will do the right thing."

Stan couldn't believe what he was hearing. "You can't justify murder for the sake of some national policy, Gerry."

"Don't use that term, Stan. And we're not just talking policy. We're about to take the first and most difficult step in reshaping the United States of America, forever. Think about it. We're on track with the plan. Within two years, Mexico will be our fifty-first state. Next, Guatemala, then maybe Cuba," he said, his face shining. Waving his hand in a grand gesture he said, "Someday the United States of America will cover two continents and have seventy-one stars on our flag."

He began to pace. He stopped in front of the east door, looking out onto the Presidential Rose Garden. "We may not be here to see it, but we will know that we got the ball rolling," he said enthusiastically. Looking back at Stan, he continued, "Think of the millions of people who we'll pull out of poverty. Think of the corruption that we'll uproot."

"You don't think the murder of two people, one of whom had nothing to do with this, is corrupt?" Kauffman countered. After a pause, he said in a voice barely audible, "You need to resign, Ger. This has gone too far."

The president held up his hand. "No, no, no. That's all behind us now. Moreno and his wife will pay the price as patriots of our great country. Their sacrifice means justice will be done. Look at where we are. No more sacrifices will be needed."

At one time, this all made so much sense to Kauffman. He had seen his friend's vision. Now it all just sounded so dirty. He stood slouching in the middle of the Oval Office, listening to the President of the United States ranting about conquering nations to build a greater power. *Is this how the Soviet Union began?* he wondered.

At that moment Kauffman straightened his back, standing as if at attention. "Mr. President, you will have my letter of resignation on your desk in the morning."

He turned and walked toward the door.

Donaldson followed."Stan, no. Don't do this. All that's behind us now. We're almost there. The hard part is over."

Kauffman opened the door and kept walking. As he went into the outer office he heard, "Stan! No, I won't accept your resigna—" as the door closed behind him.

EPILOGUE

AFTER TWO grueling months stuck in Washington, Rick finally was able to go home to Minnesota for a week. It had been one of the most challenging times in the nation's history. Rick had sent the recording to Kramer, who wasn't able to use it as evidence, but he also gave it to several reporters and news outlets. Within a week, Donaldson had resigned as President of the United States.

While progress was being made steadying the ship, Rick still had something he felt he had to do. He made an appointment with the St. Paul chief of police for the morning after he arrived home.

Before he walked into police headquarters for his meeting, he received a call from Jim Gunderson asking if they could meet for lunch.

"Good morning, Jim. Sure, I'd love to have lunch. In fact, I'm in St. Paul for a meeting. Maybe we could meet someplace near here at noon. No, make that one. There's a chance that something could come up to gum up the works, but I should be able to make that happen. You pick the place. Just text me with it, and I'll see you then."

He continued into the building and followed the signs to the chief's office. He was greeted warmly by a receptionist who offered him a seat. In less than a minute, Miles Proeber, the Chief of Police, walked out of his office and greeted him.

"Good morning, Senator Taylor. We don't often get dignitaries such as yourself in our little office. Come in, and I'll ask Jill to bring us a cup of coffee." He gestured at his receptionist, who smiled and nodded as she made her way to the coffee machine.

They sat in a small, private conference room off the chief's office. Jill brought a tray in that held packets of creamer, various sweeteners, and an insulated canister full of coffee along with two cups.

"Thank you, Jill," Proeber said, smiling. Then he turned to Rick and commented, while she could hear, "I always feel guilty asking her to serve us like that. But when we don't have guests, I try to get her coffee from time to time too."

Rick smiled. He was impressed by the chief's disarming demeanor. He could imagine that this guy had been a pretty good beat cop at one time. He suspected that he knew a lot of the people in the neighborhood he served. He looked around the dingy office and noticed some photographs of police officers on the wall. The table they sat at was a heavy wooden thing with more than a few nicks in it.

Once they were alone, Chief Proeber poured their coffee and said, "So, Senator Taylor, what can I do for you?"

With a touch of nervousness in his voice, Rick proceeded to tell the chief about Maggie's confession on the day she died. He went into every detail that she had given him —the substance put into Sands's water, how she had done it, and why. As Rick detailed his and Maggie's conversation that afternoon, the chief watched him and listened carefully, a grave look on his face.

"Chief Proeber, Maggie was consumed with guilt over what she had done," he said as he blinked his eyes several times. "The last time we spoke, she told me that she intended to turn herself in."

"Senator Taylor, you've bowled me over this

morning," the chief said. "It took a lot of courage for you to come in and share that. That death was ruled natural causes. Nobody would have ever known."

"I suspected that. At the time, I felt certain that when she turned herself in, there may have been a strong assumption that I was involved. I have no proof to offer. I can only tell you that I had no idea what she was doing at the time."

Proeber was silent for a moment, then stood and walked to his desk. He pulled a laminated sheet of paper from the center drawer, found a number on it, and made a call.

"Good morning, Cliff. This is Miles. Have you got a few minutes for me this morning? I would like to ask you some questions about the Jeff Sands autopsy.

"No, I'll come to see you if you're available," the chief said, pausing for a response. "I'll be there in ten minutes."

He hung up the phone and looked at Rick. "That was Cliff Lindloff, our coroner. His office is only a block away. I'd like to gather some information from him, and I think I should do it without your presence. Would you mind terribly if we paused for about an hour and then reconvened here?"

"That would be fine," Rick agreed.

"There's a really great bakery around the corner that pours a good cup of coffee. If it would be more comfortable for you, you could leave and come back in an hour, or let's make it an hour and a half."

Rick smiled and shook his head. "Thanks, but this is comfortable for me. I would just as soon stay here, check my email, and make some phone calls, if that's okay with you."

"Fine," the chief said. "As soon as I get back, I'll come right in. If you need anything, just ask Jill."

Rick began checking his email while he drank coffee in the chief's conference room, but his mind wandered. He thought of Maggie, his heart aching. She was such a special woman—his partner for life, he had thought. Everything they had accomplished, they had done together. He thought about her song that had brought life to his struggling campaign. She had believed in him and in his campaign so much.

How could she have thought it acceptable to do what she had done? He knew that she had done it for him. She was a wayward patriot who was so focused on the goal that she sacrificed the values that they shared, just that one time. Perhaps her death was a blessing. He couldn't imagine her living out her remaining years in prison. She didn't deserve that, and yet she did. The thought that she had been spared that life helped him to feel a small bit of closure.

He went out in search of a restroom at one point. When he returned, he found the chief sitting at the table. "That didn't take too long," Rick said.

"No, Cliff is an efficient, no-nonsense kind of guy."

Rick sat down again and took half of the remaining coffee, pouring what was left into the chief's cup.

"Senator Taylor, I did not bring your name up or the name of your wife in my discussions with the coroner. I simply told him that I had some loose ends to tie up before I closed the case."

Rick nodded and sat quietly with his hands folded in front of him.

"The bottom line is this. Jim told me that the acid level in Jeff Sands's system was elevated, but that could have been caused by a number of things. He also said there is a drug that, as you described, can cause acidosis in a person's system. He told me that for a guy in Sands's condition, increasing acidosis could very well kill him."

Rick shook his head and held his forehead in his hand. "I was hoping you would learn that she was wrong. That what she did wouldn't have killed him."

Chief Proeber continued. "He also said that any man in Sands's condition could well have collapsed on a hot day doing any activity that is more strenuous than normal. He told me that what he found during the autopsy suggested Sands wouldn't have lasted a year in any circumstance."

"Even so, Maggie didn't know that. It's still so hard for me to believe that she has done something like this."

"Look, Senator Taylor, with what you've told me, there are adequate grounds for opening an investigation into this."

Rick nodded his head, knowing that a whole new ordeal was about to begin. He dreaded what was coming.

"But what good would it do?" the chief asked. "Maggie is dead. Who do we put on trial? Sands may have been dispatched a little early, but there is nothing we can do about that now. What benefit would there be in putting his family through litigation more than a year after his death?"

Rick said nothing; he just stared at the chief and nodded.

"The same thing goes for you. Are you ready for me to open a big investigation about your wife's actions? You told me you weren't involved, and I believe you. Nothing here suggests that it's worth pulling resources away from other important casework to chase after ghosts," he said frankly. "Besides, you're doing a pretty darned good job representing the people of Minnesota in the Senate. Why create that distraction and ruin your family name?"

Rick had a difficult time holding back his emotions. He didn't know why he couldn't stop the tears. Was it relief that he wouldn't be investigated? Was it the bit of closure from Maggie's death and what she had done for him? Or was it because he had finally gotten the whole nightmare off his chest, in an official way? *Probably all of the above*, he thought.

Proeber grabbed a box of tissue from his credenza and handed it to Taylor.

"I hardly know what to say, chief," Rick said. "I'm so thankful to have had the opportunity to talk with you about this. I'll be forever grateful for your time and wisdom today."

"Does anyone else know about this?" the chief asked.

"Only one person in the world, and I trust them completely."

"Good. Well, if you'll excuse me, this has taken much longer than I had anticipated, and I've got another meeting soon. Thank you for coming forward like this. And I wish you well in your work in the Senate."

Rick walked out of the building feeling like a huge weight had been lifted from his shoulders. He looked at his watch. It was twelve-thirty, just in time to catch lunch with Jim.

#

Rick walked into the restaurant to find Jim already seated in a booth. He tossed his jacket on the bench seat and slid in, facing his friend.

"How'd your meeting go?" Jim asked him.

"It was great. Something I just needed to get taken care of. It was nice to finally get the time to do it."

"I know it's been a long time since you've been back to Minnesota. It's good to see things settling down in Washington. How do you think President Whittington is doing?"

"Boy, she had a mess to clean up," Rick said, shaking his head. "But with Donaldson's resignation and our troops now out of Mexico, the immediate crisis is averted."

He looked at Jim and chuckled. "You know she actually approached me about taking a Cabinet position?"

"Wow!" Jim said with wide eyes. "What did you tell her?"

"I told her I was still trying to learn how to be a senator and that she didn't need some wet-behind-the-ears Washington newbie in her Cabinet. It will be hard enough for her to clean house as it is. There's been a lot of trust lost by the people."

Jim nodded. "On the heels of that scandal, there's no way that the party would have kept your seat if you left. We've already seen Moreno's seat go."

"Listen, Rick," Jim continued. "The reason I wanted to

meet with you is that I've given you the year that I promised, but now it's time for me to move on. I'm a campaigner, not an administrator. Midterm races are starting to develop, and I've gotten a few calls already."

Rick smiled and nodded. He wasn't surprised. "Jim, I can't tell you how much your guidance and, even more, your friendship has meant to me. You've supported me in so many ways. I hope our friendship will remain."

"It's been a crazy two years. You've dealt with so much. I look forward to being able to meet for a beer or maybe just go fishing sometime. No politics. No drama."

"That sounds great," Rick agreed.

"Well you've got a couple of weeks before you need to be back. What are you going to do now?" Jim asked.

"I'll stay engaged," Rick said. "But I'm also going to try and relax a little and clear my mind."

"That's great," Jim said. "Why don't you come to the house for dinner tomorrow? We'll get some steaks and have a few beers."

Rick smiled and shook his head. "Thanks. I'd love to, but I've got to be in Duluth tomorrow night. I owe someone a hamburger."

COMMENT FROM THE AUTHOR

Thank you for reading *A Higher Betrayal.* I hope you found it interesting and entertaining. If you enjoyed it, I would appreciate it if you would enter a review on Amazon or another favorite online bookstore.

James Madison, the man who penned our Constitution, once said, "If men were angels, no government would be necessary. If angels were to govern men, neither external nor internal controls on government would be necessary. In framing a government which is to be administered by men over men, the great difficulty lies in this: you must first enable the government to control the governed; and the next place, oblige it to control itself."

Government positions have become significant seats of power in our nation. That is why people in those positions spend the first 25% of their term governing, and the next 75% working to get re-elected so they can retain that power. While there are many noble people in the United States Senate and House of Representatives, it seems to me that term limits would provide some restraint to this ever-increasing quest to hold on to personal power.

When comparing our two-party system to other republics around the world, it is probably better in some ways and worse in others. We need to do our best with the system we've got. I laud all of those who seek to do the right thing, with or without the support of their party, for the good of the country. What is good for the country? Now, that is something that will be debated from now until she falls.

ACKNOWLEDGMENTS

Before I recognize all who helped me in writing this book, I must apologize to my military readers. I acknowledge that a trained operator would have dispatched Rick and Cindy at the boundary waters with little problem. Also, military procedures and processes are more rigorous than depicted. I took these liberties intending to entertain my readers.

Thanks to the many people who informed me as I wrote *A Higher Betrayal*.

Jim Hahn, a dear friend of more than thirty years, was generous in sharing his experiences as a campaign manager and deputy chief of staff for a US congressman. Dr. Eric Bode was instrumental in helping me make some of the medical elements of the story viable. I would be remiss not to acknowledge Lou Anne Benson, a nurse who stood beside our table in a restaurant and helped me understand the best way to sever a femoral artery!

Ron Clanton, President of US Computer Support, dumbed down his explanation of artificial intelligence to the point of me being able to grasp it in its simplest form. Thanks also to Jake Behmer who spent several summers as a camp counselor in the Minnesota Boundary Waters. His insights helped with an exciting element of the story.

Thank you to my friend Chuck Hughes for his encouragement and help with initial edits as I wrote. Also, to Cathy Hughes, who provided early feedback and was helpful in coming up with the title that we finally settled on.

Carrie Cannella, my editor, made the finished product better in many ways. She's worth her weight in gold!

My love and appreciation to my daughter, Lori Ehlke, who worked with me on the cover design. Thanks also to that small group from my list of followers who provided input on the various cover options and titles being considered.

ABOUT THE AUTHOR

Jack Meyer is a Christian, husband, father and grandfather, retired businessman, and author.

As he writes, Jack seeks to develop characters that are based on 'everyday' people who ironically get caught up in situations they've never envisioned. He expands on intriguing and complicated circumstances that generate a variety of emotions. While the characters in Jack's books have political opinions, they are never defined as 'good' or 'bad' based upon their philosophy or views. Each person in his stories is relatable and has strengths and weaknesses of character, as all people do.

Jack and his wife, Barbara, divide their time between their homes in Colorado Springs and Tucson. Both define different landscapes, people, and experiences. He stays fit by playing golf and hiking. He is always pondering over the news of the day and how it might feed into his next book.

You can follow Jack, monitor progress on his next novel, and ponder interesting questions on government and politics by signing up for his monthly newsletter, **Patriot Aims**, at his website, **HTTP://waywardpatriotbook.com.**

Other books written by Jack Meyer are available through Amazon Books and other online retailers:

Wayward Patriot: Preserving the Vote

In Defense of the Grid - A Wayward Patriot Thriller (novella)